THE MAGICAL AWAKENING OF EMMY SUKAR

The Limitless Series Book I

Sol Kwon

Sol Kwon/SpurLight Press
solkwon.com

Publisher's Note: This is a work of fiction. Names, characters, places, and incidents are a product of the author's imagination. Locales and public names are sometimes used for atmospheric purposes. Any resemblance to actual people, living or dead, or to businesses, companies, events, institutions, or locales is completely coincidental.

Book Layout © 2014 BookDesignTemplates.com

The Magical Awakening of Emmy Sukar/ Sol Kwon. -- 1st ed.

To my loving and patient husband Christopher.

We are what we think. All that we are arises with our thoughts. With our thoughts, we make the world.

—THE BUDDHA

CONTENTS

Prologue 1

{ 1 } 9

{ 2 } 21

{ 3 } 29

{ 4 } 41

{ 5 } 47

{ 6 } 53

{ 7 } 61

{ 8 } 69

{ 9 } 75

{ 10 } 83

{ 11 } 87

{ 12 } 95

{ 13 } 101

{ 14 } 107

{ 15 } 115

{ 16 } 125

{ 17 } 135

{ 18 } 147

{ 19 } 153

{ 20 } 159

{ 21 } 169

{ 22 } 177

{ 23 } 181

{ 24 } 189

{ 25 } 199

{ 26 } 209

{ 27 } 217

{ 28 } 225

{ 29 } 231

{ 30 } 235

{ 31 } 241

{ 32 } 251

{ 33 } 257

{ 34 } 263

{ 35 } 269

{ 36 } 275

{ 37 } 283

{ 38 } 289

{ 39 } 295

{ 40 } 301

{ 41 } 309

{ 42 } 317

{ 43 } 323

{ 44 } 333

{ 45 } 341

NOTE TO READERS 351

ABOUT THE AUTHOR 352

Dear Reader:

Thank you so much for choosing *The Magical Awakening*.
The stories contained here symbolically reflect my own
journey as I found the courage to leave an old life for a new
one; it makes this novel that much dearer to my heart than any
other I'll write. I'm grateful every day to my family, friends,
and the writing community for the love and support they
provided as I birthed this novel. There is also my mentor
Summer McStravick, without whom none of this would have
been possible, and the Flowdreaming community. My
heartfelt thanks also go out to my editor, Jeni Chappelle, and
the cover artist, Dane Low.

I hope you'll enjoy the ride as much as I did writing it. If you
feel pulled to this story, I believe you were meant to be here
and we were meant to connect. However small that may be.

One more thing: if you do enjoy this novel, please leave a
review so others may also find it. Thank you again from the
bottom of my heart.

With Love,

Sol

Prologue

Sohan Sukar had never felt happier in his life. It didn't matter this was the second time this week that he'd come by the market for boiled pig's feet—this dark lump of fat, cartilage, and bones. Hello, good day, cheers, he'd say to shopkeepers and strangers with a big grin on his face, whether it was windy, cloudy, sunny, or rainy outside. His beautiful, young wife was pregnant with their first child in her mountainous belly; her latest fantasies involved spice-boiled pigs' feet and pickled hot peppers. She'd already had her fill with salted anchovies, stewed okra, and fresh strawberries. No matter what the request, each time she whispered her longings in his ear, he was fast out the door on a mission.

"I tell you," the old man said as he wiped his hands on a clean towel before wrapping up the meat for Sohan. He smiled broadly. "She sure's a lucky lady. When's she due?"

"Oh, just another month, about." Sohan's grin spread ear to ear as his cheeks turned red.

The man winked. "Hey, we're just happy she wants this stuff. Wonderful! If everyone liked them like your missus, we'd be rich." He laughed, cut a dried sausage link hanging behind the counter with a small knife, and dropped it in the bag.

Sohan thanked the man and headed home with a hefty, brown bag warming his side. He quickly walked the dusty streets of Alexandria, navigating through the oncoming people busily going their way. This was all a familiar sight, but everything felt new and crisp.

It was about time too. He was thirty-five years old. He'd been alone and without kin for a long, lonesome while until he'd met his wife, and what a blessing she had been. It was hard to believe at first that she'd chosen him, a man nine years her senior without much to claim for wealth and not much on looks.

In truth, they could not have been more different. He had a tall, slender figure with dark-brown skin and black hair, his normally serious gaze softened by a pair of thick eyeglasses. She was round in all corners of her body and of average height, with pearly white skin that shined against her long, orange hair full of thick curls. She was also an inherently unusual creature, constantly distracted by the unseen energies around her, which Sohan found fascinating and others disconcerting.

He whistled a tune as he ran up the stairs to their second-floor flat on the busy street. He could almost see her face, the excitement and unbridled joy in her eyes. Sometimes she'd start licking her lips even before he put down the delivery. In some ways, it was much easier to please her during the pregnancy and he was enjoying every minute of it.

"Here you are, love." He kissed her cheek and proudly placed the bag before her.

Her eyes widened and mouth spread into a smile, and she carefully opened the bag as if it contained something mysterious and precious. She dug in for the warm meat with her bare fingers and moaned softly as the juices slowly spread in her mouth.

Sohan leaned back in a chair and watched her, satisfied. A part of him was in awe of her sheer ability to eat, but mostly, he marveled at how beautiful, instinctive, and free his wife looked then. He was proud of her, more at that moment than ever before, and wondered with excitement about the baby inside of her. Secretly he wished for a boy, although he'd never say it out loud. It wasn't that he wasn't charmed by the idea of a baby girl, but a girl felt to him more fragile and unknown, which scared him a little.

"I can hear you, you know." Leona Piper glanced over with her sparkling green eyes, carelessly licking her fingers. She giggled. "I don't know either. Sorry. Not that I'd tell you if I knew."

He frowned. "I asked you not to do that. It's not fair."

"I'm sorry." She laughed. "I didn't mean to. I was a little distracted." She wiped her fingers on a paper napkin, tilting her head. "Should we ask Mom? She's coming by later. She's really good."

"What do you mean?"

"She can tell us. You want to know, don't you? If it's a boy or a girl?" She smiled with mischief in her eyes.

"She can tell?"

"Of course. And I'm saying she's really good at it."

"How come you can't do it then?"

"I don't know. It's usually hard for me to do my own stuff. I care too much, I'm too attached." She shrugged. "I think a girl would be lovely. I'll do her hair, and we'll share secrets."

He came over, sat behind her, and rubbed her shoulders. "I'll be happy with a boy or a girl, especially if she looks like you."

Sohan kissed her cheek, and she leaned back on him, stretching her arms and letting out a big, satisfied breath.

* * *

Leona's mother arrived in the middle of pouring rain. She took off her wet hat and coat as she entered the apartment, shaking off water from her hair and shoes. Sohan went to his mother-in-law and took her things, kissing her cheek.

Ethel Piper wore a long shirt-dress in a beautiful shade of blue. Her big and curly white hair came down to her shoulders; she wore bright red lipstick that flattered her handsome face. After checking herself in the mirror by the entryway, she walked over to her daughter.

Leona stood over the kitchen stove waiting for water to boil. She kissed her mom as she entered. "We'll get you some hot tea real soon, Ma."

Ethel picked up the cup and sniffed the dried tea leaves. "Lovely. That'll warm me up nicely." She walked over to the table and sat, facing her daughter. "I brought the valerian root you wanted. It's in that bag that Sohan took."

"Thanks. I'll check later." Leona smiled. "We have something to ask you first."

Sohan came over and stood next to her.

"Will you tell us if the baby's a she or a he?" She studied her mom's face, beaming with excitement.

"Oh, you decided you want to know?" Ethel laughed. "Is that why you really asked me to come? Well, I don't see why not. You want to do it now?"

Leona nodded and looked at her husband, who shrugged.

"All right, let's do it then." She walked over to the living room, which had a big couch and a couple of chairs around it. Leftover pork feet still sat on the coffee table, making Ethel—who'd stopped eating meat years ago—cringe. She brought the bag to the kitchen and went back, waving her arms to clear the air and lighting the lavender-scented candle on the side table. "Come on over when you're ready."

Leona and Sohan joined her. He set a cup of steaming hot tea on the table. Leona sat down on the long couch next to her mother, who wasted no time. She lifted her daughter's shirt up to just below her breasts, exposing the tight skin of her pregnant belly.

"Okay. Now close your eyes and take a deep breathe in." She spoke low and slow. "One more time, breathe in…and out." She paused. "Now focus your attention on your baby and imagine that there is a bright light shining and growing from its center. Good. Now stay with that image for a minute and breathe into it." She closed her eyes and brought her hands over her daughter's belly, not quite touching the skin but hovering just above. "Okay. Sweet little baby, show us if you are a boy or a girl. Nice and easy." She took in a deep breath.

Sohan sat aside and watched, his mouth slightly open. The room was absolutely silent.

A minute, maybe two, passed until Ethel spoke again. "Good. Thank you. All right..."

Just then Leona let out a sudden cry. The baby had made a sudden kick, and an imprint of something was visible on her skin, pushing out from the inside. She opened her eyes and rubbed her skin, saying, "Ouch. Oh, baby, it's okay. Mama's here."

Her face distorted with pain, she soothed the baby inside her. The baby moved one more time then settled. Ethel's face hardened as she kept her eyes on her daughter's belly.

"Something wrong?" Sohan asked.

His mother-in-law looked at him and exhaled deeply. But she smiled and said, "Well, she's a girl." She turned to Leona. "And," she let out a sigh, "oh, some things are better unknown."

"What? You can't do that."

"The future is never set in stone." Ethel stroked her daughter's belly. "All I'll say is that this little one is going to have some tough times ahead. She goes many lifetimes with you." She looked at Leona. "But it could be all right. Nothing's decided yet." She lowered her cheek down near the baby and whispered, "And I'll always be here for you, baby girl. You'll see."

Part I.

{ 1 }

Sixteen years later.
September 20

When classes ended, Emmy Sukar walked over to the elementary wing of her school to fetch her ten-year old sister, Nora. Emmy felt especially tired from the day and slightly annoyed at this added, although usual, task. For two years she'd been doing this.

But to this day, there were still some people who were surprised to learn they were sisters; no one would have known if they didn't say so. Nora's looks took after her mom, with light skin and curly, red hair; Emmy entirely took after her dad, with brown skin and straight, black hair. Each might as well have been a child from the respective parent but not both.

Growing up in Alexandria, the capitol of The New Republic, people thought she had been adopted whenever her mom took the girls out without their father.

"Where's she from?" they'd ask curiously, as if she wasn't there to hear them. Of course their mom quickly explained that Emmy was indeed her daughter, but what usually followed were gasps and gawks. By the time she was old enough to understand, a small seed of resentment had already started to grow, although she didn't know exactly against what.

When Emmy finally spotted Nora, she was still fumbling with her backpack that looked way too big for her. The moment their eyes met, Emmy turned and walked toward the exit, and her sister quietly followed.

It was gray outside. The wind brought a chill that penetrated their coats. The air smelled of the pungent earth; it also buzzed a little bit, as if there was an electric current moving through. The clouds were dense and dark over the mountains that surrounded them north, south, east, and west. It looked like rain had already started at one of the mountaintops, with black clouds smudging down to the pointy hills. Near the bottom, white fog hung lazily like smoke.

She turned to check on her sister. Nora was almost a full block behind, squatting on the sidewalk and focused on something on the ground. "What are you doing?"

No response.

"You have an umbrella?" she asked, already knowing the answer.

"No, it wasn't raining this morning." Nora looked up and made a face.

This was why Emmy always kept an extra in her locker. She continued to walk. "Hurry up."

Nora usually trailed her sister by at least four feet. Emmy walked with focus and efficiency; she also rarely waited, until their distance grew too much. This way she could pretend that she had the peace and solitude she longed for. Even so, Emmy was glad that the walk wasn't very long, and that Nora was now almost old enough to walk by herself.

Emmy was graduating in less than two years. Lately she'd been busy planning the grand escape, knowing that her good grades would allow her to have her pick of schools all over the country. After that, Nora would no longer be her responsibility, and her parents wouldn't be there to tell her what to do. And no more of this hole-in-the-wall town called Bath. It was exhilarating to imagine how that would be, and she was often lost daydreaming about the possibilities.

She considered going back to Alexandria. She missed the city, with all its happenings and crowds. It had all happened suddenly, and her parents hadn't even said why. One day her dad had come home and announced that he'd quit his job at the city government. A week later her mom had said they were moving away. That was two years ago.

It hadn't mattered that Emmy would lose all her friends or that the move would interrupt her studies. Sure, she'd protested. She'd even staged a hunger strike, although that hadn't lasted two days. She loved food and couldn't stand being hungry.

They called this place Bath because the natural springs here were supposed to be rich with healing minerals. It was surrounded by mountains, trees, streams, and rivers. The people, most of whom had lived there for generations, kept themselves busy through curiosity about each other's lives and gossip. Her family generally kept to themselves, though, and had done a pretty good job keeping a low profile. This was, after all, what her parents wanted.

She looked back to find Nora now almost two blocks behind and stopped to wait. To her left was a small park, from which a tree-lined main street full of small stores began. It looked quite charming at the moment, actually, with colorful awnings and yellow and red leaves of fall. The park was the center of Bath. It had a fountain that pumped out spring water at a constant seventy degrees Fahrenheit, all year around. The story went that many famous people had come from near and far for a soak, including the country's founders, back when the town hadn't been much more than a few houses behind low stone walls. Naturally it was the pride of locals and the place of communal activities.

The rain felt closer now. Suddenly, and with amazing speed, the wind picked up, hitting her face with dead leaves and grains of sand. It was getting hard to keep her eyes open.

"Hurry," she yelled back at Nora, who was busily moving her skinny legs. Emmy felt a heavy rain drop on her head then another. She ran for cover in front of the bookstore, and her sister soon followed. The rain came in a sudden gush, hard and loud, and soon it looked like a tornado moving through, wetness and cold thrashing everything in its way.

"Come on." She pulled Nora inside the bookstore.

A couple of people were quietly browsing through the stacks, oblivious of the weather. The owner—a gray-haired man in his fifties—stood behind the counter and seemed mesmerized by the scene outside, briefly nodding in the girls' direction as they entered. Nora headed straight to the children's section and settled on the floor. Emmy stood by the front window and watched. She loved the feeling of a hard rain: raw and immediate on her skin, that buzzing in the air, and such a release! Every rain drop drummed a wild beat on everything it touched.

Lost in her thoughts, she noticed something odd across the street by the park. At its entrance by the black iron gate, hung a huge banner she hadn't notice before. It said, "Breakthrough Rational Bath." It had a symbol on one side, in red on white, of two capital letters, RP, inside a square box. The entire thing felt familiar to her, except that she couldn't remember where she might have seen it before. The banner fluttered violently against the wind. People on the street held on to their umbrellas as if they were about to fly away, their clothes fully soaked in the rain. But the sign—what was it?

"Emmy, there's a new flying witches book," Nora called from the stacks. It was her favorite series.

"That's great."

"Do you have any money?" Her small head peaked from behind a bookshelf.

"Nope." This wasn't entirely true, since she had money, but it wasn't for her sister.

"Come on. Please?" Nora walked over and clutched the book to her chest. Her lips protruded and eyebrows furrowed, the way babies got dramatic about the things they wanted. "Mom will pay you tonight. You know she will."

The book cover showed an old witch with a big, pointy nose, wearing a black dress and a witch's hat. She had bad skin and a wicked expression. Next to her was a younger witch, who wore a pretty baby-blue dress and looked happy and sassy, smiling. Emmy had read those books when she was little too, and it amused her that the story had taken a different turn. Nora looked at her pleadingly.

"Fine. But you pay me tonight, okay?" Even as she said this, she wasn't sure what changed her mind.

"Okay." Her sister happily turned to the counter.

By the time they were done paying for the book, the wind was quieter and the rain much lighter. They could walk home in this. Nora carefully placed the new book in her backpack, and Emmy took the umbrellas out of hers. Stepping out onto the wet street, the cold air pricked her skin all over, making her shiver. Then she remembered.

That sign at the park was for the Rational Party, the political group that had come into power a few years back. Similar signs had been everywhere in Alexandria when her family had left the city. She stopped to look back at the sign.

It now drooped, heavy with the weight of the rain. She shrugged and picked up her pace toward home.

* * *

Rain had stopped completely as the sisters walked up the muddy hill to their house on Cattail Run Road. There were no sidewalks in this part of town, so they had to step aside whenever a car drove by, which wasn't often. Gushing streams had formed where the ground was low; the sounds of trickling and flowing water came from all directions. Skipping and hopping over the squiggling worms unearthed by the heavy rain, they slowly made their way home.

Their mother was at her garden when the girls finally reached their two-story, cobblestone house. She was hunched over a plant that had been knocked over by the wind, trying to prop it up with stakes. She was also whispering in a soft and reassuring voice, words that no one else could hear. Leona grew herbs and flowers in a small plot by the kitchen wall. As far as Emmy could tell, it always overflowed with lush life and vibrant colors. Even at that moment, so soon after a storm, butterflies fluttered around her and song birds sat on the edge of the roof, chirping, as if they had all gathered as friends. Even the honeybees were out working and buzzing about; a hummingbird whizzed away in amazing speed.

It was as if Leona had a secret language to communicate with the world around her that exchanged nothing but love. She looked like she was from another world, or so Emmy thought, and very beautiful. She had never met anyone like her mother. Even Grandma Ethel seemed more human than her mom. Her silky, orange hair; pearly, white skin; and blue-green eyes. Plus, and strangest of all, her constant happiness. Everything about her showed what Emmy would never be.

"Mom!" Nora ran toward her.

Leona turned and smiled brightly. "Hey, girls, did you get wet?"

"Nope. We stopped at the bookstore, and I found the latest flying witches book. Want to see?"

She got up and dusted off her hands and clothes. Nora hugged her, almost knocking her off balance. Butterflies and birds flew away as Emmy walked toward the door, but she didn't mind. This was, after all, the normal interaction between humans and other creatures, the way it should be.

"Oh dear, you feel cold," Leona said, embracing Nora. "Let's go inside. Did you have a good day, Emmy?"

"Yep," she responded without looking back. "Nora owes me money for the book." She glanced at her sister. "Pay up before bed. Okay?"

Nora nodded, preoccupied at the dining table and getting the book out of her bag. Before Leona could say anything else, Emmy left the kitchen.

Upstairs in her room, she dropped her bag next to the desk and took off her coat and shoes. Walking over to her bed, she caught a glimpse of her face in the mirror on the wall—a blotch of dark colors and misshapenness. She chuckled, sadly, before she crawled into bed and closed her eyes.

* * *

Emmy heard the sound of their laughter as she came downstairs for dinner. Sohan was still in his work outfit, smelling faintly of sweat and wearing dirt and debris on his pants. He'd taken a job as a gardener when they moved to Bath, very different from his previous work in the Alexandria government. She had never seen him do anything with plants before; his lean stature and bookish demeanor screamed anything but physical labor.

Nonetheless, he seemed happier and healthier as a gardener in this small town, and he was especially so at dinner. But then again, she didn't remember ever seeing him really unhappy, especially when her mom was around.

Dinner was a necessary hassle. It forced her to sit and answer questions when she'd rather be alone. She didn't mind her dad so much. But he'd been increasingly taking her mom's side whenever they argued, and that wasn't fair. If it wasn't for her generally hungry nature, Emmy would have been happy to skip dinner entirely.

"Here's my big girl." Sohan smiled and patted her shoulder.

"Hi, Dad."

Leona, who had been standing over the kitchen counter, took out a steaming pan from the oven. A delicious smell filled the air. She carefully and proudly placed it in the center of the table. It was a roasted chicken, perfectly browned and shiny with its own juices, steaming with potatoes, onions, and carrots baked around it.

"Honey, you have outdone yourself." That was what he said every time she cooked. Sohan's eyes widened. He leaned in and inhaled the savory smells.

"You haven't even tasted it," Leona protested, clearly pleased.

"I can taste it with my nose, darling. That's where it all starts." He carefully cut one of the legs off and put it on Leona's plate. Nora pushed hers forward, dancing her fork excitedly in the air. He placed the other leg on her plate. Emmy's stomach growled loudly; her face grew hot with humiliation.

"Which part would you like?" Leona asked. Sohan looked at his daughter.

"I'll do it myself," she answered. He quickly served himself and handed her the knife.

"Your birthday's coming up. Are we having a party?" He asked.

"No. It's okay. I don't want to make a fuss." Emmy placed some meat and vegetables on her plate.

"We didn't have one last year. We should have a party," Leona insisted.

"Can I have her presents, then?" Nora interjected.

"I think a party would be very nice," Sohan carefully added. "We'd love to meet your new friends."

"I don't have any friends," Emmy answered.

"But surely you've met some nice kids." Leona smiled. "Are there any cute boys?"

"No and no." She paused. "Didn't you tell me to not talk to strangers? When we moved here, you said specifically to keep quiet. Now you want me to bring people home?"

"We asked you to keep certain things to yourself. We didn't tell you to avoid making friends." Sohan paused. "But if you don't want a party, we can just have a nice meal at home as a family. How's that?"

"Fine." She chewed without looking up.

Leona sighed and studied Emmy's face. "Want to do a wishing spell? We can fetch a—"

"It's never worked before. I don't even know why you try."

"But you used to love doing it. Besides, it's not the spell that's not working. It could be many other things. Timing is always tricky, so it might still come one day when you're not even thinking about it. The most important thing is for you to really believe in it, you know."

"So it's my fault?" She gave her mother a sharp look.

"That's not what I mean. You know that."

"Please don't be rude to your mother." Sohan intervened. Before she could respond, he said, "You know how I know her magic's real?" He looked around at his daughters.

"How?" Nora nibbled on the chicken leg in her hand.

"Because she put a spell on me seventeen years ago, and I've not been free of it since." He spread his arms wide and brought both of his hands to his chest, clutching his heart. "It was the strongest love spell ever. And look, do you think I can live a day without your mother? Not in a million years."

Nora giggled, and Leona shook her head, laughing. "I did no such thing."

He continued, pointing at Emmy, "And you, my dear, are the product of that love. You remember that."

"Ew, Dad. Please." She frowned, trying not to smile.

{ 2 }

September 21

Emmy couldn't say that she felt strongly about butterflies one way or the other. She knew that there were many shapes and sizes, some more beautiful than others, not unlike people. But she remembered a certain spring day that year, when she'd stopped to notice a giant, brown butterfly seemingly asleep and hanging upside down on a bush. Just as she had stopped, a red cardinal had spotted it too. Before she'd even had a chance to realize what was about to happen, the bird had already snatched the wide-winged creature in its beak—bigger than the bird—and flown away. Watching the bird disappear into the sky, she'd felt a pang of sadness in her heart.

Click. Ms. Uchi pushed a button on the slide projector. For a second, the room went completely dark, until the next screen popped up: a tiny, white worm on the underside of a long, green leaf wiggled out of its dome-like shell. A lesson on butterfly lifecycles.

"In many species, it takes less than a week for the caterpillar to hatch from its egg," the teacher continued. "Once hatched, all it does is eat and grow and eat and grow."

Click. The next image showed a fully-grown caterpillar, with rows and rows of legs and a segmented yellow and black body, eating the green leaf as if it was a corn husk. "It's trying to build up enough resource for the next stage of life. Its weight can increase up to three-thousand times in less than two weeks."

The boy sitting behind Emmy kicked the foot of her chair. Low giggles spread across the classroom, and someone— Veronica Sanchez, she knew—whispered, "Just like Emmy." More giggles followed.

Emmy pretended she didn't hear, all the while sinking a tiny bit deeper into her chair and thanking the darkness of the room. She clenched the pen in her hand; every muscle in her body tightened.

"Quiet down." The teacher turned and paused for silence before continuing. "The caterpillar's skin resembles a wetsuit, which it cracks open and sheds whenever it needs to grow bigger, about four or five times. Its body is made up of two kinds of cells at this stage. One, called larval cells, forms the organs and other current structures of the caterpillar. The other, called imaginal cells, contains information for future components for becoming an adult butterfly."

Click. The next image showed the long body of the caterpillar attached at one end to a thin tree branch, hanging in the shape of a J.

Ms. Uchi continued, "At some point the caterpillar finally stops eating and prepares itself. It weaves a silk pad on an object, attaches its tail like Velcro, and hangs vertically. Here, it sheds its skin for the last time and forms what's called a chrysalis."

Click. A bright green and yellowish cocoon appeared on the screen.

"Historically, the chrysalis has been a symbol of mystery and the cycle of death and rebirth in many cultures. Scientifically, no one knows exactly what happens in that tiny, little box. At first, the body of the caterpillar literally digests itself to form a kind of a molecular soup, which will be later repurposed to form brand-new, adult butterfly parts, including entirely new eyes, wings, legs, and other systems."

"Ew," someone said from the back of the classroom. Kids giggled again, but Emmy was focused on the screen. What a strange concept. Technically, then, was it dead in there?

Click. A monarch butterfly—with antennae on its head, legs, and beautifully patterned orange and black wings—has just hatched.

Ms. Uchi said, "The butterfly sits on its cocoon for a while and finishes building its wings before it can fly away. But when it does, it's gone through three stages of life as entirely different organisms."

Click. The screen went bright and blank—the end.

"Lights on, please?" The lights came back on and curtains opened. The teacher walked up to the front of the class and looked at her students. "Hope you enjoyed that as much as I

did. Butterflies are truly beautiful and fascinating creatures."
She glanced the clock on the wall. "Since we have a few
minutes, how about a review?" She paused. "Veronica, can
you name a type of cells in a caterpillar?"

The girl looked up and grinned sarcastically. She tended to
be an equal opportunist when it came to bullying. "Um…live
cells?"

Everyone laughed.

"Sure they're alive, in a live caterpillar. How about we pay
a little more attention to class and a little less on others?" Ms.
Uchi looked at her coolly. "Even if one has no plans on going
to college."

The room laughed. This time, it was Veronica whose face
turned red as she sat a little smaller. Emmy loved her teacher
just then.

"Anybody else?" the teacher continued.

Emmy raised her hand.

"Emmy?"

"There are larval cells and imaginal cells."

The boy behind her kicked her chair again, and a wave of
low giggles spread, just like last time. She didn't react. She
wouldn't give them the satisfaction.

"Enough." The room quieted down. "That's right. Very
good. The larval and imaginal. They were the—"

The bell rang and signaled lunch. Everyone packed up
their things in a sudden gush of freedom and activity.

"Remember we have a test on this next week," Ms. Uchi
yelled after the departing kids.

Emmy took her time packing up her things and was the last one to leave the classroom. Everywhere in the halls, kids loudly whizzed by in couples and groups toward lunch. Serving lines were short by the time she entered the cafeteria. On the menu were noodles with brown gravy and meatballs. She loved noodles of any kind, so she piled them up high on her plate. She thought of her bulging thighs and felt guilty about the weight of her tray, but only for a second. On days like this, she felt especially ravenous. Besides, having a full stomach helped her feel warmer inside, more filled. She shrugged it off and moved on from the line, genuinely excited for her lunch.

The dining hall was a sea of picnic tables, already crowded with kids eating and goofing around. She paused to look around and saw Rose waving her arm in the left corner of the room. They'd started eating together a few weeks ago, when they had sat next to each other in art class and gotten to talking. She had saved her a seat at lunch ever since, and Emmy had gone along with it. The girl was nice enough, and it was better than eating alone.

Emmy had known who she was before but had never bothered to talk to her the same way she hadn't bothered with anybody. She knew that others made fun of Rose for being poor. She did tend to wear the same outfit on most days, but that was nothing to hold against her, as long as she kept clean and didn't stink.

It wasn't even that everyone else here was much better off; Bath was not a wealthy town. But it was just one of those things. Somewhere along the way everyone decided that it was easy to pick on Rose, and they'd been doing it for longer than they could remember how it all started in the first place.

Either way, Emmy didn't care. They fit well together, after all. Besides, she thought that she knew exactly how Rose felt sometimes, although her friend never said it out loud. The pang in her gut when Veronica walked by the table—it was like sport, how she occasionally whispered and giggled with her friends, pointing at Rose, for all the world to see. In such moments, Emmy almost felt Rose's embarrassment and fear in her own gut; these were feelings that she knew all too well.

"That smells good." Rose had her usual, a thin Bologna and white bread sandwich, in front of her.

Emmy plunked her tray down on the table and sat. "Want some?"

"Oh, maybe just a bite." Rose took the fork and swirled it around to form a ball of noodles and dropped it into her mouth. She smiled as she chewed, her cheeks full.

"Good?" Emmy chuckled. She dug in, herself.

"Mm," she mumbled and licked her lips. "That's good gravy."

"Have more if you want. You can get another fork." Emmy pushed her plate forward.

Rose shook her head and went back to her sandwich, which looked thinner and drier than before.

"My mom makes something like this, but better, with mushrooms and—" Emmy stopped.

"I hate mushrooms, but if you ever want to invite me over, that might be a different story."

Emmy thought for a moment. "Hey, how's Mr. Lois's drawing class? I might take it next semester."

"He's fine." Rose looked back at Emmy with a question on her face. She paused. "I wasn't inviting myself to your house, you know."

"No, it's not that. I'm sorry. My family's pretty weird. I try not to talk about them or bring anyone home. It's just my thing, you know?" Crap. She stopped and looked at her new friend, who looked perplexed but relieved.

"If you say so," she said, smiling.

{ 3 }

September 25

The little box on the wall screeched before the principal, Mr. McNally, came on. "Attention, everyone, attention. We have a special event today in the auditorium. All students and teachers of grades nine and up, please report to the auditorium. Again, grades nine and up, report to the auditorium now. Thank you."

Kids looked around for a moment, but soon everyone got up from their chairs and headed to the door, talking and goofing around. At the end of the hallway the popular kids congregated, waiting for still others, making the oncoming traffic move around them. They were always so visible—a good-looking group, the boys tall and handsome and the girls pretty and flirty—and looked happy. They had fun, all the time.

Emmy eyed Veronica Sanchez as she walked with the crowd toward the auditorium. Veronica was flipping her long, brown hair back and laughing, listening to a couple of boys who were, apparently, extremely funny. The scene made

Emmy sigh, although she didn't quite know why, until she felt a push on her back.

"Move, assholes."

She looked back, stunned. Behind her was Adrian, the school bully, whose older brother, everyone knew, went with the local thugs. Adrian acted like one at school too, despite his baby face and short stature, and didn't care who he threatened, kids or teachers. He seemed annoyed right then. His eye was on the group of kids, still standing in the corner and slowing down the traffic. She quietly stepped aside, as did a few others around her.

He pushed forward, screaming, "If you don't fucking move, I swear I'll punch someone."

Veronica and her friends looked over. She rolled her eyes and whispered something to the boy next to her. He laughed, but they finally moved.

Emmy spotted Rose when she entered the auditorium. She was seated in one of the last rows and had saved a seat next to her. "At least we're not in class. This is exciting. Are you going to sign up?"

"For what?"

Rose looked at her, with an 'Are you serious?' look on her face. "For the Rational Youth Brigade, silly. It was in the newsletter. What did you think this was all about?"

"You mean that political party? What about it?" She thought of the banner outside the town park, on that stormy day. Memories of her last days in Alexandria came back to her again.

"Sometimes it's like you live in a different world." Her friend shook her head. "It's only, like, the best thing that's ever happened for everyone."

"I know what the Party is. It's always on the newspapers and television and stuff."

"Where do I start?" She thought for a moment. "When my mom got pregnant with me, she lived in a different place, a few hours from here, another small town. She was young—seventeen, I think. It was a big deal there when she got pregnant, because she wasn't married and wouldn't say who the father was." She paused and frowned.

"My mom's family and the entire town were very religious, and the priest there was this horrible guy. They tried to force her to tell who the father was or give the baby—me—up for adoption. But she didn't want to do any of that, and they kicked her out. Like, her family asked her to leave. That's when she moved to Bath, and she hasn't been back since."

"That's harsh."

"Yeah. I'd never even heard from our grandparents until four years ago. That's when the Party broke up the Church of the New Republic. Remember that?"

Emmy nodded.

"Apparently that gave them a change of heart. They contacted my mom and wanted to see us. They'd known that mom had other kids because she'd been writing letters, except that before, they'd always thought we had to be punished for our sins." Rose chuckled bitterly. "So I love the Party and what it's doing," she said, sounding more upbeat. "Besides, the Party's been really good to us in other ways. They gave us a house this year, and we don't have to worry about paying rent anymore."

Her mom worked all the time, supporting the family as a waitress. If the Party had given them a house, that was a big deal.

"Haven't your parents said anything?" Rose asked.

"No." Emmy's parents hadn't mentioned the Rational Party much, except maybe in Alexandria before they moved. But that was all she remembered. She shrugged. "But I don't talk to them much."

The auditorium was now full. Kids were still talking and moving around; the stage was set with a big projection screen and a few chairs to the side. The lights went out for a moment and came back on, and the room quieted down.

From behind the right curtain, Mr. McNally stepped out, sporting his usual brown, wool jacket. Slightly balding but handsome, with a friendly demeanor, he was usually liked by everyone. He walked to the front center of the stage, looking excited, followed by a tall man in a suit. The man had a grin and moved slowly, confidently, as though he owned the spotlight. Mr. McNally took the microphone.

"Hello, everyone." He paused and smiled, looking around at the audience. "I'm sure you're all wondering who our surprise guest speaker is today. How many heard of the Rational Party?"

Nearly everyone raised their hands.

"Good. As you know, the Rational Party has become the greatest party in the history of the New Republic, opening the next chapter in our nation's future. I know you're young and couldn't care less about politics, but this is different. It's a movement, and we're going to need everyone in this. So, here to help you get on board is Mr. Sweeney Stryker, who's just arrived in Bath. Now please welcome him with a round of applause."

The sound of clapping and whistling filled the auditorium. Mr. McNally handed the microphone to Mr. Stryker, who waved in all directions. He was taller than six feet and skinny. His blue eyes sparkled against his pale skin and hair. His white teeth also sparkled, and there was elegance in the way he moved his long limbs.

"Thank you." He waited for the room to quiet down. "I've been in this beautiful town for about a week now, and the welcome has just been tremendous." His voice projected certain genteelness, like a professor. "As Mr. McNally just said, we're living in a truly exciting time in history. The Rational Party is working very hard to make important things happen for you, and we need your help."

He slowly walked to the edge of the stage. "Now most of you have heard of the Party. Who can tell me something about it?"

A handful of hands went up.

"You," he pointed to one closest to him.

A skinny, pale boy wearing a baggy, faded white T-shirt stood up. A teacher standing in the aisle handed him a microphone. He seemed nervous. "The Rational Party wants to help everyone to have a good life. My family recently moved to a new house that the Party assigned us."

Mr. Stryker nodded. "That's right. The Rational Party passed the New Citizens Rights Act three years ago, giving our people the basics for a good life. To us, that includes decent housing and sufficient food. Imagine if everyone had that, what the world would look like. Right?" He paused. "Think of the possibilities."

He thanked the boy, who sat down.

"What else?" He walked a few steps in a different direction. Other kids raised their hands, and he picked another. "You, in the brown sweater."

Mary, a girl from Emmy's art class, stood up. "The Party wants everyone to live from logic and reason. That means only believing in things tested and proven to be true. Like, in science and nothing else." She handed the microphone back to the teacher and sat down.

"Good," he said, smiling and pointing his finger at Mary. "You guys are all smart here. Makes my job much easier."

Everyone laughed.

"That was the first thing that the Party focused on, a fundamental part of what makes the Party what it is. We believed that it was time that those outdated institutions of myth and religion closed their doors."

He paused, as if to make sure everyone was listening to every word.

"It wasn't easy at first, but that's what it takes for a true revolution. If we're to move forward to the next stage of human evolution, we can't have these so-called leaders preaching lies."

Mr. Stryker slowly walked to the other end of the stage, making eye contact with some of the kids in their seats.

"Now, I'll admit that there was a place for blind faith in earlier stages of our civilization. But we're long past that now." The room listened silently. "This is something we have to recognize in order to unburden ourselves from the baggage that comes with blind faith and dogma. Do you know what dogma is?"

No one raised their hand.

"Dogma is a doctrine that is proclaimed as unquestionably true by a group of people." He paused again. "Now think about that for a minute. If there's no room for logical questioning, that also means, unequivocally, that there is no room for progress. And to not progress is just insanity, to me."

He chuckled as he walked from one end of the stage to the other.

"Only by relying on what is verifiably, undeniably, and unfailingly true, can we create the utopian society that we truly deserve. That excludes some of what human kind has relied upon in the past, such as faith, religion, and the concept of 'god.'"

Mr. Stryker made a goofy face and air quotes with his free hand. Everyone laughed.

"See, you think it's funny, and I'm laughing with you. But the truth is, many aspects of this faith-based living were detrimental to our society. Countless groups of people suffered because of it. Now that is nothing to laugh about."

The room fell silent.

"It's good to remember these things, lest we forget. It's extremely easy to forget the things we don't want to remember. Let me show you some examples of what I mean. After you see this, you'll be glad that you live in this world and not that."

His finger pointed to the screen.

The room slowly darkened, and a light came on the projection screen, starting a video. An opening picture of the Rational Party symbol, a box with letters RP in it, came on briefly, before the images started.

The first screen read, "In the Name of God." An image followed: barefooted, black men stood in rows on gravel, with heavy chains dangling between their necks and ankles. They wore tattered clothes and had big scars across their skinny bodies. A few white men in thick suits stood nearby, guarding the chained men. One had a gun on his side and a whip in his hand.

The room gasped in horror. It was footage of the slave trade. More visceral images followed, some in black and white, some with color. Some were silent, and some had sounds. An image showed an olive-skinned woman buried half way in the ground and being stoned to death, blood all over her clothes, by an angry mob. Apparently she was accused of committing adultery.

In another image, wounded men, women, and children, covered in a thick layer of white dust and bleeding from different parts of their bodies, fled buildings that had been bombed and were on fire. The images continued, but Emmy closed her eyes.

She'd never seen so many disturbing images, displayed one after the other. A tight ball formed in her throat, and she felt queasy. She kept her eyes closed but still heard everything, including the sound of people shouting, "God hates fags!"

Eventually the room became silent, and she opened her eyes. The lights came back on. Some were crying; everyone sat in their chairs, unable to move. The men onstage didn't move right away, giving their audience a moment to reflect. Slowly Mr. Stryker came forward to speak again, this time in a lower and somber voice.

"I know that was disturbing. Sadly, these are not made-up. Do you get that every single one of these acts was committed in the name of god? In the names of different gods but all the same. Emotional, physical, and systemic violence on others because of dogma. Now, who can see the insanity in that? I certainly do."

He raised his hand, slowly and deliberately, and the entire room followed.

"And this is why the Rational Party is committed to building a society without dogma, and why it's important that we have you on board. Now, can you step up to the challenge?"

The room roared in applause; many stood up from their seats.

Mr. Stryker looked around the room. "This is great. Now, to get to the action part of all this, you can do a couple of things. One, you can sign up to be a member of the Rational Student Brigade. There'll be a desk outside where you can sign up."

He pointed to the door.

"Second, and this is just as important, when you go home tonight, talk with your parents about what you just saw and ask them to go take the Oath to Reason and Rational Living, if they haven't already. It's easy, it's quick, and guess what? There might be some real big benefits for your family. Who can say no to that, right?"

The room roared again.

"Listen," Mr. Stryker continued, "You have been super. I can't remember the last place where I saw such intelligence and heart. I'm excited to be here in Bath, and I hope to see you all at the Brigade activities. Thank you so much for allowing me to be here, and see each of you soon."

He waved and exited the door, Mr. McNally in tow.

The audience took their time getting up from their chairs, still feeling the heavy emotions from the last hour.

"Wow." Rose stretched her arms. She sniffled and wiped her nose. "You signing up?"

"Yeah. Let's go," Emmy answered.

{ 4 }

"What's that?" Nora frowned, getting up from the steps where she'd been sitting.

Emmy had run a little late coming to pick her up, after waiting in a long line to sign up for the Rational Party Student Brigade. Her sister didn't seem upset at waiting, though. After all, there were plenty of other older siblings running late that day.

But she'd just noticed the new pin, sparkling brightly on Emmy's coat chest. Silver-colored and about the size of a thumb nail, the pin had the Rational Party symbol in its center: the letters RP enclosed in a square box, in red. Nora stared at it for a moment and looked around, noticing the change on all of the older kids' chests.

Of course Nora had no idea what this was all about; the presentation was only for the upper classes. So Emmy had to explain to her, with more patience and gentleness than she'd had with her sister in a very long time, all about the Party— that it was leading everyone into the next phase of human history, in which no religion and nothing other than our simple logic was necessary. In this new world, she told her, people wouldn't be able to hate others in the name of "g-o-d."

That she'd just joined the Student Brigade, herself, which Nora would be able to join in a few years too.

"But what about magic?" she asked solemnly.

"Magic doesn't exist. It's only in story books. For kids." Emmy lightly petted her sister's head.

"Mom does it."

She chuckled. "Oh, you silly. Don't you know that they never worked? It's not real."

"Liar. You're wrong!" Nora pushed her hand away with angry eyes. Without waiting for a response she ran home, leaving Emmy behind.

She shrugged and continued her walk. Nora was obviously too young to understand. The rest of her way home, she actually felt content, a feeling she'd almost forgotten.

* * *

The family sat around the dining table for supper. As was every inch of their home, their kitchen was cozy and clean. Everything was in its place, surfaces always clean. But the place was full of colors too. In one corner of the ceiling hung red and white paper figurines, marked with symbols that Emmy never understood, and fragrant dried herbs. On one side of the wall stood a tall cabinet, lined with small vials of blue, green, and brown, storing Leona's potions and elixirs. Presently a few logs burned brightly in the fireplace, giving the entire room a warm glow and a hint of woody smoke in the air.

Nora talked incessantly as she ate her plate of wild rice, squash, and lemon-caper fish. Their parents mostly listened, occasionally contributing surprise or agreement. As usual, Emmy ignored their conversation and daydreamed. That was, between catching Nora making hateful faces from across the table whenever their eyes met. She ignored that too, choosing to simply stare back at her, without expression, until she had to take another bite. She just wanted to finish eating and go back to her room.

"Emmy joined a new club today," Nora blurted out. Suddenly everyone's eyes were on Emmy, who glared at her sister.

"A club? Which one?" Sohan asked.

"Nothing special." She caught a piece of squash with her fork.

"Not what you said before." Nora sneered.

"Tell us. I'm glad you found something of interest." Leona smiled.

"It's nothing. I joined a...the Student Brigade for the Rational Party. Well, everyone joined, really." Silence followed. When Emmy looked up, both her parents had stopped eating and looked at her, with stunned faces. "What?"

Sohan cleared his throat and exchanged a glance with his wife. Slowly, he said, "Well, I don't know how to tell you this, but we don't want you to be a part of that."

"What do you mean?" She frowned.

"I don't expect you to understand right now, but there are things about the Party that your mom and I strongly disagree

41

with. It wouldn't be good for us. We don't want to worry you, but we'd like you to stay away." He looked serious.

"Why?"

"They're not what they seem. Just don't do it. Please trust us."

"I don't see how you can disagree with anything they stand for." Emmy put down the fork.

"We need you to listen," Leona said softly. "There are some bad people at the Party, and it's not for people like us. Okay? I'm glad that you feel inspired by something, but there are things you don't understand. Trust us, please."

"I think I'm old enough to decide for myself."

"I know. You're old enough for a lot of things. And we're very proud of you. But—"

"Really? It sure doesn't feel like it." Emmy looked away and sighed. She felt angry inside, like she was about to burst. "I can't do anything right by you."

"It's not that at all, sweetie," Sohan pleaded. "We just know some things that you don't, and we're still responsible for you. It's for your own good and ours."

"Whatever." She didn't want to argue anymore and didn't understand why they had to be so difficult all the time. Why couldn't she have normal parents so maybe she could feel normal sometimes?

"Is that a yes?" Sohan asked.

"Sure. Whatever," she answered, getting up. "May I be excused?"

He nodded with a sigh. She stormed upstairs to her room, making sure that they could hear her anger with every step she took. As far as she was concerned, it was none of their business what she did on her own. They just wouldn't find out.

{ 5 }

September 29

Emmy sat next to Rose in one of the chairs lined up outside the auditorium. It was initiation day for the Student Brigade, which meant that every single member got to meet with Mr. Stryker privately. It took about ten minutes for each meeting, the way each kid entered and came out of the auditorium. Everyone combined, though, this was taking all day. Emmy didn't know what to expect from the meeting. The kids coming out seemed happy and excited, not that she'd ever ask them. Rose looked happy, as she had been recently, and was very chatty about anything that came to mind.

The hallway was loud with everyone's voices, some of them bored and restless and others excited. Rumors spread about a couple of kids who didn't show up to school today. Alice Spears was a god-lover, some kids whispered, and so was her entire rotten family. They were probably holed up somewhere praying together, they speculated, which made some laugh and others shudder. It was also entirely possible that Alice just didn't feel well today. But no one would confirm that she'd signed up for the Brigade, either, and this had become an issue.

A few admitted that their parents were not keen on the idea of them signing up. Not that their parents were god-lovers or superstitious, they claimed, but because the parents thought they were too young to be actively involved in politics. But they'd just have to get used to it, they said.

Emmy didn't know what her parents were. She'd never seen them go to church or any other place of worship, even when such places existed. They never talked about god.

Of course her mom was different. She claimed to commune with spirits and predict the future. But who knew if she ever really talked to dead people? Or if she was just mildly insane? She had also seen her mom's predictions not come true—like the time when she said Grandma Ethel would live but she still passed anyway. The way Emmy saw it, if it didn't work all the time then it never really worked.

But none of this mattered any more. Since they'd moved to Bath, Leona hadn't done any of her magic things or talked about them much. She certainly didn't talk to anyone outside their family about it, like she used to. Why they'd oppose the Party was a mystery that Emmy didn't care to solve.

Emmy was finally next in line when Liz came out of the auditorium. Her face was full of smiles. Something had made her laugh in there, and she still was. Emmy's stomach tightened a little as Rose whispered, "Good luck," in her ear.

She got up from her chair and slowly entered the auditorium, breathless about having to introduce herself to total strangers. She relaxed more when she saw the school counselor, Ms. Alms, sitting behind a long desk in the middle of the stage, along with Mr. Stryker and another man. Mr. Stryker wore a dark, tailored suit and looked comfortable in his chair. He was handsome, and something about him made her extra nervous. The other man was new. He was chubby and bald, wearing a short-sleeved, white, button-down shirt and dark-framed glasses.

An empty chair waited for her in front of their desk. The rest of the auditorium was dark, empty, and huge. It gave her a strange feeling. She fidgeted over to the chair, sat, and looked up, trying to smile.

"Good afternoon, Emmy," Mrs. Alms greeted her with a smile. "This is Mr. Stryker and Mr. Brooks from the Rational Party. You met Mr. Stryker a few days ago."

"Yes. Hello." She nodded to each man. "Nice to meet you."

They smiled and nodded back.

"Pleasure to meet you, Emmy," Mr. Stryker started. He looked down at a file in front of him. "Miss Emmy Sukar..." He looked up. "Welcome to the Student Brigade. I see here that you're a very smart young lady. Your grades are among the top of your class."

"Yes. Thank you." She looked down at her hands, playing with her fingers.

"The Party really believes in nurturing talent. I hope you'll consider taking a leadership position in the upcoming election," Mr. Stryker said. Mr. Brooks observed.

"Oh, no, thank you." She chuckled. "No one'll vote for me."

"Don't sell yourself short," he said warmly. "Although if you really don't feel up to it, we can find you other roles."

"He's right," Ms. Alms intervened. "You have potential."

"Thank you," she responded mechanically. Did Ms. Alms know her? How were they drawing these conclusions?

"Well, think about it. We still have time to decide." Mr. Stryker leaned forward on his elbows on the table. "Today we have a couple of formalities to go over with you. First, you're invited to take the Oath to be formally inducted as a Brigade member. This, of course, is a requirement. Do you consent?"

"Sure." Emmy smiled.

He nodded to Mr. Brooks, and the latter took over.

"Raise your right hand with me, like this." He raised his hand, open and palm facing out, next to his shoulder. She followed, and he continued. "Now repeat with me." He paused a breath before starting, "I swear my life this Oath, that I shall from this day on denounce all lies of the unseen and false beliefs. I commit today to Reason alone, as a responsible student of the New Republic, and pledge my life unconditionally to fight for this Truth."

Emmy followed along with these words, not really registering what they meant. She tried to process them in her head, but the syllables were moving faster than her brain could at the moment.

"Do you swear?" he asked.

"I do." But Emmy was in a daze.

"Good." Mr. Brooks lowered his hand. The other two gave a short applause; Mrs. Alms looked proudly at her student.

"Now I'd like to ask you a few questions." He looked down at the file in front of him and grabbed a pen. "Have you ever worshipped a so-called higher being in a church, mosque, temple, synagogue, or a similar place?"

"No." It was true; she'd never been in any of these places.

Mr. Brooks checked off a box on the paper in front of him. "Has any member of your family?"

"Not that I know of."

After he wrote something on the paper, he continued, "Do you have any objects of worship inside your house?"

"Like what?"

"Like an altar for religious worship, for a so-called higher being."

"No, I guess not." These were easy questions.

"Have you ever prayed in your life to a so-called higher being?"

"When I was a baby." She laughed, and the others smiled in sympathy.

Mr. Brooks checked off a box on the paper without looking up. "Have you seen any members of your family doing so?"

Now this was a little tricky. She tried to think. What does she say about her mom? She swallowed. "Can you define praying?"

All three behind the desk looked back at her. Mr. Stryker answered. "As in the same definition of the word 'to pray,' with which you answered your previous question."

"Then yes." Emmy looked down at her hands, feeling a sudden awkward tension in the room.

Mr. Brooks asked, "When was the last time you saw this person pray, and who was it in your family?"

She started to answer their questions with first thoughts that came to her mind. There was no time to make anything up, and there was no reason to lie—except for the strange and curious feeling inside that felt like a thorn under her skin. The words came like a flood, and she talked until her throat started to hurt, soon forgetting the world outside of that room.

When she finally stepped out of the auditorium, Rose grabbed her arm impatiently. "What took you so long? You were in there an hour." Without waiting for an answer, she went in for her turn.

{ 6 }

October 1

The warm smell of bread baking woke Emmy up from sleep. It was the Saturday morning before her sixteenth birthday. She opened her eyes slowly, her mouth already salivating. The rest of her family seemed already up, their footsteps loud and busy on the old, wooden floors. The sun shined brightly through her bedroom window, with a clear, blue sky dotted with plush white clouds. Over the horizon, the undulating lines of mountaintops were still lush green, but her nose tingled from the cool air.

She heard someone running upstairs and toward her bedroom. The door swung open, and Nora burst in and crashed on top of her in bed.

"Get off of me." She tried to push her off, annoyed to realize that her sister was heavier and stronger than before.

"Wake up, you lazy bum. Do you even know what time it is?"

The clock showed ten.

"So what?" Emmy pushed Nora, who fell off the bed with a thump but came right back again, this time sitting on her face. She flailed her arms underneath.

"Everyone's waiting for you downstairs." Nora wrestled with her, her breath heavy with physical strain. "Mom made a birthday cake. Come down."

Emmy squeezed her face out for air. "Fine, I'm coming. But you get out, now."

Nora ran out the door, giggling and apparently happy with herself, and slammed the door. Emmy's head throbbed. What an annoying monkey.

She took her time getting out of bed and resented that they were all waiting for her downstairs, just expecting her to do whatever they wanted, whenever they wanted. Didn't she tell them that she didn't want to do anything for her birthday?

They were all sitting around the table chatting when she finally made it downstairs in her pajamas. It was warm in the kitchen from the fire. Her dad seemed relaxed and happy, sipping his coffee. Leona was at the stove, finishing up breakfast. She turned when she heard Emmy come in.

"Good morning, birthday girl." Leona smiled, embracing her daughter, who didn't reciprocate, only pausing for her mom to be done, and went to her chair to sit.

"Good morning, sleepy head." Sohan leaned over to kiss her on her cheek.

"It's not my birthday."

"Yes, but I thought we'd celebrate early," Leona said. "I made your favorite cake, red velvet. We also have eggs, bacon, fresh bread, and some fruit too. Want some tea?"

"No, thanks. Not hungry right now."

"Oh, come on," Sohan said, "I know you're hungry, and we waited for you." He poured a cup of hot water and handed it to her. "Now tell us, how does it feel to be sixteen?"

"Not at all different." Emmy sighed and placed a tea bag in her cup. She still could use more sleep; their active energy rattled and annoyed her.

"I can't believe it," Sohan said, almost to himself. He smiled, taking in the sight of his daughter. "It feels like yesterday that I saw you walk for the first time. Amazing how time flies."

Leona placed fried eggs, bacon, fresh bread, and a bowl of fruit salad—raspberries, blueberries, and sliced apples from her garden—on the table. A cake waited on the counter too, plainly decorated but shiny with white, cream cheese frosting.

Suddenly Emmy felt a sharp pull of hunger, and her mouth salivated. Her mother finally sat down and served herself with little bit of everything. Everyone ate. The bread was still warm, crusty on the outside and soft and sweet with nuts and dried fruit baked inside. The bacon was thick, savory, and salty, and crunched in her mouth. She felt better.

Her parents recounted stories from when she was a baby. This, they did every year. She'd had a weak heart when she was born, and they didn't know if she'd survive until she was almost two. It was Grandma Ethel who often took care of her when she was sick, trying to give the young couple some relief, and doted on her until she passed away.

Leona's eyes moistened as she talked about her mother, one hand placed over her chest. At least she felt her presence all around them, always looking out for them, she said.

Emmy missed her grandmother too but kept her mouth shut. She hated it when her mother said things like that. If grandma's spirit was really around, shouldn't the rest of them feel her too? It was simply nonsense.

When they were almost finished eating, Leona got up and grabbed something from the other room.

"Hope you like it," she said, a little shyly, and put a small paper box in front of her daughter. Emmy put down her fork and opened it slowly. Last year her mother had gotten clothes for her that she didn't like and never wore.

Inside the box, a small, silver locket shined. The oval locket was about the size of her thumb and had an intricate design engraved on top. On the back, it said, "To Emmy with Love, on her Sixteenth Birthday." There was even a small picture of the family inside, along with a tiny, purple sprig of dried lavender flower. For such a small thing, its strong fragrance spread around Emmy and tickled her nose.

"How did you get that in there?" She was impressed.

"Do you like it?" Leona's face was full of anticipation.

"It's pretty."

That was enough for her mother, who had been recently unused to positive reactions from her. Her face beamed with pleasure.

"I'm glad. I wanted you to have something like this. I had a bad dream a couple of weeks ago. You were all alone in this forest, and I couldn't get to you. Don't ask me why." She laughed and shook her head. "Just being an anxious mother. But I didn't know if you'd like it. I'm relieved."

"Thanks." Emmy smiled.

"What about me?" Nora protested, pouting.

"We'll get you one on your birthday." Sohan smiled and petted her head.

"A bigger one, okay? Bigger and shiner," Nora said. Emmy rolled her eyes.

"Here, let me help you put it on." He took the necklace from her, stood behind her, and put it around her neck.

Leona watched from across the table, beaming with happiness. "Do you know what lavender means?"

"Nope."

"Love and devotion. The fragrance also helps you relax and connect with your heart. It's my favorite from the garden."

"Cool."

"Well, who's ready for cake?" her mother asked, looking as happy as she had seen her in a long time.

There were candles, a birthday song, and a birthday wish that Emmy only pretended to make. She was old enough to know that birthday wishes were nothing more than just a silly ritual for children. But she went along with it; it was easier and made them happy.

The cake was delicious, and she was feeling content when Leona wanted to give her a reading. They'd done this before on birthdays, for fun, to see how the next year of their lives would turn out—even though it hadn't made sense to Emmy for years.

Everyone's excitement and cheer—it'd been a long time since they'd felt like the old, happy family they used to be, like they were in Alexandria—persuaded her to consent. Her mom grabbed a candle and lit it on the table between them, the routine was familiar. As Sohan and Nora watched silently from their seats, smirking and whispering to each other, the mother and daughter held hands across the table. They closed their eyes.

"Okay. Take a deep breath in," Leona said, "and out." Emmy followed. "One more time... All right. Let's look at you, in that place where I see the possibilities unfolding."

The room fell perfectly quiet, except for the crackling fire. Emmy followed as best as she could but became bored. She opened her eyes just a sliver to peek. The candle in front of her flickered, its flame dancing around as if in a breeze. Sohan and Nora both quietly watched Leona, who looked like she was in a trance, like she was somewhere else. Her fair skin glowed warmly in the candle light; a couple of strands of her hair over the side of her face sparkled in red. She was stunning.

The year before, the reading had merely been that she would do well in school and make a new friend. Her mother has also said that Emmy worried too much and would benefit by trying new social settings and hobbies, which would help her feel lighter.

Emmy didn't take any of this seriously. Anyone could say those things about a girl her age, it seemed to her.

Leona suddenly let out a big sigh.

"You can open your eyes," she says softly, slowly letting go of her hands.

"So?" Sohan asked first.

"I'm not sure what I saw, really. It was fuzzy." She blew out the candle. Everyone looked at her tense face.

"What is it?" Emmy asked.

"Well." She hesitated. "You were walking in the woods, alone, like in the dream I had. I couldn't tell where, but it didn't feel close to home. You looked sad, and I'm not sure you knew where you were going or what you were looking for. But you kept on walking and your heart was heavy." Leona's eyes filled with tears as she covered her mouth with her hand.

"You're kidding, right?" Emmy asked. Never before did her mother say anything like this from these readings.

"No, sweetie, I'm not. It's what I saw."

"Well, that sounds pretty bad."

"I'm not sure what to make of it. I'm probably wrong. I'm worried about you nowadays, so it's probably just be that. I'm sorry, honey." She smiled apologetically and reached across the table to rub Emmy's hand. "You know how it can get all mixed up when I care very much about something, right? It's just that."

"Maybe it means that Emmy could appreciate her family more," Sohan teased. "She wouldn't want to be living alone in the woods, now, would she? Maybe they're telling her to listen to her parents." He winked at his daughter.

"Come on, Dad." She frowned.

"I'm just saying that if I was to interpret that scene, that this could be a possibility." He laughed. "But you're right. I'm just teasing. Don't worry; it's probably nothing. You cheated, anyway. I saw you looking around the room during the reading. True?"

Emmy nodded. "True."

"Do it again," Nora said.

"No, let's not," Emmy said, getting up from her chair.

{ 7 }

October 3

Dark clouds filled the sky, and the wind rattled Emmy's old, wood-framed window. But she felt content; it was her birthday. She was glad that she could expect a normal, quiet day, having already had a family celebration over the weekend. The Student Brigade elections were after school, and she looked forward to it as the first function of the group. She was curious, most of all, who was running and who'd win. She got ready quickly and in her good mood, put on the silver necklace from her mom before running downstairs.

"Happy birthday." Leona smiled from the kitchen table with a cup of coffee and a notebook in front of her. "The necklace looks great on you."

"Thanks." Emmy meant it. She liked the necklace. She grabbed an apple from the fruit bowl on the kitchen counter. "I'm going over to someone's house to do homework after school today, okay?"

"Oh? Who?" Leona looked curious. This was the first time that she was spending time with someone outside school since they moved to Bath.

"A girl named Rose. She's my partner on a project. I'm not sure when we'll get done, so I may not be home for dinner."

Her mom believed her without a second thought. It was another reason why Emmy didn't believe she could really see things.

"Do you need any money?" Without waiting for an answer, she reached into her wallet and handed some money to her daughter. "For snacks and such."

"That's a lot." Emmy looked at how much was in her hand.

Leona hugged her and kissed her cheek. "Hope you have a good birthday."

"Let's go, Nora," Emmy yelled, turning toward the door. Nora hurriedly fumbled down the steps and into the kitchen, struggling to put on her backpack.

"Coming." She kissed Leona good-bye.

* * *

Rain started after lunch, and Emmy mostly stared out the window through math and literature, watching the raindrops fall. Time passed at a snail's pace, and she had a tough time concentrating all day. She didn't know why she felt this way, but her mood had shifted from good to bad several times already. This was highly unusual, even for her.

It was still raining hard when classes finally ended. She went by Nora's locker to make sure that she had an umbrella for her walk home alone. Sure enough, her sister had forgotten to bring hers and was very happy to see her. She loudly showed off in front of her mates, making a small scene and embracing her for her thoughtfulness. Emmy rolled her eyes but obliged, and sent Nora on her way.

Only then did she take her Rational Party pin out of her pocket and put it on. She headed to the auditorium for the Brigade elections, where everyone had their shiny pin on their chests as they filled the seats.

Up for popular vote were the leadership positions, and several candidates—two boys and two girls—were about to give their campaign speeches. The candidate with the most number of votes would become the president, and the runner-up would become vice president. After those positions were decided, then the two appointed other students—most likely their friends—to the other positions.

Normally no one took these things seriously. But given that most of the older student body were now Brigade members and the active involvement by real Rational Party representatives, this was turning out to be a big deal.

On the right corner of the stage, two ladies from the Party sat and observed the proceedings. Sweeney Stryker was nowhere to be found, but the ladies were making an impression on their own. One wore a tailored navy skirt-suit and had short, blond pixie hair that framed her blue eyes and milky skin tone. The other, in a light gray pant-suit, had olive skin and long, straight, brown hair that came down to her back, with big, brown eyes that were alert and soft at the same time. Each had a shiny RP pin on. They were at once looking out of place in Bath's school auditorium, making the older boys gape and grin awkwardly.

Mr. McNally hosted the proceedings. One by one, each candidate took the podium and talked about how they wanted to lead the Student Brigade. The first speaker talked about going door-to-door to explain Party ideals—to embrace logic and denounce myth—and benefits of taking the Oath to Reason and Rational Living and to get family sign-ups.

Another talked about organizing a concert at the downtown park where information and materials would be freely distributed and Party registration would also take place. But the stories became repetitive after a while, and it was soon clear that the votes would go to the most popular candidate running.

This was deflating for Emmy, who always preferred the underdog. She hated to think that things were usually, if not always, predetermined by qualities like good looks, social confidence, or who your friends were. So her vote for the underdog was actually an active defiance against the status quo, even if it made no difference in the end.

She voted for Dwayne, the tall and skinny, dark-skinned boy who seemed nervous to talk about himself and whom she'd known to be genuinely a nice guy. She knew there was little to no chance he'd win, but she did what she usually did.

By the time all votes were counted, it was Veronica Sanchez—the mean, popular girl who played the heroine in all school plays and the one that Emmy least wanted to win—who won. She was now the president of the Student Brigade. Jon Randolph, a football player who always had a clean haircut and liked to skip classes, was the vice president. Veronica and Jon ran in the same circles; she vaguely remembered that they'd dated at one point in the past.

Rose and Emmy watched with bitterness as Veronica and Jon celebrated with their friends. Veronica's tall boyfriend, another football player, tossed her up in the air, sending a round of applause and laughter from those around.

"I hope he drops her," Emmy whispered. Rose laughed, but Veronica came down safely into his arms.

Emmy left the auditorium feeling confused and disappointed. Was the Student Brigade going to be just like anything else—a waste of time and energy? She couldn't bear the thought of having to watch Veronica call the shots; she'd rather lick the toilets clean, if she had to. Rose certainly had not lost her enthusiasm after what had happened. Election results were no fault of the Party, she agreed, but still. She'd just have to wait and see.

Outside, the rain had stopped when she started to walk home. Dark clouds had long gone, and the sun set low over the horizon, covering everything near in brilliant hues of orange and red. Clouds just above the mountains hung like soft cotton balls, reflecting beautiful waves of yellow, orange, purple, and blue.

Emmy was officially sixteen years old this day. It was strange that she didn't feel any different from the day before, considering the meaning people assigned to one's turning of their sixteenth year.

But certain was the fact that, with every passing moment, she was getting closer to leaving this town and closer to something else. She just wanted to be different—feel different.

She had to. There had to be a way.

It was dark by the time she reached home. The sun was setting earlier and earlier now, noticeable by the day, with the changing season. She didn't notice that her house was completely dark until she entered through the kitchen door, as she usually did. Only silence filled the space between the walls, the fireplace notably empty and cold. This was strange. Even the lamp in the front room, which Leona usually kept lit when the house was empty, was off.

"Hello?" Emmy turned on the kitchen light. She walked through the hallway, into the study and the living room, peering into every space. "Mom? Nora?"

"Hello, I'm home." She went upstairs to the bedrooms, only to find them also empty.

She came back downstairs and turned on all the lights. Nothing seemed out of place. Sohan's work jacket—always smeared with plant debris—hung over the chair in the front entryway, which meant that he'd come home after work. But the car wasn't there.

This had never happened before, but she decided not to worry. They obviously all went out somewhere. She'd told her mom that she wouldn't be home for dinner, after all. It was actually convenient not to have to explain what she did after school.

Emmy went to the kitchen and made herself a turkey sandwich. With a glass of water and an apple, she ate in silence and enjoyed every bite. She hadn't realized how hungry she was. When she finished, she brought the dirty dishes to the sink and brushed crumbs off the table in one big swoop of her forearm. She turned off all the lights except for the front room and headed upstairs to get ready for bed.

It was a mystery where they could be. Her parents used to go out from time to time, to dinner or the theater, back in Alexandria. They'd had friends who'd come over frequently too. She remembered those days, when they'd come home late, tired but happy, her mom especially chatty. Nora had often fallen asleep before they returned.

She looked at the clock as she got into bed. It was fifteen past ten. She lay snuggled under a soft cotton quilt and listened to the silence in the house. The wind rattled her window, and dogs barked in the distance.

{ 8 }

October 4

Emmy woke up to the warmth of the sun tickling her face. She'd overslept, she immediately realized, and the clock confirmed eight-thirty. Why hadn't anyone woken her up?

Her memory slowly coming back, she lifted her head and listened for a moment, searching for the usual sounds of morning in her house: her mom clacking in the kitchen downstairs and Nora running around between her bedroom and the bathroom. Her dad would be long gone to work by this time.

Instead, all that existed was silence. Moments went by— but nothing.

She jumped out of bed and walked through the hallways, checking every room. They were all empty. This didn't make any sense. She went downstairs for any sign of life, but everything was exactly as she'd left it the night before. Even the dirty dishes in the sink. She picked up the phone, not exactly knowing what to do with it, and hung up when she heard the dial tone. She felt the chill of morning on her skin.

Emmy sat by the kitchen table in her pajamas and tried to think. Maybe something had happened. Or maybe they were still coming back from somewhere and just forgot to call, although that didn't sound like them. Or maybe they were doing this on purpose. Whatever it was they were up to, she was determined to give them hell when they got back.

Then she had a thought. She quickly ran upstairs and got ready. She grabbed her book bag and ran out of the house, walking as fast as she could to her dad's workplace, McLeary Gardens, in the center of town.

It was a quick walk. The muddy ground from the previous day's rain was mucking up her shoes, but she didn't stop. Her head was filled with endless scenarios of what could have happened, although none of them made any sense. She just knew that something was wrong—that weird feeling she sometimes got, like a constant drumming in her gut or a knocking on the door that wouldn't stop—and she was alone.

A small bell chimed above her head as she pushed the door open to McLeary Gardens. She'd never been here before. It was an old office. A couple of old posters with sun-faded colors hung on the walls; the desks and chairs gave the feel of an old movie. But it was clean and bright, with a big, glass front facing the street.

An old lady with short, white hair looked up from her desk. She wore a green sweatshirt with a picture of a howling wolf. "May I help you?"

Emmy stepped forward with a nervous smile. "Hi, I'm Emmy Sukar, Sohan's daughter."

"Well, hello." The lady smiled wide as she leaned back in her chair to take a good look. "So you're Emmy. I've heard so much about you. How nice to finally meet you. Are you here for your dad?"

"Yes. Is he here?" Her eyes searched around the place.

"No. I thought you came to tell us where he was. He hasn't shown up today and hasn't called either. He's usually not like this so we were getting worried. Is everything all right?"

"Um… I was hoping he was here." Her body loosened in disappointment.

"What do you mean? You don't know where he is?"

"Well, I haven't seen him since yesterday, and no one's home…" How could she explain this to a stranger?

"What about your mom?" She frowned.

"No one's home." Emmy shook her head and faked a difficult smile. "They probably went somewhere. I'm sure they'll be back soon. But if, if you hear from my dad, would you please tell him that I was here?"

"Of course, honey. I sure hope everything's okay. Let me know if anything turns up, all right, sweetie?"

"I will. Thank you."

Emmy left the office with the chime jingling above her head once again. Outside, she stood still for a minute. This was all wrong. Something must have happened, but what? She didn't know what to do.

But noticing the lady inside McLeary Gardens, still watching her through the window, Emmy slowly walked toward school. Maybe, hopefully, they'd be home when she got home that evening and explain that there was a big screw-up but everything was okay. She played with her fingers and cracked her knuckles as she mindlessly walked toward school, all the while aware of the heavy feeling inside. She was nervous and anxious but didn't know what else to do.

She was walking by the park near Main Street when a black car pulled up next to her. Distracted, she didn't even notice until the back window lowered, and a voice called out her name.

Sweeney Stryker sat there alone, smiling. He said hello, and she was glad to see a familiar face. She was surprised and flattered that he recognized her there, in the middle of the street, and stopped to say hello. He offered her a ride to school, as he was on his way there, and she accepted.

She'd barely closed the door behind he when he asked, "So, how was your first night alone?"

Emmy squinted. *What did he just say?* "Excuse me?"

"Your night alone?" he gently repeated.

"How would you know that?" She frowned as her heart began to beat fast.

"It's my job to know these things." He smiled, looking out the window. "But you were okay? Not too startled, I hope?"

"I was fine... I *am* fine. But what do you know about it?" This man knew something, and she had a feeling she wasn't going to like what she was about to hear. She nervously pressed on the leather seat under her.

He looked at her, still smiling, and slowly said, "Your family's fine. It's the least I could do." He studied her face and cleared his throat. "Of course you have a right to know what happened. They were paid a visit yesterday by the Party. We determined that they required some reprograming for Rational thinking. They reported for transport immediately."

"Transport? Where? What does that mean?" Emmy didn't understand. Her brain felt to be firing in all directions, and it was difficult to think clearly.

"It means that they're going away for a while, but they'll be back as soon as they see the light, so to speak."

"But where? What about Nora?" Her stomach knotted up inside.

"Your sister went with them since she's a minor." He smiled, all confidence and leisure. "She's a feisty little girl, your sister. She'll be reeducated too. They have excellent classes for the young. I can vouch for that because I was one of the architects of the program."

She felt nauseous and rubbed her ears to clear the buzzing in them. "But for how long?"

"That's up to them, but as long as it takes for them to take the Oath." He looked at her again. "I only tell you this because I know you to be a good member of the Brigade and the Party. You took the Oath, didn't you?"

"Yes, I did. But—"

"There is no 'but.' They're in good hands. I'm doing you a favor telling you this. I realize that you're still a young lady and didn't want you to be scared." He looked at her curiously, as if she tested his patience.

"I'm not scared." Her voice was sharp. She hated him then. Her breath quickened, and something balled up in her throat. She looked down at her hands, clenching the seat under her. Every inch of her body was tight and tense, and her nausea— she wanted to throw up.

"Good. I knew you'd be. I want you to let me know if you need anything. Money, food, whatever. Actually, why don't you take some right now?" He took out his wallet, handed her a wad of cash, and patted her arm as if to say, *We're on the same team.* "When you run out, go to the Party office at the town hall. We take good care of our own."

Emmy nodded, her eyes on the cash in her hand. The car stopped in front of school and they all got out. She barely thanked Stryker and ran inside, heading straight to the bathroom where she burst into a stall, dropped her bag on the floor, and puked into the toilet.

What had she done?

Part II.

{ 9 }

The smell of vomit stayed with her when she arrived halfway through class. No one asked any questions. The teacher, Mrs. Reed, only nodded when Emmy came in through the door and watched her sit as she carried on with the lesson. Rose gave her a brief look, as if to say, *What happened to you?*

Emmy tried to act as normal as possible. But her head spun, and her stomach squirmed. She wasn't sure what she was feeling, except the numbness in her chest. She pretended to pay attention to class, but her mind raced.

What did it all mean? The Party had taken them away to an unknown place. What was going to happen to them? Why wouldn't Stryker tell her where they were? Why were they taken and not her?

This was all wrong. They weren't religious. There was nothing about reeducation in Stryker's presentation. Maybe they'd be back before she knew it. If they were smart, they'd take the Oath right away, if only to come home. But her dad never did anything he didn't want to, and her mom!

Nausea returned full-force, and she put her head down on the desk and closed her eyes, trying to breath. When the bell finally rang for next class, she slowly got up to leave.

Rose waited for her by the door. "Are you all right? You don't look well."

Emmy looked away, feeling her friend's eyes on her. "I don't know. My family's gone. They're gone." It felt strange to hear herself say it—more real, somehow, but also still hard to believe. Tears formed in her eyes.

"What do you mean?" She looked confused.

"They've gone to be…reeducated. The Party took them."

Her eyes widened, and her face soon froze in a blank look. "Well, I'm sure that they deserved to go then. Don't you think so? The Party… They wouldn't have sent them if they didn't have to."

"Right. Probably. I just hope they're okay."

"Of course they're okay. What do you think the Party would do to them?" Rose sneered. "Seriously. It's like you live in your own little world. I'm sure they'll be back soon, once they show that they're with the Party. You could be thankful that the Party is providing them with this opportunity, don't you think?"

"Right. Well, I have to go. I feel sick right now. Talk to you later?"

She nodded. "I understand the shock. See, aren't you glad that you joined the Brigade? You just never know who you can trust. Apparently not even your own family."

Rose shook her head as Emmy quickly walked toward the exit.

Someone had to be able to tell her something.

She ran until she reached the town hall building near the center of town and stopped to catch her breath.

The day was cool and sunny, like a real fall morning. The leaves had changed colors, with bigger spots of yellow and red, all along the tree-lined street. It was strange that it should be beautiful, as if there was nothing wrong in the world. Everything felt unreal, like one of those vivid nightmares that sometimes woke her up sweating and screaming.

Inside town hall, a young lady sat behind a long desk busily reading something and didn't look up when Emmy entered. Up on the wall behind her was a directory of offices in the building.

Emmy quickly scanned the lines and found the Rational Party office in room 217. She walked past the long desk without making a sound. The woman only briefly looked up before sinking her head down again.

Room 217 was a small office, with only a few desks in it. A wooden door on one wall was closed and had the name Sweeney Stryker on a plaque. A young man with blond hair and glasses sat behind one desk; next to him was an older lady in a bright, blue jacket, peering over the papers in front of her.

The blond man looked up first. "May I help you?"

Emmy slowly walked forwarded to his desk. "Hi. I have some questions about my family, and I was hoping you could help me."

"Have a seat." His eyes pointed to the empty chair across his desk. He waited until she sat. "What can I help you with?"

"My family's gone since yesterday. Mr. Stryker, I know him from the Student Brigade at school, he said that they were sent for reeducation. But he didn't tell me where they went or when they'd come back. Could you tell me anything more?"

"Unfortunately, no," he answered, without a change in tone or emotion. "I can't. If that's what Mr. Stryker said, that's really all we could tell you. Besides, we don't deal directly with reeducation efforts. The Ministry of Mental Hygiene office deals with all that. They're the ones you should talk to."

So that's why Mr. Stryker couldn't tell her more. She felt a faint surge of hope. "Where do I find them?"

The lady in the blue jacket looked up from her book and stared at Emmy curiously without saying anything.

"Room 301," the man answered. "Upstairs and to your right."

"Thank you." Emmy smiled. "Thank you!"

She got up, carefully slid the chair back to where it was, and walked out of the office. She went up to the third floor, just as instructed, and found the Office of the Ministry of

Mental Hygiene. Through the open door she saw a bigger office than the last one, with about a dozen desks and a number of private offices along the walls. More people were on the phone, walking around, typing, and filing. She took a deep breath and stepped inside.

The man at the front desk looked up and when he heard her question, directed her to an older woman sitting near the window in one corner of the room. Emmy maneuvered through the busy office, feeling a bit out of place from her environment.

The woman was on the phone, looking out the window with her back to the room. Emmy quietly waited for her to finish. She was wearing a dark gray skirt suit; her light brown hair was short and wavy. She looked to be in her sixties, maybe, and on the heavy side. Her desk was very organized and clean, with color-coordinated file folders lined up on one side and tall metal cabinets filling the wall behind her desk. A folder with a red stamp of the word, *Confidential*, on the cover sat on her desk.

She turned around, put the phone down, and glanced at Emmy. "May I help you?"

Emmy stepped forward. "Hi. They told me to come to you about a question. My family's been sent for Rational Party reeducation, and I'd like to find out more information. Can you help me?"

"Possibly." The woman, who had a strong jaw and bright blue eyes, let out a short sigh. "What's your name?"

"Emmy Sukar. My dad's name is Sohan Sukar, and my mom's Leona Piper. My sister's gone too, and her name's Nora. She's only ten. They've been gone since yesterday."

The woman pulled one of the color-coordinated folders from the side of her desk and flipped through the pages. She looked through a list.

"Sukar, Sukar, Sukar." She reached the end of her file and flipped it back to its beginning, again saying to herself, "How about Piper?"

After a couple of minutes searching, she finally looked up.

"I don't see those names. These are the names of all Bath residents who've been recommended for reeducation this month." She tapped on the folder. Emmy looked at her helplessly, her anxiety getting bigger in the pit of her stomach. There had to be someone who knows. "We usually give the families prior notice, like a final chance to take the Oath to avoid the trip. Most don't end up going to the camp. Did your family get that?"

"No, I don't think so."

"Well, I'm sorry, but I don't know what to tell you. I don't see those names on my list. Maybe there's been a mistake. You sure they were sent for reeducation?" She leaned forward with elbows on her desk.

"I'm sure. Could you check one more time? It's Sukar with a K."

"That's what I looked for," the woman said, unmoving. "It's not here. Who told you that they were sent for reeducation?"

"Mr. Stryker, the Party representative, told me."

"Mr. Stryker." She pondered. "Well, then you should go ask him because we don't have anything here, young lady. It doesn't look like it went through us. That happens sometimes." She shrugged, closed the folder, and placed it back neatly among the others. "I'm sorry I can't help you any more. But good luck."

The lady picked up the phone, dialed a number, and turned to face the window.

{ 10 }

October 8

C urled up in a fetal position in her bed, Emmy couldn't tell if the darkness helped or made her pounding headache worse. Faint moonlight came through the window and filled her room with shadows. It had been four days since her family disappeared. She hadn't stepped outside or left her bed, except for the occasional trips to the bathroom and the kitchen, although she couldn't get herself to eat much of anything. Instead, she'd mostly been sleeping.

She still felt deathly exhausted. It was the voices in her head. They were constant and deafening, often running in a repetitive loop that trapped her for long stretches of time.

Is this what you wanted? How will you live with yourself now?

Maybe they'll be back soon.

But something's not right. Why the secrecy?

Don't be so dramatic. Everything will be okay. They'll be back.

You have to go back to school. Maybe if you're more active in the Student Brigade, you'll be able to find them.

The Student Brigade? You really are a fool. It's all your fault, you know. If you'd only listened.

They're never coming back. They're probably already dead.

No. The Party wouldn't do that.

Do you really believe in the Party? What about a world without magic? What will happen to them if they don't take the Oath? Do you even know?

What does it matter, what I believe? I'm stupid and useless. This is my fault. If only I'd kept my mouth shut... So stupid—ugly too.

Hours passed like this. Only sleep gave her a break, and sometimes, she rested peacefully like everything was okay. When she awoke from such sleep, though, she startled to hear the voices come back, one by one, as if someone was slowly turning the volume up on a radio. The dread spread over her body like thick molasses, forming a tight, heavy ball in her gut and anchoring her firmly onto bed, unable to move.

Other times, which was more often the case, sleep wasn't peaceful. There was a recurring dream in which she was in the house, watching her family being pushed and shoved away by burly men without faces. The men each had a Rational Party pin on their coats, just like the one she had, and beat her dad with thick, black batons as he crawled on the floor.

She tried to yell and scream, but no could see or hear her. She tried to pull the men away, but it was as if her hands lacked physical form and couldn't make contact. There was nothing she could do as she watched her mom trying to cover her dad with her body, only to be shoved aside, and Nora, crying and pleading the men to stop. She was a ghost in the room, crying out of pain and helplessness. Then, Nora would look straight at her with furious eyes and let out a long, high-pitched scream. That's when she woke up, still crying and unable to breathe, taking too long to realize that it was just a dream.

{ 11 }

October 13

The sound of footsteps woke Emmy up with alarm. A flash of hope passed through her as she slowly regained consciousness that maybe it was Nora, back and rucking about.

When she opened her eyes, however, it was Sweeney Stryker standing in the middle of her room, his tall stature seemingly filling half the space and hovering over her. She shook her head hard, trying to wake up if it was another dream. But there he stood, looking around the room.

"How did you get in?" She frowned as she sat up, covering herself with the blanket. She felt weak, tired, and heavy all over, but his presence was piercing.

"Finally awake," he said in a friendly tone, as if nothing about this picture was out of place. "Pardon my intrusion. But we were getting worried. You've been absent from school for more than a week."

"Has it?" She slouched and pressed each of her temples, now throbbing, with her fingers. "But why are you here, and how did you get in? I locked all the doors."

"Your dad gave me a set of keys." He grinned and patted his pant pocket, making it jingle. He pulled her desk chair next to the bed and sat down, leaning back and crossing his legs. "I have to say, I'm a little disappointed. I'd hoped you'd handle this better. I thought you were an adult and a committed member of the Party."

"I am," she said, still pressing on her temples. *Why the hell do you care?* She looked down at her lap.

He continued, "But your behavior leads me to question my judgment about you. I mean look at this place. It's filthy."

"I had food poisoning. You know, cooking for myself and all." Her voice was sarcastic.

"Is that so?" He paused. "So I'm mistaken that you came by the Party office and the Ministry of Mental Hygiene office to make inquiries?"

"That's only natural." She lifted her head slightly. "Besides, it's not like they had any information. Apparently nobody knows what happened to my family except you."

"I told you that you wouldn't get any more information. Was I unclear?"

"Really? I thought you said you didn't know."

He uncrossed his legs and leaned forward, placing his elbows on his knees and looking closely at her face. "Well, let me make this even clearer to you then. Your family has reported for reeducation, where they'll stay until they decide they're ready to be citizens of our new world. That's all you need to know, and that's all you *will* know. Your job is to continue with your life as a young member of the Party, unless you think you'd rather join your family at the camp."

"Don't you worry," Emmy replied quickly. "Like I said, I've had food poisoning. I'll come to school as soon as I feel better, and you'll be the first to know, I'm sure."

"Good. And yes, I *would* be the first to know." He eased his posture and leaned back in the chair.

"Can I have our keys back?" Emmy asked.

"I'll give them back when I feel certain that you've got it under control. Show up to school and the Brigade, and if you're acting responsible by then, I'll give it to you." He paused to look at her and sighed. "You don't realize how I've gone out of my way to spare you. I hope it wasn't a mistake."

She bit her lip and looked away, so angry she wanted to slap herself. He got up from the chair and walked toward the bedroom door, nodding before he left. She sat completely still until the sound of his footsteps disappeared. Outside the window, a car waited for him along with a couple of men in gray uniforms who looked exactly like the ones from her dream.

* * *

The next morning, Emmy got out of bed long before the sun came up. All night she'd gone back and forth between sleep and being awake, a couple of hours at a time. She felt tired and wanted to stay in bed but also anxious to go back to school, now that it was clear that Stryker was watching her every move. She didn't know what this all meant. A part of her wanted him to send her to reeducation too, but she was afraid. He scared her, and so did the Party. She was just a young girl, now practically an orphan. What else could she do?

She had plenty of time before school so she moved slowly, went to the bathroom, and washed. It felt nice to be clean, on one hand; on the other hand, she went through the motions without any thought or feelings. She looked in the mirror above the sink and brushed her wet hair. Her eyes were sunken in and cheeks hollow, her face looking much narrower than she last remembered. The person in the mirror looked like a leftover version of herself, dejected and empty.

Emmy went back to her room and put on a pair of wool stockings—which now hung slightly lose on her skin—a skirt, and a clean shirt. She also put on a sweater, and as she pulled her long, straight black hair from under it, she noticed the silver locket on her desk. She touched it with one finger, feeling its shape and thought of the Saturday morning before her birthday, when Nora had come to wake her up, and the delicious, warm breakfast they shared.

Was this what her mom had seen in her vision? Why didn't she see anything about herself being taken away?

She picked up the locket and opened it. Inside, a tiny picture of her family stared back at her. It was an old picture, when Emmy was about Nora's age in Alexandria. She looked happy, standing next to Nora about half of her size and holding her hand. Leona and Sohan looked happy too, with his arm around her.

Emmy smelled lavender, the sweet, flowery fragrance, just like she had that morning. She missed them all so much that it hurt in her gut, as if someone punched her there, and tears came.

But she took a deep breath and shook it off. She deserved this, after all. For all the tantrums she'd thrown, for ignoring her parents, and... She didn't want to remember. For everything she'd done, the choices she made, the only thing she was left with was herself.

Her miserable, ugly, stupid self. That was fair.

She closed the locket, wore it around her neck, and slipped it under her sweater.

When the time came, she showed up to school as if nothing had happened. She first headed to the teachers' office and told the secretary that she'd been sick with food poisoning. The secretary didn't question further or ask for a doctor's note; she just smiled, nodded, and acted awkward around her.

Something was off. It was possible that they were in on it with Stryker, after all. So what did they know that she didn't?

Emmy left the office and entered the hallways, headed to her locker. She felt everyone's eyes on her. As she moved forward, the area around her got quiet, only to fill with whispers after she'd walked on. When she looked back, the kids quickly looked away and pretended to go on with their business. She spotted Rose behind a crowd, but her friend avoided making eye contact. But she didn't have the energy to care. Instead she went on to her locker and then to her first class, all the while feeling like an animal at a zoo.

She went through her first three classes without interacting with anyone, not even with the teachers. No one talked to her or looked at her straight. Just before lunch, though, a group of boys—the troublemakers who always traveled in packs and got into fights—surrounded her at her locker.

The air behind her changed, and things got even quieter. Even though she really didn't want to, she turned to look. Adrian, the baddest and meanest of them all, stood right behind her so that when she turned, his face was right up against hers. She could smell his breath.

"Hey," he said.

"What are you doing?" Her heart thumped against her ribs, and she wanted to crawl into a hole.

"Heard your mom was a witch."

"No." Emmy took a step back for some space and looked at him straight in his face. She didn't know what to do. Her breath quickened.

"Really? That's not what I heard. I heard that your family members were all loonies and your mom was a witch. Isn't that why they're gone now?"

Her heart beat like a war drum. No words came out of her mouth. Her hands were sweaty, and she tried to think of something to say. When she looked away to the crowd she saw Rose, watching like everyone else was, with a blank expression on her face. It was her, who'd told. No one else knew.

"Hey." Adrian raised his voice. "I'm talking to you, dummy. Your mom's a witch, right?"

"I said, no," Emmy yelled back louder.

"Liar." He smirked and pushed her shoulder, and she fell back hard against the locker, making a loud noise.

Her shoulder blades were on fire. She gathered herself slowly, got up, and looked at him in the eye. "My mom's not a witch."

"Oh, yeah? Then why's she gone? And why are you still here?" He was about to push her again when a voice disrupted him.

"Break it up." Mr. Blake, the science teacher whose classroom was right across from her locker, stood in his door. He was tall, with a physical presence that towered over the boys.

"We're just having a conversation here," Adrian said with a smirk.

"Break it up anyway," Mr. Blake said, "Everyone. Go on to your next class, lunch, or wherever. Move—now."

The crowd slowly moved, including Adrian and his friends. They laughed and snickered as they walked on, as if all of this was a joke.

Emmy stood there a moment and tried to catch her breath, but Mr. Blake motioned her to move too. She grabbed her book bag and walked quickly to the bathroom. Other girls scurried away and left as they saw her enter. She went into one of the stalls, locked the door, and leaned on to a wall.

Tears streamed down her face, and she couldn't stop. What was she supposed to do? What *could* she do?

She knew one thing: she had to leave.

{ 12 }

October 14

The next morning, Emmy went into her parent's bedroom and searched for her mom's address book. She'd thought through this all last night. The only people she could think of to ask for help were Jimmy and Cynthia Marten, her parents' closest friends in Alexandria.

She found what she was looking for in one of the drawers and sat on her parents' bed near the phone, flipping through the pages. She dialed the number. It rang once, twice, as she waited, but on the third beat, a message came on to indicate a wrong number. Emmy dialed one more time, this time making sure to press the right numbers, but the same message came on. She hung up the phone and sat there, thinking. She couldn't give up now; she had nowhere else to turn. Besides, even if she couldn't find them in Alexandria, she surely couldn't stay in Bath.

Back in her room, she emptied her book bag and filled it with some clothes, clean underwear, and toiletries. She found all the money she could find—the wad of cash that Stryker had given her, her saved allowance, and the family emergency cash from the kitchen jar—and put it in a deep pocket of her bag. She did a final check in her head: did she have everything she needed? After a moment of hesitation she sat down to write.

Dear Mom & Dad,

I'm leaving Bath. I don't have many places to go, but if you're back and reading this, it won't be hard to figure out where I went. I hope they still live in their old house.

I'm really sorry that I didn't listen to you before, and for everything else. I miss you all so much and hope you're okay. I won't write much since they might find this letter. I hope that one day we'll meet again. I promise I'll be better then. I love and miss you so much.

Emmy

P.S. Please give Nora a hug for me.

Emmy folded the letter and placed it under Sohan's pillow. She wasn't sure it would reach them, but hoped it would. She made their bed as nicely as she could before leaving the room and closed the door behind her. Then starting from upstairs, she went around the house locking every window and door and turning off the lights.

When she was done, she gave a final look around and put on her coat. The Rational Party pin still shined on her chest; she'd forgotten about it completely. She snatched it out and walked over to the trash can, but put it in her pocket instead.

She grabbed her bag and walked out through the kitchen door, locking it behind her.

The sun was coming up outside. Leona's garden looked saggy and sad in the faint morning light; weeds had grown over many of her herbs and flowers. It'd been less than two weeks, but it was as if they all knew she was gone. No birds, bees, or butterflies fluttered by.

Emmy didn't look back as she walked away. The air was sharp and cold, prickling the skin of her face. She fixed the collar of her coat and looked up. The mountains still loomed all around, tall and heavy, and unsympathetic. It was about time that she left this place.

* * *

The nine o'clock train to Alexandria was scheduled to reach its destination by two. She chose a seat by the window and tossed her bag in the compartment above her. The car was mostly empty except for a short, round man in a suit a few rows away, who was fast asleep and falling onto the seat next to him, snoring. She covered her face and body with her coat and sank deep into the chair, closing her eyes and letting out a deep sigh. It felt safer and warmer like that—cocooned and hidden.

The train moved in that rhythmic vibration of heavy machinery, and Bath was slowly, finally, getting away from her.

Everything still felt unreal. That her family was gone, since her sixteenth birthday of all days, felt like a lie. Sometimes it was difficult to tell what was real and what was not. On her way to the station, she'd admired the color of the mountains—now really in their fall colors in full-force—in the quiet of early morning. She'd gotten lost in her thoughts and had completely forgotten where she was going and why. When she'd come to it, she'd hated herself a little more—this time for forgetting, even just for a minute.

Emmy wished she had her mother's magic now. There was a time when she longed for such things, a long time ago, even though she never admitted it to anyone else. If she did, things might have been easier for her. She was supposed to have magic, after all, as the firstborn daughter in her mom's lineage.

The legend was that, at least for six generations, which was just how far back the memory went, every firstborn child of Leona's family was a girl who grew up to be a powerful seer, an intuitive, a psychic, a fortuneteller. Each of them had a unique gift, an ability to communicate with the unseen and know the unknowable. A few others in the family had also been known to have such powers, but never as strong as in the firstborn girls.

Emmy was a firstborn daughter, just like Leona was. But she'd never seen any evidence of the extraordinary. She'd never felt powerful or special in her life.

She'd believed it when she was a child that she was destined for magic. She'd wished and longed for it to come.

Every year on her birthday her anticipation grew and climaxed into a sad disappointment, as she realized that nothing was different, once again. She'd stopped wishing and waiting when she'd turned thirteen, the same year that her grandmother died. She'd already known that she was an anomaly in the family. She'd certainly looked it—and still did. Or maybe it was all a big joke that she'd never understood.

Emmy didn't know if Grandma Ethel and her mom could really see things that others couldn't. When she was very young, the family had many visitors who sat with either of the women—sometimes both—and asked all kinds of questions. She used to hide under the table and listen to everything that went on above, fascinated by the stories of strangers. Some cried and some sighed, but in the end, all left thanking Leona and Ethel for their help. Many of them came back multiple times, so that Emmy became intimately familiar with their secrets, worries, and joys.

But the people stopped coming when she was about ten, and she didn't know why. She'd suspected that it was because they were found, somehow, like they were exposed and no one wanted their help any more. That was just a story in her head, of course, and not necessarily true. She'd just never questioned it before.

{ 13 }

Jimmy and Cynthia Martens' house stood empty when she arrived, and even though Emmy wasn't sure that the they still lived there, she sat on their front stoop in the cold and waited. It was already evening; she hoped someone would come home at any minute.

The hours passed by until darkness descended and the street lights went on. She was exhausted and hungry but determined to stay and find out. She moved her legs and rubbed her arms to keep warm, all the while thinking what she'd do if the house no longer belonged to her parents' friends.

When they finally arrived, they were shocked to find her at their doorstep, not even recognizing who she was at first. Not only did she look like a runaway, shivering and squatting on their steps with a bag next to her in the dark, she also looked significantly older, thinner, and more dejected than they remembered. It had been a few years, and she'd changed much more than they had.

They understood immediately that something was terribly wrong and quietly let her into their home. Just as Jimmy locked the door behind him and closed the curtains to the street, Emmy blurted out, "They're gone," and fell onto the living room couch.

Feeling the cold all around the young girl, Cynthia covered her with a blanket and hurried into the kitchen, looking for something warm. By the time she returned, however, Emmy had already fallen deeply asleep.

Unbeknownst to the Martens, it had been a long time since she'd been able to sleep without waking up for more than a couple of hours. She slept more soundly that night, perhaps because of exhaustion from travel or perhaps from knowing that she could under the Martens' roof.

When Emmy finally woke up, the house was still dark and quiet, and it took a minute for her to remember where she was. Careful not to wake the Martens, she went to the kitchen to get a glass of water and sat by the table. Her entire body felt limp and formless, like a deflated balloon, but the blanket was soft around her shoulders. Their home was cozy and not very different from what she remembered. On one side of the kitchen stood tall, glass cabinets showing colorful china and cookbooks; on the other side, little green plants adorned the windowsill over the sink.

Soon Cynthia came down—neither of the couple could sleep deeply that night, worried about their friends—and Jimmy soon followed, both still in their pajamas. She fixed tea and coffee, brought Emmy some bread, and carefully asked her to tell them what happened.

They both listened in silence as she told them about the Rational Party coming to Bath, how everyone disappeared on her birthday, which according to Sweeney Stryker, meant that they'd been sent to a reeducation camp. She told them no one at town hall could give her any information, about the harassment at school, and why she had come to them.

Cynthia sat next to her and rubbed her back. Her voice trembled, and her eyes were wet as she said, "I had no idea. I talked to your mother just a few weeks ago, and she didn't say anything. But how could she have known?"

Jimmy let out a big sigh. "I was afraid this would happen. I told your father that he couldn't hide forever. I told him it'd be better to just take the Oath and get it over with. But he and your mom… I guess it was just a matter of time." He shook his head and then slammed his fist on the table. "Bastards!"

"What do you mean, you told them? When?" Emmy asked.

"You don't know? That's why you all moved to Bath, to get away from this nonsense. That's why he quit his job here. For years he tried to help the opposition, but nothing worked, other than getting himself squarely on the Party's radar. And your mom, you know, thought that it would get worse, which she was right about. So they decided to move to Bath and take you all into hiding." He paused. "They thought that if they lived quietly there and didn't raise any eyebrows, they might be okay."

"But they never said anything." She frowned and shook her head in confusion. "Why didn't they say something?" Tears started, and a tight ball formed in her throat. "I was angry with them for moving us there. I was angry…for everything. But I didn't know."

She put her head down on the table and cried. If only they'd told her… She might have understood and listened.

Cynthia hugged her and whispered in her ear, "It's okay. It's not your fault. They wanted to protect you and Nora from all this ugliness. None of this is your fault."

"But it is." If only this woman knew what she'd done when she joined the Brigade…

"You know, your mom has always been proud of you," Cynthia continued, gently brushing Emmy's hair.

"But I was really mean to her. And now I may never see her again." Her tears didn't stop, and she wanted to disappear into darkness. "This is all my fault."

"Oh, no, sweetie, don't think like that. It does no one any good. Your mom understands, you know? She knew you were sad about not having the gift yet, that you were heartbroken about it."

Emmy looked up. "She did?"

"Yes. She also knows that you're a teenager, and it's a sensitive period in life. She just doesn't like to see you suffer." She smiled and gently brushed hair out of Emmy's eyes. "You know what else? She's confident you'll get your gift when you were ready, at the right time."

"I don't know about that." Emmy wiped her tears.

Jimmy, who'd been thinking quietly, asked, "Why didn't they take you?"

His question came at her like a slap in the face. She looked down at the cup in her hands. "I don't know. I wish they took me too."

"Right. How would you know? But don't think that way." He petted her head briefly. "I'm glad you came. We'll try to find any information we can and see what all this means. Let's not think the worst. For all we know, they can come home tomorrow, right?"

Cynthia squeezed her shoulder. "You poor thing. You've lost some weight since I saw you. Is it all from the past few weeks? We're going to have to fatten you up. "

{ 14 }

October 18

The Ministry of Mental Hygiene office in Alexandria was huge, with its stately six-story building on top of a hill surrounded by big, tree-lined lawn. The sun shined brightly, and the air was crisp; the lawn was well-groomed and still green, the trees yellow and red. A stream of people went busily up and down the long pathway to the main building. Emmy panted as she walked quickly up the long, wide steps.

She hoped to find some information about her family here. This was the national headquarters of the Ministry, and she figured it was worth a try. Cynthia and Jimmy were looking for information on their own through their contacts because they didn't believe official channels would lead to anything. But Emmy wanted to start doing something if only to occupy her time.

The long pathway led to an open, paved area surrounding the building. Several security guards with long rifles stood watch; there were a couple on top of the building too. At the building entrance was a security check where guards looked through the contents of everyone's bags, making her a little nervous. Why did they need such heavy security here? She got in the long line formed by the checkpoint.

"Can you believe that nuns still exist? I mean, in this day and age. Just what is she doing?" a young woman in front of Emmy said.

"I think she's praying. Praying! Oh, they better do something," her friend said, excitedly looking over the other's shoulder.

"I wonder how long she's been there." The first woman shook her head, her eyes steadily watching something.

Emmy followed her gaze and saw a tiny, old woman kneeling on the edge of the pavement, with her hands clasped together by her chest. Her eyes were closed shut, but her head looked up to the sky, although the expression on her face wasn't clear. She wore a long, black garment with a white collar that surrounded her face, neck, and shoulders. A black cloth covered her head and fell behind her back. She was absolutely still.

She had never seen a nun before in person. She knew of them, of course. But the church had been dismantled years ago, and she hadn't seen a proper nun, ever.

The nun was a curious sight in front of the ministry. Some, like the two women in front of Emmy, watched the old lady like a spectacle; others simply ignored her and went about their way. The guards watched her closely, although they weren't doing anything to move or stop her, giving a strange tension in the air.

The nun fascinated and scared her. What *was* she doing? Emmy hoped she'd go away, for her own sake. Nothing was worth the danger, and for what? She could be taken to a reeducation camp too, in her old age, or maybe they'd punish her some other way.

One way or another, she had that strange feeling again— like a drumming in her gut or a constant knocking on the door that she couldn't open. It was telling her that something was wrong, but she wasn't sure what. She kept her eyes on the nun while she waited in line, occasionally glancing at the guards.

The line moved slowly. When the women in front of Emmy finally reached checkpoint, they chatted with the guard.

"How long has she been there?" the young woman with brown hair asked.

"Since this morning, kneeling like that all day," the guard said, methodically opening the woman's purse and looking through its contents.

"Wow, that's a long time. She hasn't moved once?"

"Nope, not even once." He closed the woman's purse, gave it back to her, and looked her up and down. He motioned her to pass and her friend to stepped forward.

"I guess she doesn't need to go to the bathroom?" the brown-haired woman said to her friend, and they both laughed.

"Why aren't you doing anything about it?" the friend asked the guard as he looked through her purse.

"We're just following orders, ma'am. We apologize for any inconvenience this may cause," he said, a hint of annoyance in his voice. The women left it at that and moved on to their destination.

What were they supposed to do? Looking back one last time, Emmy hoped that the nun would be gone by the time she left the building. Either way, the situation made her feel even more uneasy and nervous.

She passed the security check quickly and found the information desk in the middle of the big, busy room with high ceilings. Everything echoed in there, and every movement she made seemed to make a loud noise.

"Excuse me," she said to the lady behind the desk. "Where would I go to find out information about people who went to reeducation camps?" She had practiced this many times in her head, but it came out all muddled when she actually said it, as she was nervous and distracted.

The woman looked back sharply through her glasses. "That depends. What are you looking for?"

"I'm looking for some people. Where they went and anything else I can find." Emmy fidgeted.

"We don't give that information out to anyone, young lady." She grabbed a pamphlet from behind the desk and handed it to someone behind Emmy. "Are you immediate family?"

"No, it's for a friend. A young girl and her parents, I'm looking for them." It felt warm and stuffy in there all of a sudden.

"Sorry, that information is confidential unless you're immediate family. And if you were immediate family, there is paperwork you'd need to fill out." She motioned the next person in line to come forward and joked, "But your friend might be back soon if she decides to be a good citizen."

Emmy stepped aside and considered what to do—go back and ask more questions? Tell her that she was, after all, immediate family?

But she didn't want to raise suspicion either. She certainly didn't think it was a good idea to fill out any paperwork, announcing her whereabouts in writing. It was another dead end.

A loud chorus echoed through the entire building: "I swear my life this Oath, that I shall from this day on denounce all lies of the unseen and false beliefs. I commit today to Reason alone, as a responsible citizen of the New Republic, and pledge my life unconditionally to fight for this Truth."

The voices came from a room at the end of the hall, behind the double doors that were slightly open. It was the same oath that she had taken when she'd joined the Student Brigade, the oath that her mother and father were likely refusing to take. A shiver went down her back, and she was desperately out of breath; she'd begun to sweat all over. She wanted to run as far away as possible.

Emmy almost ran out of the building and, glad for the cooler, fresh air, fell onto the closest empty bench. She closed her eyes and took deep breaths, listening to the harsh, strained sound of her lungs. It took a couple of minutes for her to feel better and orient herself. When she finally opened her eyes, the sun looked brighter than before and the sky, higher. She sighed in relief.

The nun was still there, kneeling at the far end of the pavement, in direct view from where Emmy sat. Her body moved just a little, as if she swayed in the wind. Her face looked serene, still toward the sky.

Emmy felt mesmerized by the nun's presence. But she also wanted to yell at her, to tell her to get off her high horse and get out of here.

It was shame she felt. She couldn't even ask honest questions about her family's whereabouts, afraid she too would be sent away, yet this old woman had gotten into her full gear this morning and came to protest before all these people and soldiers—in front of the Ministry of Mental Hygiene building.

Where did she get her courage? Where was Emmy's? She felt hateful; she also wanted to grab the nun and run away. This simply couldn't end well.

As if on cue, a loud voice came on through the speakers, snapping her away from her thoughts. "Attention, all security personnel. Attention."

Guards on ground level suddenly stood up straight and held their rifles uniformly across their chests.

"The lady in black," the voice continued. "We order you to clear out now. I repeat: you have to leave now. What you're doing amounts to an act of terrorism, and you will be prosecuted accordingly unless you leave now. This is your last chance. You have two minutes, or you will be prosecuted."

Everyone stopped in their tracks. All attention was on the nun, who gave no indication that she'd even heard the announcement. Most everyone stood still, waiting for her to move, except for those who had just exited the building and didn't know what was happening.

A full minute passed, and Emmy held her breath. She clenched one hand and nervously tapped her fingers with the other. She didn't want to watch the nun get hurt, but she couldn't bring herself to get up from the bench. In her mind, she was already up and grabbing the nun to walk away from the scene. But with every second that passed, her body tensed more, and she felt heavy and frozen to her seat.

Still the nun did not move. No one did. Only the flutter and chirping of birds filled the space, with cars honking in the far distance.

"Thirty seconds," the voice from the speakers erupted again.

Emmy finally stood up from her chair and looked around. Up on the roof, a man had a rifle pointed at the nun. She looked between him and the nun, her heart pounding and desperate.

Move! Why don't you move? She wanted to cry.

"Ten, nine, eight..."

Some observers braced for what was to come, frowning or covering their mouths with their hands.

"Three, two, one."

In silence, absolutely nothing moved. The nun remained completely still.

Then the gun fired, the sound overtaking everything for a brief moment, and a bullet pierced through the nun's chest. She fell, a bright red stain spreading slowly on her white collar. Even on the ground, her hands were held together in a prayer.

{ 15 }

October 22

The image of the nun's hollow face and the dark, red blood that pooled under her lifeless body haunted Emmy when she wasn't paying attention. She saw it walking up the stairs; she saw it when she lifted the fork to eat.

Unable to move after the nun was shot, she had sat on that bench and cried, watching as soldiers came to collect her body and washed the blood off with several buckets of water. Only hours after, when the sun had gone down, had she finally been able to move.

Cynthia and Jimmy were both surprised and worried that she had gone to the ministry. They were relieved that she hadn't revealed her identity. But they wanted her to be extra careful and not to do anything unusual to attract attention.

Emmy didn't mind. There was nowhere to go, anyway, and she was now afraid to go out. She slept a lot—sometimes with nightmares and sometimes not—and waited for Cynthia and Jimmy to come home, in case they found any information about her family.

Jimmy still worked for the city government, where he'd met Sohan many years ago. Cynthia ran a school as an administrator. They had friends who might know things, just from the positions of their work. They had to be very careful to not draw attention to themselves, but it helped that they had already taken the Oath and were considered model Rational citizens in the Party's eyes.

For Jimmy and Cynthia, taking the Oath was more a practical choice than a moral one. They weren't religious anyway, and they understood that, oath or not, no government or another person could really dictate what one believed. It was simply unnecessary for them not to take the Oath and become targets, so they got it over with as soon as it was expected of them. Things would have been much simpler had her parents shared a similar philosophy.

But then again, Leona could never hide who she was. She was never good at pretending to be normal or anything other than what came naturally. To her, there was never a good reason to pretend or say things she didn't mean or to spend a minute of her time with people she didn't like.

Grandma Ethel had been much like her in that way. Maybe it was a necessary quality in the family because they were always so different from others. Sohan, too, was a natural fit in this respect. He was stubborn and uncompromising about the things he believed in. And Leona was the biggest belief in his life.

Emmy missed them. She missed her dad's smile and geeky jokes and the way it felt safe in his arms. When her dad was near, she'd never questioned how much she was loved. She missed Nora and hated the silence without her. Sometimes she thought she heard her sister's chatter, only to realize it was only her memory. She missed her mom too, perhaps the most. It was simply her presence that she missed. Whatever her mom was saying or doing, or even if she was quiet and still, Emmy knew she was there. She always felt it. The emptiness she felt without them was bigger than she could've ever imagined. She'd never known she could feel such regret.

The window of Martens' second-floor guest bedroom faced the street. Outside, past the dwindling, brown leaves of a sidewalk tree, cars drove by, and people went about their business. It had been almost a week since her trip to the Ministry of Mental Hygiene, and she hadn't left the house, choosing instead to mope around the room and watch out the window.

A ray of orange light pierced her sight as the sun set over the rooftops, and Emmy squinted, pulled her head back a bit to get out of the sun, and noticed Cynthia coming down the street through the window. She had her briefcase in one hand and a brown paper bag full of groceries in the other, walking toward the house. She was a handsome lady, petite with fair skin and dark, straight hair that came just below her ears. She looked tiny from where Emmy was.

She was about to go downstairs to greet Cynthia when a couple of men got out from a parked car across the street. The men—who each wore a suit and a hat that covered their faces—walked toward her and appeared to call her name. She turned but didn't seem to recognize them. They chatted for a moment and walked toward the house together. As she led, she briefly glanced up to Emmy's window with a nervous look.

What was this? Emmy quietly walked to the bedroom door and closed it most of the way, leaving a small crack. She leaned in and pressed her ear against the door. Downstairs, keys jingled, and the front door opened.

"Please, come in and have seat. Let me just bring these to the kitchen. Would you like something to drink?" Cynthia spoke more loudly than usual.

"No, I think we're all right for now, but thank you," a man said.

The voice sounded familiar, and Emmy's heart began to beat faster. Cynthia walked toward the kitchen and back to the living room. Emmy held her breath as a brief silence followed.

"You have a lovely home," the man said.

"Thank you." Cynthia's voice was animated. "We've been here fifteen years. It's hard to believe. We've had to do a lot of work but love it." There was a short pause. "So what was it that you said you were looking for?"

"Of course. We don't want to waste your time any more than we need to. Like we explained outside, we're from the Rational Party and the Ministry of Mental Hygiene. We're looking for a young lady, a runaway. You have friends by the name of Sukar?"

Emmy's heart jumped. Now it made sense. None other than Sweeney Stryker stood downstairs, looking for her.

Shit. How had he found this place? She tried to hold still, but her hands trembled.

"Yes," Cynthia said. "Sohan and Leona and their two girls. Of course. Is everything all right?"

"The family's been sent for reeducation, but one of the girls, Emmy, is now missing. Have you seen her? It's likely that she's come to Alexandria, since she lived here before."

Bastards, Emmy thought, holding her breath.

"She's run away? That's horrible… But no, I haven't seen her in years. I talked to her mother a few weeks ago. What have they done?"

"Did you know that they were spiritualists?" It was the other man, who had a harsher voice. "The mom, especially. She actually thought she talked to ghosts."

He laughed as if this was the funniest idea.

"No, I didn't." Cynthia also laughed. "I knew she was kooky, but I always appreciated it as her sense of humor."

Stryker continued, "I'd known about her husband's ideologies back when he was in Alexandria at the city government. It was a real treat when I found them in Bath. Of course when we talked to them, they refused to take the Oath and expressed all kinds of deviant ideas about the Party."

Emmy covered her mouth, afraid she was breathing too loudly. Stryker had known her family from Alexandria. No wonder her family had become a special, secret case. There was more to this than she'd known, of course.

"Did they? Well, I had no idea. So, where are they now?" Cynthia asked as naturally as she could.

"The Ministry has them at a place where they'll go through some mental retraining. But the reason for my visit here is about the daughter, Emmy. We need to take her in too. You sure you haven't seen her?"

"I really haven't, although I guess I may not even recognize her now, even if I saw her. But she certainly hasn't come to us."

"You're aware that hiding runaways or an agitator is a serious crime, considered punishable by Party principles?" the other man said.

Shit, was it? Emmy looked down at her feet, incredulous that it hadn't occurred to her before.

"Yes, of course. But what can I tell you if I haven't seen her?"

"Well, here's my card," Stryker said. "If you see her, please let me know. I don't think she has many places to go."

"What will you do with her when you find her?"

Emmy pressed her ear closer against the door.

"She'll have to be reeducated too, but it depends. For now, she's a runaway. Please do call if you see her."

"I will. It's too bad, what happened." Cynthia sounded eager for their departure.

"Yes. You'd think that everyone would be ready to evolve, but no. Dealing with the masses can be tricky." Stryker chuckled.

"Sure, I can imagine. Thank you for all you do." Her footsteps headed for the door.

"Actually, do you mind if we take a look around?"

Emmy's stomach dropped. She panicked, looking left and right. Her breath quickened even faster as she tried to think.

"Well, sure. It'll be messy, but you're welcome to, if that'll help."

"It would just be a formality, you understand. We promise to be quick."

Emmy stood frozen behind the guest bedroom door, not knowing what to do. Stryker and his partner walked around downstairs, opening doors and making small talk with Cynthia.

She had to move. Slowly, with her trembling body, she made herself lift one foot after another, being extremely careful not to make any noise, moving toward the closet. Her heart raced, and she held her breath to steady her movements.

They were now coming up the stairs. She continued her slow journey toward the open closet door, listening to every word they said as they came closer and closer. After what felt like eternity, she finally reached the closet, with just enough time to crawl into the dark corner when the men reached the top of the stairs.

In a moment the door squeaked as it opened, followed by heavy footsteps on the wooden floors. Her heart sank, and she covered her mouth with both hands, painfully aware of her loud, thumping heart.

"This is our guest bedroom. The master is on the other side," Cynthia explained.

"Do you have a guest currently?" Stryker's partner asked.

"A guest? No, why do you ask?"

"The bed is unmade. Someone slept in here."

Crap. She'd never made her bed. It was something that her mother used to nag her about, and now she hated herself for not listening.

Someone walked around the room and stopped in front of the closet. Emmy was tightly balled up in the dark corner under old coats and suits. The man's shadow darkened the closet. She could see the toes of his shoes and smell his cologne. She pressed her lips together and held her breath.

"Oh, that was me," Cynthia finally said. "My husband and I had a fight last night, so I slept in here. We sometimes do that, and I never make my bed. I may sleep here again tonight, though, depending on his behavior." She laughed.

"Well, isn't that a shame?" Stryker chuckled. Emmy remembered that sound. "I hope you won't have to, Mrs. Marten."

"Please, call me Cynthia."

The man by the closet poked around the hangers a couple of times and looked inside. He turned around, facing the room again. After looking around for another moment, he walked away. Their voices moved down the hallway, and holding very still, Emmy let out a breath.

It didn't take them much longer to finish. They exchanged a few pleasantries, as well as a reminder to be alert, when the men left the house. Only after she heard the front door close and lock did Emmy come out of the closet, and even then, it was slowly. Her heart still pounding, she tiptoed over to the window and peeked outside, careful not to be seen.

Stryker and his partner walked away from the house on the street but paused before they got into the car. They seemed to be having a tense discussion. Stryker looked back at the house, and Emmy saw his face for a split second before she jumped back. He did not look happy. Soon the car doors closed, and it drove off.

Emmy ran downstairs to Cynthia, who sat by the kitchen table with a glass of wine in her hand. Her hand trembled as she lifted the glass to her mouth, and she forced a smile when she saw Emmy.

"Are you okay?" Emmy sat across from her.

She chuckled. "Yes. You?"

"Yeah. But that was…"

"I know. I recognized his name when he introduced himself."

"I'm sorry that I brought him here." She lowered her head, wanting to cry.

"Oh, honey. It's not you. It's them. This is just…all wrong." Cynthia shook her head and sighed deeply. She took a long sip of the wine. The two sat for a while in silence. Emmy knew that she couldn't stay here forever. But where would she go?

Keys jingled at the door, and it opened.

"Hello." Jimmy dropped his things and walked over to the kitchen. "I'm home."

"We're in here," Cynthia barely yelled.

"I have good news." He entered the kitchen excitedly but stopped when he saw the two ashen faces. "What's wrong?"

Cynthia told him about Stryker's visit. Emmy sat with her hands covering her face.

"Well, you're not going to believe this," he said when she was done. "But I found out where they might be."

{ 16 }

October 23

The full moon hung bright and high at three in the morning. Emmy walked through the dark house like a cat, carefully and softly, trying not to make any noise. She left a note on the kitchen table for the Martens, remembering that this was the second goodbye note she'd left in the last couple of weeks. At least this one was sure to be read. She slowly opened the back door, which led to an alley.

It was pitch-dark outside, and no one was up; the yellow street lights gave a warm glow to the shadows of the night. The air was cold against the tip of her nose, which made her sniffle. She quickened her pace, hoping it would help her get warmer, and walked through the alleys a few more blocks before turning to the main road. She didn't know if Stryker's people would be watching at this hour, but she wanted to make sure, if only for her friends.

Jimmy's sources had told him that there was a reeducation camp operating in a town called Berryville. The Ministry of Mental Hygiene was currently building more sites to expand capacity, but for now, this was the only one. Jimmy planned to go see it for himself. He'd go alone, he said, under the guise of a hiking trip. Besides, it was too dangerous for Emmy to be out and about, especially after knowing that Stryker was looking for her in Alexandria.

But she couldn't let her parents' friend take any more risk on her behalf. They'd already done so much. Stryker or others from the Ministry would return, and if she stayed in that house, they were sure to be found out as traitors and agitators. It would be safer for everyone for Emmy to be on the move. Besides, she wanted to do this herself, looking for her family. Doing something, she hoped, might give her a reason to not feel guilty any more.

With a single address written on a piece of paper in her pocket, she took the seven o'clock train to Berryville. It was ironic, how harmless the name of the town sounded.

The train was only half filled but loud for such an early morning. A group of young men, not much older than herself and dressed in grey uniforms, were being rowdy at the end of the car. They seemed excited and full of energy, horsing around and having a great time. They were all wearing the small, silvery pin of the Rational Party. Emmy still had hers somewhere in her bag, it occurred to her, and suddenly she couldn't stand the sight of these boys.

She turned to the window and looked outside, where the sun was rising, wanting to crawl up into a ball and disappear. Were they like her, when she didn't know better? How stupid this all was, and how stupid people were. She hated them all. But she hated herself even more.

Emmy burrowed into her seat, sitting in a fetal position with her knees pulled to her chest. She took out the silver locket from under her shirt and looked inside at the picture of her family. Everyone looked happy. She brought the locket to her nose and took a long whiff of the lavender.

"Love and devotion," her mother had said.

A pang of sadness pulled on her heart. She closed the locket and put it back under her shirt. At least she was on her way.

* * *

The train pulled into Berryville in midafternoon. Emmy got out of the car and walked along the dusty terminal, following the crowd of people. Inside the station was a big hall with high ceilings, with large, wood-paneled windows all around. It was an old-fashioned train station, looking as if it had been built many decades ago.

Just inside the main entrance, she found the local map displayed on the wall, took out the piece of paper with the address, and looked between her hand and the map, soon realizing that the map only covered the downtown area. She needed to search further.

Outside of the station, Berryville felt much like Bath. It was a small town at the foot of the mountains, surrounded by the same ridge that ran vertically through western New Republic. If she followed the mountains and headed north, she would reach Bath eventually.

But unlike Bath, the streets of Berryville were peppered everywhere with Rational Party signs. A huge Party flag fluttered at the three-story pole in front of the train station, side-by-side with the national flag; every streetlamp was decorated with a small banner bearing the Party sign. They took the Party very seriously here. It also felt much colder here, compared with Bath and Alexandria. The air was damp, despite the full sun, making Emmy tighten the scarf around her neck.

Her stomach growled, and she realized she hadn't eaten anything all day. She took out the few bills left in her pocket. It wasn't much, after having paid for train fares and spending money in Alexandria, but it was enough for a meal. She passed a book store, a flower shop, and a hotel. Many of the buildings were made with the same big stones of dark gray that made the place seem ancient and even colder.

She soon found a small restaurant with a bright yellow awning. A couple of outdoor tables stood empty; it looked warm and homey inside. She stepped in. The restaurant was quiet, with only a few tables filled with people. A young woman, who wore a short apron and had her hair up in a ponytail, led her to a small table by the front window. Emmy ordered a cup of hot tea, a bowl of mushroom soup, and some bread.

Her hunger grew as she waited, which amused her. It had been a while since she had any appetite. When the food came, she devoured the last drop of soup and every piece of the bread. Her body warmed up from the inside, and she felt more energized. She took off her scarf and placed it on the chair next to her.

When the server came to collect the empty dishes, Emmy took out the piece of paper from her pocket. "Excuse me, do you know where this is?"

The server stopped clearing the table and looked. "Hm."

"I'm headed to my uncle's house, and it's my first time here."

The young lady tilted her head. *1435 Chamber Street.* "I can tell you how to get to Chamber Street."

"That works. How do I get there?"

She drew a map on a clean paper napkin that showed the route from the restaurant. Watching her draw the lines and the arrows, Emmy's heart began to beat a little faster. It felt close, whatever was waiting for her when she got there, and she was eager to find out. She was eager to find her family. At least she'd be able to say, *See? I did something.* And maybe this would be all over. She didn't know how, but getting there was the first step.

Emmy thanked the server and paid the bill. It was about three in the afternoon when she stepped outside and followed the map. She walked quickly. It was still bright outside, but the sun was getting shorter now, with winter coming, and she didn't want to be lost in the dark.

Chamber Street was just a few blocks away and easy to find. But the number on the address, 1435, was nowhere to be seen—the closest was 23. That was fine, and she turned toward the direction of higher numbers. She just had to walk until she got to the number, and that was easy enough. She picked up her pace, her hands in her pocket and eyes forward. Berryville was a quiet town. Not many people walked around, and only a few cars passed by.

She'd walked about an hour when the street number became 1400, on the outer edge of town. Ahead of her, the road wound up the side of the mountain, and the houses began to be much farther apart from each other. The sun was starting to set, but she might as well go on.

The road became steeper, going up the mountain, and it took more energy to keep moving at the same pace as she was before. Her breath became heavy, and she was hot and thirsty but excited to finally see for herself, this mysterious place.

Emmy passed a small, abandoned house with a missing wall, whose barely visible numbers said 1433. Up ahead, a side road that turned left had a little sign that said 1435 Chamber Street. There it was.

She ran to the sign and made the turn. A winding, dirt road that led up the mountain stretched in front of her, with deep tire marks in the dirt. As she made her way, being careful not to step in small puddles that had formed in the soft earth, she noticed the absolute silence of the place. The only other thing in motion was the wind and the falling leaves. The tall trees dancing in the wind gushed like waterfalls.

It was strange, how dead quiet it was. After all, if there was a government-run facility at the end of this road, there might have been more activity—or at least the road would have been paved. But maybe this was part of the façade, so that people wouldn't know what was there. It certainly wouldn't attract any attention, this place. Listening to the sound of her footsteps and feeling a little strange, Emmy walked on.

The road eventually opened to a clearing at the edge of the mountain. In the middle stood the ruins of what must have once been a two-story building of red bricks. The foundation was still there, along with a half-standing side wall and piles of broken stones and bricks. Tall grass grew in and around it. She walked around to continue on her way, but the road stopped there. Behind the ruins was only a rocky wall of the mountain, across it, a sharp fall onto a cliff.

She tried to figure this out. But her head was foggy, and she couldn't think clearly. She slowly walked around the area, surveying, to make sure that she hasn't missed anything, as if taking her time to look and make sure would change what was in front of her. But all that greeted her was the ruins, and an ashy fire pit that had been lit recently. Empty bottles scattered around it.

It wasn't here. *They* weren't here. She should have waited until Jimmy Marten checked it out first.

Suddenly her knees felt weak, and her body felt limp all over. She stumbled over to the edge and fell onto her knees near the rocks.

What do I do now?

She didn't have the energy to go down the mountains. She was also out of money, so going back into town wouldn't do her any good. The chill from the ground below sent shivers up her bones. The last sliver of orange sun hung over the horizon, coloring the sky with deep red and golden light. Above her, the sky was already deep, dark blue, bejeweled with flickering stars. Down below, the town of Berryville sparkled with lights. It all looked beautiful.

What do I do now?

Darkness quickly descended like thick molasses. It was especially so in the mountains, away from civilization and electric lights. Emmy had learned that during her first days in Bath, when she'd walked home one night with her mom and sister. The girls had gotten scared, unused to the real darkness of the mountains and the noises of wild animals near and far. Leona had held each of them in her arms and told them stories of her childhood as they walked. When they'd neared the house, she's told them to look up, and Emmy had never seen such bright stars. It looked as if someone had strewn a bunch of sparkling jewels on a bed of dark and blue velvet.

She missed them so much. Disappointment and shame tore at her gut like a hungry beast. She'd failed again. That's all she seemed to do.

What do I do now?

Tears streamed down her face, and her breath quickened. She broke down in a sob.

Emmy cried out for her mom, dad, and sister. She wanted to tell them that she was sorry. What a grand mistake she'd been, all her life.

If it wasn't for her, they'd probably be home safe. It would have been better if she didn't exist. It hurt all through her gut and heart, and her head throbbed. She wanted it all to stop, but a part of her said that she had to stew in this—that pain was what she deserved.

You ugly, stupid child. You can't do anything right. You deserve this. You deserve to be alone. Just look where you are. You are the seed of everything bad.

The voice screamed in her head, over and over, and she just wanted it to all stop. She was sick of crying, sick of feeling guilty, sick of being not enough. She didn't want to feel anything anymore.

Emmy stood from where she sat. She didn't want to *be* there anymore. There was something she could do, after all. Maybe that would make everything better, for everyone.

It was pitch-dark past the edge of rocks in front of her. That made it a little easier. She closed her eyes and took a deep breath, clenching her trembling hands.

Forward, just forward.

It was only a couple of stumbling steps before her ankle twisted and her body was in the air, until a loud thump made everything go dark and silent.

{ 17 }

L ight emanates from all things—trees, animals, rocks, and streams—that the human eye can't see. People need the sun, for its rays to bring shape and color to the world we live in, but just because the eyes can't see, doesn't mean it's not there. The world glows and undulates in this light ceaselessly, whether we know it or not, and it is the most beautiful thing one can ever see.

On the side of the mountain, each and everything was alight in a soft glow. Pinks, greens, blue-whites, and golden lights formed the outlines of everything and radiated out to each other, mingling and interacting. Everything was conscious, even the light itself. It was a dark night before, but there was no darkness here.

Emmy floated, like a feather blowing in the wind, and it felt right and good. She was captivated by what she saw and felt, because she was sure that she was in another world. There below, her body lay in the woods—bloody and limp— and a soft light emanated from that too.

She'd left her body and didn't have a form. She didn't have an arm to raise or a leg to kick. She didn't have eyes to see or ears to hear, but she sensed everything. Whatever she focused on, she could zero-in with laser-like clarity.

A cricket chirped, and she looked for it. In a split second, she'd become the cricket.

Instantly everything was different again, and her mind felt all jumbled. Her body vibrated head to toe with the rhythm of her sound. She panicked—it was too intense—and was kicked back to the floating awareness, above the side of the mountain. She could do this with just about anything she saw or could think of.

Am I dead? Is this what dead *is?*

The question did not worry her. Emmy didn't know why, but she knew that everything was okay. This was right, and all was well. It felt like home. She was connected to everything near and far, with a sense of total belonging. She *was* everything and, everything was her. Distance was only an illusion, and she could be here and up near the stars at the same time. The immense beauty of it all overwhelmed her; all was well-being, joy, and possibility.

In time—she didn't know how long; she was enjoying herself too much, and time was different in this world— Emmy felt something approach her. It didn't have a form, *per se*, but it was a being like she was now, a conscious awareness.

Immediately she knew who it was: Grandma Ethel. She knew just because she knew, just like one could pick out her family in a crowd of people. And because this was the pure essence of Grandma Ethel, like home, acceptance, and love, just like Emmy used to feel when her grandmother had been alive.

"My darling," the entity seemed to say, though no words were spoken. It felt warm and open.

"Is it really you?" Finding it hard to believe, she studied the presence, surreal yet unquestionable.

"Sure am." Grandma laughed. "Do you know where you are?"

"I think so. I'm dead, right?" The thought brought her mixed emotions, of excitement, wonder, and a pang of sadness.

"Not quite, but almost there."

"Have you come to take me?" If so, she was glad that it was her grandmother.

"No. I've come to give you a choice." The spirit embraced Emmy, enveloping her in a field of safety and love.

"I missed you so much." It had been a long time since she felt this way. She could have wept with relief, except that she didn't have any tears to shed.

"I know, dear. But would you believe that I've always been with you?"

"You have?" Emmy suddenly wanted to hide. "But how?"

"Just like you could see everything here, I can be with you wherever I want. You just couldn't see me."

"Oh." She felt heavy, ashamed, and sad. She wanted to run away. "You saw everything I did then?"

"Of course," Ethel responded, matter-of-factly.

"Do you hate me?" No one could love her after what she did, she was certain.

"No," her grandmother answered softly, almost cooing.

"But I hate myself." There was no way to hide anything from her grandmother, after all. At the same time, it felt good to unload and get honest about the ugly things inside of her.

Ethel was still soft and warm. "There's no need."

"But it was me. You know it if you saw it." Didn't she understand?

"I do."

"So you know it was me who told Stryker about mom, that she talked to spirits?" Emmy wanted her grandmother to agree with her, how bad and stupid she'd been, to confirm what she'd known all along.

"Yes. By the way, what do you think you're doing now?" It was as if Emmy's heavy feelings bounced off of her grandmother, unable to penetrate.

"But this is different. I'm dead, almost."

"So who says everything ends when you die?"

"Fine. But how can I not hate myself when it's my fault that they're gone? When it was me who told. Now I don't even know if they're okay." Emmy wanted to sink into the deepest, darkest part of the world and stay there, hidden.

"You didn't know this would happen. If you did, you wouldn't have. You were only doing what you thought was right. You didn't know they'd take your family. It wasn't your fault."

"But I should've known better. I should've listened." If only she had…

"You could have. But if I had a dollar for every time that Leona didn't listen to me, I'd be rich." She laughed.

Emmy laughed too. It'd been a long time since she'd been able to laugh. It felt good, like a release of some sort, and to hear from someone that at least it wasn't all her fault, as if she had been given permission to feel better.

Ethel continued, "If you want to know about your family, we can see them now. You want to?"

"We can?" Surprised, a part of her lit up with soft hope and curiosity.

"Well, that's why I'm here."

Her grandmother gently guided her—it was as if she was just shown things, taken to places, even though she didn't do anything—and in a split second, they were both floating above an island. They quickly zoomed into a big compound with high walls, topped with barbed wires. Inside stood a number of four-story buildings of red brick walls, with rows and rows of windows. People walked around on the grounds, some talking and others working.

"Let's get closer," Ethel said, and they were in a room.

Nora lay in a bunk bed with a ragged doll in her arm. She was skinnier than when Emmy had last seen her and wore a white, cotton dress that seemed two sizes too big. Emmy wanted to touch her but couldn't, for she didn't have a form. She sang a lullaby to the doll, in a wispy, low voice. The song sounded so sad that Emmy could hardly listen; she wanted to cry—her heart ached.

"She's not hurt, at least," Ethel said. "Let's go see your dad now."

They found themselves in a dining hall full of weary-looking men with trays of food in front of them. Sohan sat with a few others, wearing a shirt and pants that Emmy recognized from home but were dirty and worn. He looked tired, and his cheeks were deeply sunken in. His hair was too long. Emmy knew that he'd hate being this way, unclean and unkempt.

"Dad," she called out. He was hunched over his tray, chewing, although with no enthusiasm.

"He can't hear you," Ethel said.

Emmy watched him in frustration. He was right there in front of her, but she missed him more than before. If only she could talk to him and touch him...

The scene suddenly changed, and they were now in a different room, filled with rows of bunk beds covered with white sheets. Leona was on a bottom bunk, lying down. She, too, looked weary and skinnier than Emmy remembered.

Ethel moved closer, hovering just above her left shoulder. Leona, who was reading a book, sat up and blinked. "Mom?"

She does talk to spirits! After all that had happened, Emmy still found it hard to believe.

Grandma Ethel whispered something to her, and Leona smiled. Ethel turned to Emmy. "I told her I was watching over you."

"Can I talk to her?" She was desperate to connect with her mother.

"Sure. But don't tell her you're hurt."

"Mom?" Emmy tried to say—she just did what she did with her grandmother, kind of like a projection of meaning and feeling. Leona was right in front of her, looking into her eyes. It looked and felt as though she was looking back at Emmy, but it was hard to tell.

"Emmy, my girl, are you looking for me?" Leona's lips did not move, but Emmy heard her all right. They communicated through thoughts and emotions. She focused and information came across even more clearly. "I'm okay, sweetie. I'm fine. But I see you in my dreams and worry about you. I see you all alone, like in that dream I had before. Are you okay?"

Emmy's heart filled with tenderness and longing for her mom, who looked more beautiful and fragile in that moment than ever before. She wanted to hold her and for her mom to hold her back, but she was without form. She wasn't even here, technically. "I'm okay, Mom. I met Grandma out here. Can you believe it?"

Leona smiled. "You always had it in you. I knew it would come."

Emmy didn't tell her that she might actually be dead. "I love you so much."

"I love you too, sweetie."

She felt the warmth of her love through her whole being, like a glowing, beautiful light. "I'm sorry that I was so difficult."

"I know. It's okay. I always knew." Leona smiled into space.

"Time to go," Ethel said.

Before Emmy could protest, she was already growing in distance from the scene. She said goodbye to her mom reluctantly.

In a snap they were outside the kitchen window of the Martens' house. Cynthia and Jimmy were sitting at the table, with Emmy's letter between them. Cynthia said something with tears in her eyes, and Emmy could feel her worries. Jimmy looked worried too, as he listened. Ethel nudged her to another direction, where Sweeney Stryker stood lurking in the dark alley, watching the scene inside.

"Will they be okay?" Emmy asked her grandmother, who affirmed.

"You're not there anymore, are you?" Ethel said, "You left at the right time. You did them a favor."

She felt relieved and surprised she did something right. Then, just as suddenly, they were back above the mountains of Berryville.

"Now listen," Ethel started, "I showed you all this because I want you to make an informed choice. You haven't completely transitioned yet and can now choose whether to stay or go."

"But why would I go back? I'm done. I feel at home here, and I have you."

"It's up to you. It was your choice to step off that edge, but your body's holding on. So you can go back. And if you do, you'll remember everything you saw here, including me and what I'm about to tell you. You'll find that the powers you've been waiting for your whole life will soon be available to you. You'll have to work at it, and it won't come overnight, but it'll come. Then you'll be able to help your family with my guidance. A way will be shown to you if you trust." She paused. "But none of this matters if you choose to stay. Staying means that you can come with me to the deeper realms and do whatever you want next."

"Are you telling me that there is really no right or wrong choice here?" Could it really be? It was difficult to wrap her head around it.

"That's right. No right or wrong. It just is. It's how it's always been. But it is your choice to make," Ethel explained with gentle patience.

"Will they suffer without me?" It seemed to her that there was much to consider. This was a major choice.

"They may suffer *with* you. Besides, they're responsible for their own lives, at the end of the day. Everyone goes through life with that opportunity and responsibility, for themselves and others."

Emmy felt torn but only for a brief moment. She knew she had to go back. If there was anything she could do to help them, if there was something she could do to make up for her mistakes, then she had to at least try. They all looked vulnerable there. Besides, she wanted to be able to ask for their forgiveness in person and see their smiling faces again. The mere thought made her happy and light. "I'll go."

"Good." Ethel smiled. "Now listen carefully. When you go back, things will be shown to you one by one, step by step, so have faith and pay attention. Most importantly, practice quieting your mind. Everything starts from there. It will help you guide your thoughts. The thoughts you choose to have in your head, the ones you indulge in, create the emotions you feel. And emotions are like the language of the Universe. They bring and guide what shows up in your life. If you hold on to thoughts that make you feel good, things will happen that will reinforce similar feelings. It's the same for the thoughts that make you feel bad. Choose your thoughts with intention."

This boggled her mind. "But how do I control what I think or feel? If my family's gone, I'm going to feel bad about it. If I'm alone, I'm going to feel lonely. If I'm ugly, I'll feel ugly."

"Is that really true? What you're describing are mere reactions to what seems to be. And what seems to be depends on perception. As humans, we can always choose our story. For example, some of the most attractive people are not the most handsome or pretty according to social ideals. Rather, it's how they feel inside about themselves that makes them irresistible. Because they believe they're attractive and feel so, the world reflects that back to them."

Emmy listened quietly. It was a lot to take in, although it made sense.

"Experiment, if you'd like," Ethel continued. "You'll see. The world is merely a mirror of your stories, thoughts, and feelings. But the first thing you have to do is practice quieting your mind. Meditate. Find a quiet place, close your eyes, and be still. Don't fall asleep, but watch your thoughts as they drift in and out of your mind. Practice letting go. In stillness, breathe into your heart."

"That sounds hard."

"It'll take practice at first. But the more you do it, the easier it'll be. It'll teach you that you're not your thoughts and that you can choose what happens inside of you—in thoughts and emotions. It will also help you stay connected to this realm more, where all things originate. Eventually you'll want to do it just because it feels good."

"Really?" It was hard for her to imagine actually liking sitting quietly for a long time, not doing or thinking anything.

"Yes. It will start with mere glimpses, but you'll get there."

"What's my intuitive power?" That was the more important question, as far as Emmy was concerned.

"Oh, sweetie, you'll see. You've always had it. You've just been so preoccupied with not having it, you just never saw it before."

Part III.

{ 18 }

October 27

"Stop. You don't even know what you're doing."

A girl's voice echoed above Emmy's head, and she was suddenly awake, with excruciating pain all over her body. Shooting pain reverberated through her limbs.

"I'm just checking," a young boy's voice said, defiantly.

"Don't wake her." The girl hushed him.

Emmy couldn't open her eyes. It hurt too much. Where was she? She tried to say something, but her mind was foggy. All that came out was a moan.

"Wait," the girl said, "she's awake."

Everything went dark again.

* * *

A delicious smell tickled her nose. All of a sudden it was as if every cell in her body was awake and urging her to move, telling her it was time to eat. The right side of her body still hurt, but the sensations were much quieter than before. She slowly opened her eyes and was surprised to see the rocky walls of a cave. A small fire burned a few feet away in a black, stone-lined pit, creating a warm glow to the space.

Emmy felt around her hands and found herself laying on a bed of straw covered with a blanket. Near her head was her book bag, looking untouched; on the other side of the fire was another straw bed, just like the one she was on.

Her stomach growled, like the cry of a wild animal, and pulled at her for action. Laughter came from one direction of the cave, along with the smell of food. Slowly she lifted herself to sit up, barely managing to not scream in pain. Her clothes were torn in places, with dried blood stains, but the wounds had been bandaged and cleaned underneath. Whoever had brought her here had saved her life.

She had no idea how long she'd been out. But considering that she saw her dead grandmother on the other side, she was relieved that this was the extent of her injuries. All her limbs were intact, after all, and the hunger she now felt was a good sign. Her mouth felt dry, but she smiled as her memory from the other side flooded back and she realized that she came back to life, just like she was supposed to. If what happened there still felt like a dream, this at least was evidence that it might have been real. Now only if she could find some water and food.

Painfully she got up and slowly limped toward the smell. About twenty feet of cave stretched in front of her. As she neared the opening, the walls closed in a bit and opened up again, dividing the place into two separate rooms. Two more straw beds and an unlit fire pit were in the other room, with a tall pile of wood against the wall.

It looked dark outside, and tall trees in the shadows surrounded a small opening in front of the cave. As she approached, a scene slowly unfolded before her: a steaming pot hung over a big fire surrounded by three kids and a small, white dog. They seemed relaxed and happy, talking and laughing together, until the dog raised its head and growled low at her.

Suddenly the boy who faced Emmy's direction jumped and fell backwards, spilling the contents of his bowl onto his lap.

"Holy shit!" He stared at her with his mouth open.

The other two turned, also surprised. The dog stood up and barked.

"I'm sorry." Emmy's voice came out weakly. She tried to smile. "Didn't mean to scare you. The smell woke me up."

"Down, Chester," the older boy said to the dog.

The dog stopped barking and scurried over to the younger boy, who tried to gather the food from his lap and spoon them back into his bowl. It stole some of the meaty chunks and swallowed without chewing.

"No, Chester," the younger boy protested, trying to push the dog away. He looked a little younger than Nora and had olive skin, with brown eyes and hair. He was a little chubby and had a face full of mischief.

The other two were a boy and a girl: the boy looked a little older than Emmy; the girl was about the same age. The older boy put his food down and walked over to Emmy.

"Here," he said, holding out his hand. He was at least a foot taller than she was and had soft, brown curls that fell around his blue eyes. He smiled gently and helped her walk toward the fire to sit.

Without saying a word, the girl got up and disappeared into the cave. Her chocolate-colored skin was darker than Emmy's; she had short, puffy, black hair and big, brown eyes. She looked athletic and nimble, the way she moved quickly and gracefully about. She came back with a cup of water, which Emmy took with both hands and gulped it down at once. The cold liquid spread down her throat, chest and stomach, satisfying a deep thirst that she didn't know she had.

"Thank you," Emmy said and put down the empty cup. She wondered for a moment if she should be guarded of these strangers, but they had, after all, saved her life. They couldn't be all that bad.

The girl handed her a bowl of hot stew. Chunks of meat and vegetables looked glossy and steamy, making Emmy's mouth water. She was about to attack the bowl with the gusto of a hungry bear when she noticed the others still looking at her, motionless and mouths ajar. She must have been a sight. But there was nothing she could do.

The girl handed Emmy a spoon and studied her face. "Eat slowly. You haven't eaten anything in days, and eating too much could make you sick."

Emmy nodded and slowly dug her spoon into the bowl. The girl walked back to her place and sat, resuming her dinner, as the others did the same, including the dog.

This girl sounded wise—what they might call an 'old soul'—which made Emmy feel a little self-conscious in comparison. But she also felt grateful that a girl like that would worry for her, not even knowing anything about her. Emmy liked her immediately. She couldn't remember ever liking someone her age so quickly. But then again, a lot of strange things had been happening recently.

It took effort for Emmy to not empty everything into her mouth at once. The stew was delicious, whatever it was, maybe the most delicious thing she'd ever eaten. Slowly her insides warmed, and she relaxed more, the muscles and tissues of her body feeling the incoming nutrients.

"What's your name?" the older boy finally asked. He was curious, trying not to gawk but periodically glancing in her direction.

"Emmy Sukar." She smiled. "Thanks for saving my life."

{ 19 }

November 3

A set of lucky coincidences had helped them find Emmy. The younger boy, Pablo, had gone to check on a trap he'd set days before, far from their usual paths and tracks. He'd taken Chester—a West Highland Terrier, who loved to chase little animals—with him that day, even though Chester usually followed Finn, the older boy, everywhere. The dog had wandered away and found Emmy's beaten-up body in the bushes, alerting Pablo with incessant barking. The boy had been spooked at first; she'd looked more dead than injured. But having found a pulse on her, although a very weak one, they'd brought her to the cave and nursed her for three days until she regained consciousness.

Life with the kids was pretty quiet. For a week after she woke up, Emmy spent much of her time sleeping, eating, and sleeping again, and already her body felt much stronger. She was able to walk freely, at almost her normal pace, and the pain was mostly gone, except when she moved her arms a certain way.

More remarkable, though, was how she felt inside. Strange was this quiet happiness, a contentment she didn't remember ever feeling before. It wasn't that she'd forgotten her mission, to find and help her family. But she felt and experienced many more things that made her smile and feel joyful inside, in unsuspecting moments. The flock of birds flying in the sky, the flutter of a moth near the fire at night, and the falling leaves of bright orange and yellow—all these things moved her and made her happy.

She also loved the company of her hosts. They had their own rhythm of life that she was still trying to get used to. It was a lot of work to survive out there in the wilderness for a group of three, now four, kids. Even though Emmy hadn't been able to do too many things to help out, she'd volunteered to keep the fire going, which, on these cold November nights, was still an important job.

Pablo and Bree, the girl, were usually out all day setting traps for small animals and foraging for food. He was a goofball, an energetic eleven year old, who took his job very seriously. She was sixteen, just as Emmy was, and very protective of Pablo. Bree and Pablo had run away from an orphanage a few years back, and she had been his surrogate big sister ever since.

Bree slept across the fire from her every night. She also helped take care of Emmy's bandages and wounds, though she didn't say much in words. Emmy tried to make conversation every chance she had, but she was usually short in answers.

Emmy admired her, though. Not only was she wise beyond her years, she was also a fierce hunter. Bree often went out alone, whenever there was a need, and was able to bring back a small kill. She also taught the others which plants were safe to eat and which ones killed, a skill that reminded Emmy of her mother.

Finn was seventeen. He'd been at the cave the longest, with Chester the dog, long before the other two had joined him a couple of years back. They'd found each other in the forest, in the middle of winter, when Bree and Pablo were living like hermits and looked like wild animals, barely surviving in the snow. Finn had invited them to stay with him until spring; when the weather warmed, there was no question they'd stay.

He was also mostly away from the cave during the day, with Chester usually by his side. Sometimes he went to find food and firewood, but more often, he went into town to do odd jobs for people for money and other necessary things, such as clothes, bread, and salt. It was this connection to civilization that had enabled the group's survival in the woods.

With everyone keeping themselves busy, Emmy often found herself alone at the cave, quietly watching and feeding the fire. Sitting in front of the warm, dancing flames and listening to the crackling of the wood, it was easy for her to drift and practice quieting her mind.

As her grandmother had instructed, she closed her eyes and placed her attention on her breath, feeling the air moving in and out through her nose and lungs. The hard part, always, was catching herself in the middle of thought and remembering to let go.

Who would've thought that I'd feel this way? Something's definitely different. It's as if I'm lighter and cleaner inside. And it just feels good... Ha! I'm glad I came back. It's like I came back to a different world.

...

How long am I supposed to do this? I could be gathering more firewood or do something else that's helpful. They've all been nice to me. I was lucky. Wait, I'm not doing this right. I'm not supposed to be thinking.

Emmy brought her attention back to her breath. In and out, in and out.

...

That's right. Like that.

...

There. That was a moment of silence. Oh, yeah. But I'm thinking again. Okay, breathe.

She came back to her breath, going deep down into her lungs and out.

Her stomach growled. It was still a couple of hours until dinner.

Wonder what we'll have for dinner. Hopefully something good. Wish we had some sweets. Hot chocolate with whipped cream would be nice, like Mom used to make.

Her mouth watered.

Stop. Go back to your breath.

She inhaled deeply.

Ugh. Itchy nose. Should I scratch it? Am I supposed to? And my butt hurts. Why is the ground so hard? Well, I guess it's a rock after all. This is harder than I thought.

She scratched her nose and shifted her bottom.

Ah. That's better.

…

Come back to the breath. In and out, in and out…

Watching her breath move slowly in and out of her body, with each breath a little different than the one before, she became aware of the quiet around her. Far away the wind whistled a low tune; the firewood in front of her crackled and popped. Bringing her attention back to her body, she heard the beating of her heart, loud and ever present. It surprised her that she'd never heard it this way before. She felt the rhythmic vibration moving through her lungs, ribs, skin, and all around her chest.

...

She took another deep breath in. A huge space opened up inside of her, in her heart and through her head—a huge, empty space, warm and clear, open and accepting. Chills started from her back and moved up through her chest and neck then up to her head and out through the top of her scalp. She had goosebumps all over her body. It was a pleasure that she felt all over her skin, a tingling sensation. A smile spread on her face.

It's like a glimpse of that place, where I was with Grandma.

...

But would I really be able to help them? I don't even have a plan. But she said everything will be shown to me. I guess I need to trust. For now.

...

I wonder if Bree and Finn like each other. Oh, shoot. Stop and go back to your breath.

{ 20 }

November 25

Time passed at a strange pace at the cave. There was no calendar, to start with, and since no one went to school, one day was just as another and without clear markers.

One thing that was impossible to ignore, though, was the changing of seasons. It had become much colder, and the wind, more piercing. Even though Finn had brought Emmy new clothes—warm pants and a thick sweater, with much more practical value than aesthetic—from town, it was almost too cold to leave the comforts of the cave when the sun was down.

Everyone was busy trying to get the cave ready for winter. There was a lot to tend to, such as stocking up on firewood and food. But the days were getting shorter, and pressure was mounting. She gladly participated wherever she could, eager to help and relieved that she'd healed enough to do just about everything that was needed.

She knew, in the back of her head, that she might have to leave this place before the weather really turned cold. But she didn't know yet where she had to go; she certainly didn't want to go back to Alexandria and put the Martens in any danger. There was no reason to believe that Alexandria was where she had to go, either—it wasn't as if they could help her find her family in any special way. After all, Jimmy's sources had failed him miserably already.

So she waited. She didn't know what she was waiting for—maybe a sign, an idea, or a dream—but she waited. There wasn't much else she could do.

They had all set off on a foraging tour that morning. Inside her canvas bag were a few, small mushrooms. This was simply pathetic. She'd had her eyes on the ground for a few hours now, looking for plants that Bree had instructed as edible. Emmy really wanted to do something useful for the group, but it wasn't as easy as she thought. Pablo and Finn were not far away, joking around and playing with Chester. Still, their bags were much fuller than hers.

She tried to focus and remain patient, walking through the woods with her eyes wide. One benefit of regular meditation—sitting quietly and turning off the loud voices in her head—was that she now sensed more of everything around her. For example, when she looked at a tree after a long session, the outlines of every single leaf, every branch, and every crack of the bark jumped out at her at the same time, as if it emanated an unseen light from within. Unfortunately, however, such clarity had not been much help in finding food thus far.

The sun was bright, and the sky was blue. But the cold air turned her breath into white steam. Most of the trees had already lost their leaves; only their thin branches pierced up to the sky. A thick layer of dried leaves rustled under her feet. She was determined to fill her bag. She pushed harder, walking faster and away from the others to cover more ground.

About half an hour later, she noticed a certain fragrance in the air. She looked around to see what it was, but there were no flowers nearby. It was certainly too late in the season for flowers, making her even more curious. She sniffed the air like a dog and realized the smell was that of lavender. Patting her chest, she confirmed that the silver locket still sat under her shirt.

Then where—

This was an unusual place for lavender too, given the thick woods and heavy shade most of the year. Lavender loved the sun and the wind and grew naturally on warm, open fields. But the smell became stronger and tickled her nose, leading her to follow it without thinking.

The smell led her through a patch of thorny bushes, and she came upon a clearing that had been untouched for a very long time. Big boulders protruded out of the ground on one side, and as she stepped forward, a bird flew away in a flutter. She searched for lavender but found nothing, although the fragrance was all around her, stronger than ever.

What caught her eye next was a patch of tall, yellow flowers that thought it was still summer. She thought they were sunchokes, whose flowers looked much like yellow daisies, but the stems grew as tall as she was and had lean, pointy leaves. Bree had shown her a dried plant a few weeks ago. The value of it was that its roots could be eaten much like potatoes, although these were sweeter. Even though most of them had already died out from the cold, these were still thriving in their vibrant yellows and greens.

Could it be? Emmy walked over and looked at it more closely. They were sunchokes, all right. She dug at the roots with a sharp rock. Soon the ground was full of fat tubes that looked like oversized ginger roots. She carefully dug them out and dusted dirt off before putting them in her bag. There was more than enough to make her fill.

"Hey, guys," she yelled before turning to continue digging. "Look what I found."

Chester came first, his tail wagging excitedly, followed by Finn. "What is it?"

"Look." She held out the roots in her hands.

"No way," Pablo said, peering into the hole in the ground.

"Sunchokes." Finn smiled, kneeling by the hole as well. "Oh, man. I love these things. Wait 'till Bree sees it."

Soon they were all on their knees, digging and celebrating their find, as Chester sniffed the area and investigated.

"Remember how you got really sick last year?" Finn teased Pablo.

"What do you mean, me? You got sick too, and so did Bree." Pablo explained, "This can give you diarrhea if you don't cook it right."

Emmy laughed, imagining how they must have suffered, and the others did too.

"We were sick and stuck at the cave for a couple of days. All of us," Finn said, "but it was the hardest for me, I'll say, because Pablo was really gassy the entire time. And I had to share the room with him."

"I was," Pablo admitted, matter-of-factly. "Really gassy. But so were you."

Everyone had a good laugh. Emmy raised her head from digging and sniffed the air. The smell of lavender had gone; nothing seemed out of the ordinary. She shrugged and went back to digging. It didn't make any sense, but it also didn't matter anymore.

All of their bags were soon filled with fat sunchokes.

"Let's stop here," Finn said. "We can dig out more later. We shouldn't take everything, anyway, so they can grow again next year."

He stood up and dusted off dirt from his clothes. Pablo and Emmy pushed dirt back into the hole and dusted themselves too.

"I'll show Bree first," Pablo yelled, running ahead.

Emmy lifted her bag in her arms. It was now too heavy to hold with one hand. Just as she started to walk, something tickled her upper lip. Being careful not to drop anything, she balanced her bag in one arm and scratched her face.

"Wait. You have—" Finn leaned in, looking closely at her face. Slowly, he raised his arm and brought his forefinger and thumb close to her nose. She stepped back instinctively, but he stepped forward too. "There's something on you."

He now focused on her left shoulder. She stayed still, and he carefully picked something off. Soon a small spider wiggled between his fingers. Emmy gasped.

"These bite." He flicked it away.

"Thanks." Her face was hot, and her heart pounded.

He picked up his bag, grinning, and walked after Chester, who quietly sped in front of him, his ears alert.

What was that about? She sighed and slowly followed.

* * *

Finn and Emmy stopped to check on a couple of traps on their way back. Walking together, they talked about where they'd come from and how they'd gotten to the cave. He'd found the cave many years ago, soon after his grandmother passed away. She was a very religious Catholic and the only family he had. When the Rational Party started dismantling the Church and persecuting its orders, she'd found herself unable to set foot anywhere near her favorite place and become increasingly anxious, until one day, she'd died from a sudden heart attack.

He didn't take after her love for the Church but had come to hate the Party nonetheless. When the entire town became maniacal about it all, he came to live in the woods, all alone, away from the signs and the slogans. A few months later, someone gave him Chester as a puppy after a job he'd done, making the dog his family number one. Then, a couple of years back, he'd also taken in Bree and Pablo as his kin. Emmy, he teased, had made the grandest entrance by pretending to be dead.

The first trap they checked was empty but the second had caught a fat rabbit, which Finn skillfully placed into a bag despite its violent protest. It was such a cute animal, the white rabbit, and Emmy was thankful she didn't have to be the one to kill it.

"How about you?" Finn asked when they started to walk again.

She told him the story of her family, how they disappeared and that she intended to go look for them soon. She told him about her mom, dad, and Nora, even as it made her miss them so much more. She didn't tell him that she'd walked off that cliff on purpose or what she'd experienced while half-dead on the other side.

"You might as well wait for spring," he said, "I've heard about the camp, but no one knows where it is. It'll get really cold pretty quickly, and it snows a lot here. You should spend winter with us and go when it gets warmer." He looked at Emmy with curiosity. "Are you all better now?"

"Thanks to you guys." She smiled and took a deep breath. "I don't have a plan yet. I'm waiting for a sign."

She didn't know what he'd think of such statements and felt strange saying it. *But Grandma said things will be shown.*

"A sign?" He lifted his eyebrows.

"Yep, a sign. Something that'll make me jump, telling me to go here or there."

"What does that mean?" Finn tilted his head.

She laughed. "I'm not sure yet."

* * *

Approaching the cave, something felt off. Chester whined and headed straight for Pablo, who was hunched over next to a tree near the cave entrance. Bree stood over him with her hand on his back, her face miserable with worry. He puked and coughed violently, in turns.

"What's wrong?" Finn dropped everything and ran over. Emmy followed.

"I don't know," Bree yelled.

Finn lifted Pablo and tried to get a better look at him. His face was white, his eyes couldn't focus, and he strained to breath, making a wheezing sound.

"What can I do?" Emmy asked.

"Bring some water and a towel," Bree said.

Emmy moved. When she returned, Pablo's clothes were drenched with sweat, and he lay on the ground, moaning and clutching his stomach. Worried, Finn watched from the side; Chester lay quietly with his head on the sick boy's ankle.

"He must've eaten something bad." Bree cleaned Pablo's face with the wet towel. She looked like she was in pain herself, caressing his head on her lap.

Unable to do anything else, Emmy waited for other instructions as she nervously watched the poor boy. He breathed quickly, his chest moving violently up and down. Emmy felt her own breath quicken too and became nauseous. A pang of pain shot up from her stomach, and she let out a small cry, clutching her stomach.

"He had these in his hand." Bree pointing to some crumbs of what looked like mushrooms on the ground. "I always yell at him, but he's constantly putting stuff in his mouth. Stupid boy."

"It's not your fault," Finn said in a low voice. "But this looks bad."

Emmy's nausea continued, and she sweated. Soon it became difficult for her to breath. She stumbled over to a tree a few feet away, holding onto it for balance as she lowered her head and got ready to throw up. Her head was foggy, but she tried to focus on her breath as she did during meditations. *Breathe in...and out. In and out.*

"Are you okay?" Finn asked as he looked over.

"Fine." Emmy was still leaning over a tree, trying to breathe. But why was she feeling this way suddenly?

Breathe in, and out. Gradually the pain and nausea subsided, but her throat and mouth were parched. She slowly lifted herself to get some water.

Suddenly Pablo spoke, meekly, his eyes still closed. "Water—"

"Here." Bree brought a cup to his mouth. He drank some and stopped moaning but shivered instead. The sun was now setting, the air getting colder, and his clothes were wet. "Let's bring him inside."

Finn picked up Pablo's round, little body and brought him inside the cave, laying him next to the fire. He looked on with worry, not knowing what else to do. Bree covered him up with a thick blanket and settled next to him, her eyes full of tears.

Emmy got herself some water, feeling relieved that the strange sensations subsided. It was weird, how quickly it came and went.

But there was no time to wonder. She felt the evening's chill to her bones as she walked over to Bree's side and hurried to restart the fire for Pablo.

Emmy woke up to a shaking of her shoulders and saw Bree's face. Still half asleep, she shook her head and inhaled deeply, feeling the sharp chill in the air. The fire had been out for a while; only a few dying ambers in the pit were glowing in the dark. She could hardly see the girl's face.

"Hurry, we have to go."

"What's going on?" Confused, Emmy rubbed her eyes and lifted herself up.

"Pablo needs a doctor, and you'll have to come." Bree quickly went back to her side and busily shoved whatever she could into her bag. "Quickly."

Emmy jumped from her bed and looked around. There wasn't much to pack. She just had her bag—which she'd brought from Bath and still hadn't unpacked—and the clothes she was wearing. She put on her coat and bag and walked to the other side of the cave to check on Pablo, leaving Bree to finish packing.

The little boy lay on his side, frowning in pain but face devoid of color. He still sweated and shivered at the same time and occasionally let out a soft moan. She knelt next to him and stroked the hair on his forehead, feeling anxious for the little guy. Bree stumbled into the room, clutching a bag on her side. She knelt next to Emmy and peered into Pablo's face. Emmy's heart ached for Bree too—she didn't look like she'd gotten any sleep during the night.

His breath heavy, Finn rushed inside. "Okay, I got it. Hurry."

Chester looked confused too and nervously watched the tall boy's every move. Bree helped getting Pablo on Finn's back, and they rushed out of the cave. Emmy and Chester followed.

It was pitch-dark outside, but a full moon shined brightly in the sky. The four followed the path that led down the mountain and toward town. A trek like this could be dangerous, but they knew these woods well, and their eyes adjusted easily to the darkness.

"Where are we going?" Things were happening faster than Emmy could keep track of.

"Finn knows a doctor. But he's far away," Bree explained, her breath heavy.

"What about the doctor in town?"

"We can't trust him. They'll take us if we're caught." Bree wasn't interested in sharing any details. There was no time, and her head was filled with Pablo.

"What do you mean?"

"The orphanage. We're fugitives."

"Is he that sick, you think?"

"I've never seen him like this before." She looked back at Emmy, her face tight with tension and worry.

Emmy nodded and followed in silence, even as her head brimmed with even more questions. Should she stay? She could stop right here and let them know that she'd be waiting for them at the cave. She wondered if she was doing the right thing by going with them, considering that her priority was to find her own family.

But she didn't know when they'd be back, and being alone out here didn't seem like a good idea either, no matter how many sunchokes they had in reserve. Besides, she didn't want to leave her new friends now, when Pablo was sick. That simply wouldn't be right.

Was this a sign? She didn't know.

An old feeling returned, like that knot in the pit of her stomach. Now she knew it as fear. She was scared of being alone, of not being ready for whatever was about to begin. This was all nonsense, since all she was doing was following her friends to see a doctor. But how could she explain the sudden restlessness inside?

Emmy stopped walking, closed her eyes, and took a deep breath.

These are just thoughts, she reminded herself, and thoughts, she could let go. She placed her attention on the cold air as it went in and out of her body. She also focused on the rich sounds around her: Finn's and Bree's footsteps crunching against the dead leaves, moving away in the distance; an owl hooting on a treetop, somewhere up above.

The air was sharp and smelled of the earth. Quietly, she became one with that part of herself that observed, the part of her who was, and the huge spaciousness she was connected to.

The knot inside her loosened and slowly disappeared. A faint smile spread on her face. She heard the voice of her grandmother clearly in her head: *A way will be shown to you if you trust.* She opened her eyes wide.

"Emmy," Bree yelled from ahead.

"Coming." Emmy walked quickly, determined to focus and pay attention.

* * *

The car jumped and briefly jerked Emmy in her chair, bringing her back to consciousness. She'd fallen asleep again. She sat up and looked around the quiet car. Finn drove, his tired eyes focused on the road.

In the back, Pablo lay sideways with his head on Bree's lap; Chester sat quietly next to him, his furry little body leaning on the boy's legs. Pablo's eyes were closed, and his breath strained. She could hear his wheezing from the front passenger seat. Bree sat quietly with her hand on his side, looking out the window.

The sun rose over the horizon. They were on a country road between the mountains and big, open fields. To their right, wide, grassy lots were divided by low, stone walls covered in moss. Cows and horses idly grazed in threes and fours; the ground looked wet with morning dew. Huge rolls of hay occasionally marked the otherwise empty fields. The early sun sparkled against everything, giving the scene a golden glow. A big, black bird with wide wings flew up above, gliding toward the mountains. They were headed north.

"How much longer?" Emmy asked.

Finn glanced over. "Almost there. Maybe half an hour."

"How's Pablo?" She looked at the backseat through the rearview mirror.

"About the same." Bree's voice cracked. She lowered her window, letting in a gush of wind into the car. It smelled like grass and sweet flowers.

"Where did you get this car, anyway?"

"It's a secret." Finn smirked.

"Where *did* you get it?" Bree asked, shifting her body under Pablo's head.

"Let's say it was a loan."

"Did you steal it?"

Finn remained silent.

"Are you crazy? They'll be looking for it." Bree looked angrily at him.

"Don't worry." He seemed strangely confident. "Where we're going, no one will know. And if they do, they won't be able to do anything."

"But where are we going?" Emmy looked at him.

"Wait a minute," Bree said. "Let's go back to the part about you having stolen—"

"It's a secret place," Finn interrupted, still smug. "I met a doctor a while back who was headed that way. He said I could come for help."

"So why is it a secret?" Emmy looked back at Bree, who had given up and was studying Pablo's face.

"You'll see." Finn smirked.

"You sure we'll find it?" Bree asked, now looking out the window.

"We will." He paused. "If we don't, we'll think of something else. We need to find a doctor. We're far enough that they won't recognize you here...hopefully."

"Shit." Bree didn't question further.

The car became quiet again, leaving only the sound of Pablo's heavy breathing to fill the silence. Soon Finn slowed the car and fumbled a piece of paper out from his pocket. It had a hand-drawn map.

"There it is," he mumbled, looking at the next street sign.

The car turned onto the small road toward the mountain. It was a winding road, full of small hills that went up and down and reminded Emmy of riding in a boat. She swallowed to keep herself from getting sick.

They drove through a valley and turned a couple of times. By the time they reached a dead-end street with an abandoned, white church at the foot of the mountain, she couldn't even remember how they'd gotten there from the main road.

The church looked about a hundred years old, with some walls looking like they'd been eaten through by insects. Most of the windows were boarded up; a broken cross, which now looked like a mangled T, poked the sky on top of the front roof. Finn drove around this church and parked behind. It was a strange, old place, but the countryside was full of such landmarks.

"We'll have to walk from here," he said, getting out.

Emmy opened the heavy car door and stepped outside. It was still early morning, and the air felt crisp and clean. As she stretched her arms and legs, birds chirped and sang in the trees. Finn also stretched and then walked around the area, seemingly looking for something.

"Here." He turned to the others, his finger pointed to a path up the mountain. "That's where we have to go."

Bree and Emmy helped him get Pablo out of the car and onto his back. They grabbed their bags and walked.

"Is it far?" Bree asked, as she followed Finn through the wooded path.

"Not sure," he answered, gasping for breath.

{ 22 }

November 27

Doctor Yang responded calmly, despite the chaos of their urgent arrival. Both Bree and Finn had started talking to him as he appeared in view. After a moment of confusion about who the kids were, he'd listened and understood everything they'd said, which Emmy found amazing. He had a kindly, round face, with olive skin and short, black hair. He was about average height and wore glasses, with eyes that seemed always to be thinking.

"Bring him in. Quickly," he instructed, lifting the canvas door to the tent that served as the place's infirmary. It was a small operation, with just two cots and a couple of machines and equipment cabinets.

As Finn rushed Pablo to the cot, the doctor put on a pair of rubber gloves and grabbed his tools.

"How long has he been like this?" He looked at Pablo's eyes, one by one, and into his throat.

"Since last evening." Bree stood at the foot of the bed, a little breathless. Emmy looked on by the doorway; Finn hovered behind the doctor.

"What happened?"

"He ate some poisonous mushrooms yesterday," Bree answered. "But we couldn't take him to the doctor there. We'd hoped he'd get better, but all night, he was sweating and throwing up." She paused, watching the doctor handle the sick boy. "Will he be all right?"

"Well, you were right to bring him. This kind of poisoning could be fatal." Dr. Yang moved quickly around the tent, gathering a needle connected to a line and a bag of clear fluid. He lifted Pablo's arm and wiped a small area of his skin with a cotton ball soaked in alcohol. Skillfully, he pierced his skin with the needle and secured it in places with tape.

Emmy let out a small cry. She'd felt something prick her arm, exactly where Pablo's needle would be. Suddenly her knees felt weak, and her mind became cloudy, as if the energy in her body was draining. She leaned on a post of the tent wall and closed her eyes.

Deep breaths. She breathed in and out, feeling the air move through her nose and lungs.

Suddenly she felt a rush of emotions that was foreign to her. It was as if she was lost and desperately searching for someone...

Bree. She was searching for Bree.

I have to find Bree, the voice in her head said. *Then everything will be okay. Where are you?*

Emmy felt as if she was all alone in heavy fog and unable to find her way.

This didn't make any sense. Bree stood just a couple of feet away from her. Emmy's head was all jumbled up, enfolding her with a sense of panic and dizziness.

Taking a deep breath in, she focused on the cool air and how it felt against the tip of her nose. She clung to that sensation as if it was a lifeline to a boat, as she found herself drowning in the sea.

A minute passed, maybe two. Gradually she felt better, her mind becoming clearer and her body, firmer. She snapped back to the room with the doctor's voice.

"We have good news and bad news," Dr. Yang started. "The good news is that he seems to have ingested a small amount. This injection will replenish the lost fluid in his body, and it'll help him flush out the poison and fight the poison better." He looked up from the chair. "The bad news is that that's really all we can do for now. Now it's up to him to recover. All we can do is to hope for the best."

Bree's eyes filled with tears. "Thank you."

"You've done all you can. He would've died for sure if you didn't bring him here."

"Thank you, doctor," Finn said.

"Glad you found me." The doctor smiled, getting up from his chair. He motioned them to the door. "Why don't we get out of here and let him rest. You hungry?"

"I'll stay." Bree moved to the chair and sat down, putting her hand on Pablo's arm. Dr. Yang nodded and led the others out the door.

{ 23 }

"Do you think he'll pull through?" Finn asked when they were outside, briefly petting Chester's head. The small, white dog had been waiting patiently outside near the tent's entrance.

"I can't say. But he looks like a tough little guy. I'll know more by tonight, see how he responds."

Finn became silent as he walked next to the doctor on a path through the woods. Chester walked ahead, constantly looking back to confirm where Finn was, and Emmy followed them.

"Try not to worry. It does no good." Dr. Yang patted him on the back. He proceeded to recount how he'd first met Finn in Berryville, almost a year before, on his way here.

Emmy listened as she followed, but her mind was deep in thought. She was still trying to understand what had happened in the tent, when she'd felt sick out of nowhere and had those unexplainable feelings. This was the second time it had happened, that she felt ill while looking at Pablo. She even felt the pinch on her arm this time as she watched him get a needle in the exact same location. What was happening to her, and what did this mean?

Innisfree was interesting. The woods were thick with old trees that were tall and dense at the top. On the ground, wood cabins and large tents made of white canvas dotted the area connected by walking paths; chimney stacks let out thin strands of white smoke rising to the sky. The scent of burning wood tickled her nose. People nearby smiled brightly and exchanged hellos with the doctor; a few had guns and other weapons on their bodies, causing her to stare as she passed.

Dr. Yang and Finn suddenly stopped, causing Emmy to bump into Finn.

"Sorry," she said awkwardly.

The doctor leaned in and looked at her, as if he was about to say something important. "I don't know if Finn told you about this place."

She looked at Finn, who smirked. "No."

"We call it Innisfree, and it's a secret place. That means that, no matter what happens, you can't tell outsiders about this place."

Emmy cocked her head. "Why?"

"I'll explain over lunch. But you have to promise, yes?" Dr. Yang held out his pinky finger.

"Okay." She smiled and shyly shook his pinky with hers.

"Good." The doctor smiled back and turned to start walking again.

The three turned in front of a small log cabin. A dog with brown, curly hair and long, flappy ears came running toward them, and Chester let out a low growl. But the brown dog lowered his head, and the two sniffed each other and were instantly friends. The brown dog jumped on Dr. Yang and excitedly wagged his tail. He stopped to pet the dog.

"You be nice to our guests," he said. He looked back and explained, "This is Tony. He loves everyone."

The dog jumped over to Finn and then to Emmy, slobbering all over their outstretched hands. Dr. Yang walked on toward the cabin and opened the door.

"Hi, honey," He yelled as he entered.

A woman with long, straight, black hair and a pretty face, with a sleeping infant in her lap, slowly stood up from a big chair. A little girl, whose face looked exactly like the combination of her parents, about two years old, looked back curiously with one hand on her mother's leg.

"We have guests?" he carefully laid her baby in the crib and walked over to the door.

The cabin was simple spacious and cozy, with a big bed on one side and a kitchen on the other. Dr. Yang walked over to the kitchen and washed his hands. "This is my wife, Aram."

"Welcome." She smiled at them and shook their hands. "Make yourselves at home."

As Emmy and Finn sat around the dining table, the couple moved busily to set the table for lunch. The little girl came over and pulled on Emmy's leg. She had something in her hand.

"Book."

Emmy laughed and put the girl on her lap, and began to read to her. The girl let out a giggle. Soon they were all listening to the story, which was about a little bird who'd lost his mother.

"Hope she's not bothering you," Aram said.

"Not at all," she said. "She's adorable."

"She knows it too," Dr. Yang said, shaking his head with a grin.

Just as she finished reading the story, lunch was served: baked root vegetables, roast chicken, and buttery rolls. They all sat down to eat, and Mrs. Yang took the little girl to feed her. Finn and Emmy were especially eager. They'd not eaten anything since yesterday afternoon.

He quickly finished eating and volunteered to take a plate to Bree. Soon he was out the door. "Be right back."

Aram helped her daughter eat. "He looks nice. How do you know each other?"

Emmy told her the story of Finn, Bree, and Pablo. "I only met them a few weeks ago. I was looking for something on the mountain, but it wasn't there, so…"

"Oh yeah? What were you looking for?" She wiped her daughter's mouth with a napkin.

"Um, the reeducation camp." Emmy looked down at her plate, suddenly self-conscious. Dr. Yang and his wife exchanged a glance. "Anyway, I had an accident and fell, and they found me—saved my life."

There was a knock at the door.

"Come in," the doctor yelled.

A tall, light-skinned man with heavy boots entered, footsteps were loud on the wooden floors. A pistol hung on his side. His light brown hair was cut close to his head, and he had a short beard that framed his blue eyes.

"Hey, Chris," the doctor said and explained to Emmy, "This is our security captain."

Chris gave a slight nod and walked to the table. An older lady followed behind him.

Dr. Yang got up from his seat. "Madam Alande."

She was about average height and wore a long, sweater-like coat. She had long, straight, salt-and-pepper hair, and her beautiful face had deep wrinkles, with soft eyes and chin. Something else about her struck Emmy. Maybe it was her expression. Her eyes were calm and gentle but serious and strong at the same time. Emmy felt drawn to her instantly.

With a gentle smile, Madam Alande touched Dr. Yang's arm and gave Aram and the little girl a kiss on their cheeks. The girl broke out into laughter, her arms stretched out for the lady. Everyone in the room laughed. Mrs. Yang petted her daughter's head gently and kissed it, telling her it wasn't playtime.

"Please have a seat." The doctor pulled out a chair for the lady and cleaned some of the plates off the table.

"Hope we're not disturbing you."

"We just finished."

"We came to meet our visitors, of course," she said, looking at Emmy. Chris quietly stood behind her with his arms crossed, watching.

"We were just doing introductions, actually. There are three more. The sick boy and a young woman are at the tent, and Finn went to bring them some food. He'll be back shortly."

"What's your name?" Madam Alande asked.

"Emmy Sukar." She felt shy and nervous.

The door opened, and Finn walked in, his breath heavy. His eyes searched the room, noting the new people.

Dr. Yang made introductions. "I asked them to meet you, Finn. Madame Alande is the elected leader of our group and the movement. Chris goes everywhere she tells him to."

"More or less," Chris said with a flash of a smile.

"Very nice to meet you," Finn said and glanced over to Emmy, who smiled back to let him know that everything was okay.

"Innisfree is a community of people who want to live outside the current climate of the New Republic," Madam Alande started. "We're still growing but bigger than what you see here."

She studied the young guests' faces.

"There're many of us who disagree with the Rational Party and want to fight back, and we're organizing." She paused. "As you can imagine, we don't usually let people in here without due process, but Dr. Yang here is willing to vouch for you."

"I knew it!" Finn exclaimed. "I thought that was what he was talking about when we first met, but he never straight-out told me."

The doctor laughed. "Hey, I didn't say anything."

"But how did you know you could trust me? You told me I could come to you."

"The story about your grandmother. It was easy to see through you. Gee, you hated the Party."

"He has a good eye for people," Aram chimed in, smiling and rocking her daughter on her lap. The little girl now seemed sleepy, leaning her head on her mother's chest.

"How's the sick one doing?" Madam Alande asked.

"Pablo's breathing better, I think. Bree's with him."

"That's a good sign. I'll go check after this," Dr. Yang said.

"I hope he recovers quickly," Madam Alande said, "We're glad to help. Also, if you'd all like to stay after your friend gets better, you're welcome to. I don't know what your plans are, but Dr. Yang tells me that you were on your own before."

Finn and Emmy looked at each other.

"We could find a place for you so you can stay as a family," she said with a smile and looked around the table. "It'd be much safer for you here, and I'm sure we can find you a job to do."

"Well," Finn said slowly, his eyes on Emmy's face. "Thank you. But we'll have to talk about it, if that's okay."

"How about you, Emmy?"

"Thank you." She smiled. "But I'd only planned to stay with them until spring. Then I have to get on the road as soon as I can, to find my family. They were taken to a reeducation camp for…reprogramming, I think they call it. I'd like to at least try."

Madam Alande looked at her curiously. "Alone? That's very dangerous… We've been looking for the camp too but haven't gotten anywhere yet. Of course I understand your worry."

She looked up at Chris, who'd been quietly listening.

"They leak false information so no one can find them. We've drained a lot of our resources that way." Chris paused, looking at Emmy. He said, somewhat apologetically, "We don't know of anyone who's come back alive from those camps."

"Well, I *know* they're alive," she said sharply. She wasn't about to let some stranger say what she could or couldn't do. "And I've seen them alive at the camp. I couldn't tell you how to get there right now, but I've seen it. I know I can find it."

"How'd you see this place if you never found it?" Chris chuckled.

"When I fell, I almost died and went to the other side. I saw them then." *He thinks I'm crazy.* But she didn't care. She knew it wouldn't be easy for them to believe, but how else would she explain?

The room fell silent. Everyone's eyes were on her.

{ 24 }

December 2

Emmy walked slowly through the woods. It was quiet around her, except for the wind and the birds, on a trail away from Innisfree. She breathed and focused on the movement of her body, how her arms, torso, legs, ankles, and feet all had to move in specific and perfect balance to take even a small step forward.

She'd never had to think about orchestrating the different parts—to pull her thighs a certain way or flex the bottom of her foot this way and that—in order to walk; but when she tried to do it on purpose, she immediately lost balance and had to take a step back. Now that she tried to do it on purpose, it felt like learning to walk for the first time in her life.

How did she do it so smoothly, then, when she wasn't thinking about it? Who was conducting the music, without her conscious thought?

Even as she asked the questions, she knew, inside. It was the same part of her that observed, in those moments of silence and clarity, during meditation. It was the same force that beat her heart at every moment of her life, the same force that brought her to the spirit of her grandmother when she'd left her body.

The realization moved her deeply and filled her eyes with tears. Life had always been a wonderful mystery. How asleep she'd been.

She took another deep breath and continued to move, trying to notice everything that happened, in and outside of her body, to be only and completely present to the moment. Thoughts about people and things came and went. And each time she came back to her senses, she heard her heartbeat, steady and strong.

It made her feel stronger—there, in her heart, no voice told her she had to be or do anything else than she already was. She could just be, when she was in her heart and not in her head.

Occasionally she looked around and felt as though she was waking up to something new every time. It was now officially winter, but patches of dark green moss reached up for life on low stones and roots. She knelt down and ran her hand against its velvet, soft and moist under her palm. It made her giggle.

When she lifted her head, the rough, deep lines of tree barks looked beautiful to her. It was as if a whole different world existed there. All of this made her happy for no reason. It was the feeling of openness and freedom, of clarity and beauty, and of connection. She smiled until her face hurt.

Emmy came to an open area where tall grass grew on one side and low bushes on the other. Something moved in the distance, and she stopped. A doe raised its long, brown neck and looked back at her, her eyes black and constant. It was just a few feet away. She stood completely still and watched, fascinated and curious what it'd do next. The doe flicked her ears and tail, staring back. It was, apparently, not scared of her.

The two stared at each other for a couple of minutes until finally Emmy moved again, to continue her walk. The doe slowly turned its head to follow her with its eyes. After a while she looked back, and there it stood, totally still.

She took a step forward. It flinched a little. More slowly, she took another step. Suddenly the doe lowered its head, hissed loudly, and jumped away. She burst out laughing, watching it go.

"What's so funny?" a voice said.

"Good gravy, you startled me!" Emmy laughed harder. Chester, who'd followed Finn there, nudged her leg with his nose and surveyed the area like a hunting dog. Emmy bent down and petted his soft, white head, still laughing.

"Are you okay? What's so funny?" He looked around for a clue, but the deer was long gone.

"There was a deer, and we were just looking at each other until it yelled at me," she tried to explain.

"It yelled at you?" He looked at her, perplexed, and chuckled. He wasn't getting it.

Giving up, she stopped laughing. "What are you doing here?"

"Looking for you. The Council wants to see you."

"The Council?"

"The leaders of this place."

"What for?" she asked, turning around.

"They want to talk to you about reeducation camps."

* * *

The space was tight for the number of people in the cabin not much bigger than Dr. Yang's, who wasn't present. As she sat, Emmy counted eight new faces plus Madam Alande, Chris, and Finn. Many stood, and others sat where they could. Some looked at her curiously, or suspiciously, and others chatted unaware of her presence. Some were old, and some were young; there were men and women.

A fireplace on the wall roared with flames, and it was hot in there. Emmy took off her scarf, loosened her collar, and fidgeted with her fingers. Someone gently patted her shoulder from behind. It was Finn with a reassuring smile. She smiled back a little nervously.

Madam Alande clapped her hands twice, and the room quieted down. "Okay, let's begin. I asked you all here today as we have a young lady who says she's seen, or has been to, a reeducation camp."

No one said anything, but something in the room shifted. Some looked surprised and more curious that before, and Emmy could feel their eyes on her skin.

"Here she is, and as she'll tell you in a moment, this was not an ordinary sighting. I know what you're about to hear will be more easily acceptable to some than others, but I ask you all to keep an open mind."

She paused and looked around the room.

"You know that I consider myself a seeker when it comes to matters of the unseen. It's not that I'm without skepticism. But we also absolutely cannot afford to miss anything when it comes to these camps. And that's what we're here to decide today, if we want to take any action based on this information.

"I present to you, Miss Emmy Sukar, so she can tell you her story." She moved and stood next to Emmy. "Would you kindly tell us what you saw?"

She hesitated. *Where do I start?*

The entire room silently waited, all eyes on her.

Will they even believe me? Her heart beat fast. She took a deep breath.

"Okay, I come from a long line of seers—intuitives, psychics, whatever you want to call it." She took another deep breath. "My mother had it, my grandmother had it, and others before them. Now I'm starting to have it. We can see certain things that others can't, the energies behind form, if you will."

Emmy swallowed and looked around the room. Everyone was still.

"My mom, dad, and sister were sent for reeducation a few months ago. I was looking for them in Berryville…" She told the story of her fall, how she left her body, and how her dead grandmother became her guide on the other side. She described what her grandmother showed her, the big compound where her family was held.

No one said anything when she finished. Some exchanged looks of disbelief. She held her breath, envisioning herself curled up in a fetal position right there on the floor. The silence remained longer than she felt comfortable with, but she breathed and brought her attention to her heart, trying to get quiet inside.

But her mind soon became busy and filled with thoughts—unfamiliar voices, unfamiliar words. It was as if people were shouting at her but silently.

She's lying. Do they really buy this?

That girl is possessed. There's nothing in the Scripture that would allow this.

Fascinating, but how to know if this is true?

Who is this girl?

Her breath quickened, and she panicked.

What's happening? She closed her eyes and gripped her chair with her hands. But suddenly it all made sense. These thoughts were coming from others in the room.

She could hear their thoughts.

Before she could think of anything else, something pulled her attention toward a specific point in front of her. Emmy's mind became quiet again. She opened her eyes, and there, an older, black man with short, gray hair sat in an armchair next to the fireplace. He had big, brown eyes and a kindly face full of wrinkles. Their eyes met, and he nodded with a smile.

Slowly he rose from his chair and, balancing each step with a wooden cane, walked to the front.

"Mr. Nolan." Madam Alande bowed in his direction. The man waved his hand lightly in the air, as if to say there was no need. He stopped near Emmy.

"Thank you, Miss Emmy. You are a brave young woman." His presence calmed her. He turned to face the Council. "I believe her."

Some gasped.

"There's no guile in her. Her heart is pure and open. She's telling the truth." He looked at Emmy, and this time his eyes said, *I see you.*

She smiled brightly back, surprised and grateful to have this unexpected ally.

"How can you tell?" a young woman with short blond hair, who stood in the front row with her arms folded across her chest, asked.

Mr. Nolan chuckled. "Call it an old man's gut feeling, but I know when people are lying."

"If you're wrong?" an older, light-skinned man asked. He had white hair and beard and wore a long gray coat.

"I've been known to make mistakes." Mr. Nolan shrugged.

"But there'll be serious consequences if we're led astray by wrong forces. She may've seen what she saw, but nothing in that story indicates that it came from our one and only God," the man in gray coat said with a serious face.

"Now, now, Father Cassano." Mr. Nolan laughed. "I thought we agreed that there were many doors to the house of god. That kind of talk is not, in my opinion, welcome here."

He glanced over to Madam Alande, who nodded back. Father Cassano's mouth clenched.

"May I say something, in the wisdom of the Council?" Chris said, taking a step forward. His face was tense.

"You may," Madam Alande said.

"This is too serious of a matter to act on a mere fantasy of a teenager."

"It wasn't a fantasy," Emmy protested in a low voice.

"I know you think it wasn't." He looked straight at her. "But that doesn't mean it wasn't." He turned to the room. "All I am asking you to consider is that we've already lost many lives searching for these camps. Those efforts were based on real intelligence from legitimate sources. If we lose more people because we can't tell fiction from facts, I'd hate to be the one to tell their family that we sent them to their graves on the whim of a fanciful teenager."

The room was quiet. Emmy wanted to protest further, but there was no way for her to prove anything. She looked down at her feet helplessly.

Mr. Nolan gently raised his right hand toward Chris. "I understand your concerns and commitment. We're indeed lucky to have a leader like you. But what makes such 'real intelligence from legitimate sources' more believable to you than this? Did they not turn out to be false?"

Emmy looked at the gentle old man, curious at what he was about to say.

"Yes, but we did the best we could. This is different."

"How?"

Chris remained silent. Emmy looked between the men.

"What if you're wrong this time?" the old man continued. "What's the cost, then?" He looked around the room. "What would we lose by choosing not to believe? Or to not have an open mind?" He took a breath and continued in a firmer voice. "An opportunity to fight the very forces that brought you here? The lives of countless people held hostage, as we speak?"

"Are you asking me to act on faith?" Chris asked.

"It'd be the same faith that made you act on all other 'real intelligence.' You don't have to believe, but we have a choice. I merely ask you to be open."

"What do you propose?"

"Go with her and find out. Where it is, if it exists. Once you've done that, we can make a better plan." Mr. Nolan looked around.

A moment passed. Chris seemed out of arguments.

"Is the Council ready for a vote?" Madam Alande asked. Some nodded, and some said yes. Others looked at each other, uneasy. "All those in favor of sending a search, please raise your hand."

Four, including Madam Alande and Mr. Nolan, raised their hands. There were nine members in the Council.

"Is this all? A final call." Madam Alande waited for a moment. "If there's no—"

"Wait," the young woman with golden hair said hesitantly. She raised her hand. "Yes."

"Then it's settled. Chris James, you have our command." He lowered his head respectfully. Madam Alande looked at Emmy. "Are you up for the task?"

"Yes."

A way will be shown, her grandmother had said. She felt excited and nervous. *But what if I don't find it?*

Her stomach tightened, and her mind went blank. Butterflies fluttered inside. Then a hand gently tapped on her shoulder and brought her back to the room.

It was Finn, looking down with a smile. "I'd like to go too."

{ 25 }

December 3

Things moved quickly after the Council's decision. That evening, Chris and a couple of others had taken Emmy to a tent with lots of maps and asked all kinds of questions about what she saw on the other side. It didn't take long to narrow down a starting point, though, since what she saw was a small island off of another, massive one. It turned out that there was only one such area in the entire New Republic, although that was where the simplicity stopped. There were many small islands south of the main one, Catalan Island, and they'd have to go island by island to find the right one.

This did not please Chris. Although he didn't say anything—he was generally a quiet man—it was obvious that he simply wanted to get it over with, in order to comply with the Council's request and to prove the leaders wrong. The sooner they were done, his attitude implied, the better it would be for everyone involved. He decided in the end that they'd leave at the break of dawn.

The next morning, everyone, including Emmy and Finn, was up at the break of dawn to help get ready for the trip.

"I can't believe you're leaving when Pablo's still sick." Bree looked sad and angry, her eyes on the ground.

"It'll only be a couple of weeks." Finn busily loaded the back of the car. "Pablo's much better, and you have Dr. Yang here."

Emmy minded her own business, trying not to eavesdrop. She sat not far from the car, petting Chester's head. It was cold outside. The sky was still mostly dark, although a hint of light emanated over the horizon. The shadows of tall treetops pierced upward like black ink; the steam from her mouth rose and disappeared like smoke.

Something tiny fluttered deep inside of her. Call it excitement or fear, and both would have been true. It was like a constant whisper: *Pay attention; something's coming.*

"I'll be back before you know it," Finn said to Bree. "You'll be fine here. It's not like back at the cave—"

"But I thought we were a family. I thought—"

"We *are* a family. But it's my chance to do something. I'm not much use here, but if we find the camp..." He didn't finish his sentence and instead puts his hand on Bree's shoulder and smiled. Her head still lowered, she didn't say anything.

"Are we all set?" Chris called out, walking toward them with purpose. He looked like a soldier no matter what he was doing, but it was his focus that made him stand out.

Emmy knew that he didn't believe anything she'd said, but she had to admit, he always seemed competent, reliable. No wonder the Council trusted him so.

Finn quickly hugged Bree. "Take care of Pablo and Chester."

She hugged him back, trying to smile, but it was obviously hard for her. Emmy gave her a hug and said goodbye too.

"You take care of him, okay?" Her friend whispered, hugging her.

She squeezed her with her arms. Finn tussled with his dog for a moment, saying goodbye to his beloved companion, and handed him over to Bree. If she didn't hold on to him, Chester would try to get in the car too.

"We'll be back soon." He opened the door to the front passenger seat but couldn't look at Bree and Chester. Bree lifted the little dog in her arms and walked away, not looking back. Emmy got into the backseat, and they waited for Chris.

After a moment of silence she asked, "Why are you going?"

"Don't you want me to go?" He turned to look back, with a blank face. Emmy stared back. He glanced out the window, his eyes following Chris's movements as the latter walked around the car. "I mean, do you trust this guy?"

"I think so," she said, but she knew she did. "I know he doesn't believe me. But he's loyal to the Council, and he seems sincere."

"Well," Finn said, "I'm going along to make sure." He looked up at the sky. "Besides, it's an adventure. At the cave, we were always busy surviving. It'd be stupid to go back. What they do here, it means something."

"Do you believe me? What I saw?" She wasn't sure if she wanted him to answer, but she asked anyway. He remained quiet for a moment.

"I don't know. But I saw you unconscious for all those days. And the way you woke up and got all better, it was strange. For someone who got hurt so bad..." He took a big breath. "One way or another we'll find out, won't we?"

He turned back with a teasing smile.

"Fair enough." Emmy smiled, relieved. *Was it really that simple?* "But remember that I may not be able to save you every time you're in danger, okay?"

Finn let out an exaggerated, fake laugh, and stopped abruptly. "Yeah, right. You make sure to stay out of the way, young lady."

The driver's door opened, and Chris got in.

"All right." He settled in his seat and started the car. "I hope you're ready for a long ride."

It was indeed a long ride. Without stopping for breaks, Finn and Chris took turns driving all day. Too bad that Emmy didn't know how to drive; she'd never had to learn since she'd walked everywhere in Bath and had her parents to take her places. It was fine between the two, though. The tired driver could get in the backseat and sleep.

Sometimes no one said anything for long stretches, allowing Emmy to meditate with nothing but the bumps on the road to distract her. The small flutter in her gut stayed with her the whole time, but being still and breathing into her heart helped. Eventually she got used to the flutter.

The weather was clear and sunny. As they drove away from the mountains and headed northwest toward the sea, the air got warmer. The sounds in the car, when they had the radio on, constantly changed; every time they lost a signal it became a challenge to find another that everyone could tolerate.

Otherwise they often rode in silence. It was easy for Finn and Emmy to chat, sitting side-by-side when he drove, which mostly meant that he made fun of her for something she did or didn't do and she protested. Chris kept to himself and tolerated their presence.

They neared the city of Petersburg around six o'clock, and it was already pitch-dark outside. Petersburg was about halfway to Catalan Island and where they were to spend the night. The car was quiet. Feeling tired and sleepy, Emmy closed her eyes and put her head back. The music on the radio ended, and the local news came on.

The female announcer's voice was confident and serious. There had been a fire that day in Petersburg, which had unfortunately killed a mom and her son. Causes of the fire were unknown, but the police was investigating. The news continued.

"The Ministry of Mental Hygiene and Social Order concluded today its five-month investigation into underground religious groups, which had been suspected of holding illegal gatherings in opposition to the Rational Mandate. The report found serious security concerns, especially from groups that identify with the Hindu sect. The Ministry encourages any citizen with information of suspected activity to—"

"Turn it off," Chris yelled from the back seat.

Emmy sat up and looked through the rearview mirror. He was leaning back in the back seat with his eyes closed. She turned the radio off, reminded of the nun in front of the ministry building in Alexandria, the image of her limp body over a pool of blood across the sand-colored pavement.

She took a deep breath and shook her head. Everyone kept silent for a while.

"Chris," Emmy asked, looking back. "Can I ask you something?"

"What?" His eyes stayed closed.

"How did you get to work with the people at Innisfree?"

"A long story." He brushed off her question. After a long moment, he said, "Because it was the right thing to do. I don't believe in god, if that's what you're asking."

"Were you a real soldier before?" Finn jumped in.

"A real soldier?" Chris chuckled. "I was a soldier for the Republic...until I found myself doing things that I couldn't stand."

"Like what?"

"You don't want to know."

"Do you have a family?" Emmy asked. He was such a ball of mystery, this man.

He finally stirred, sitting up and taking out a map to study with a small flashlight, absorbed in the activity. "Far away."

Finn and Emmy looked at each other and shrugged, unable to ask any more questions. Outside the window, the scene had changed from dark, open fields to an urban area, with crowded buildings and storefronts lighting the streets. They had reached Petersburg.

"Make a right there," Chris said. "Go five more blocks to Sunnyside and turn left."

"Roger." Finn turned the wheel.

Petersburg looked nice, with many brightly colored stores and people walking around in heavy winter coats. Emmy noted a chocolatier, which she hadn't seen in years. She thought of Alexandria and her family, feeling a pang in her heart.

At least I'm on my way. She took a deep breath. One, two, three blocks.

Emmy felt odd. Sunnyside Road appeared, on a corner crowded with people and cars. But the tiny flutter grew in her gut, making her uneasy—she hadn't felt this way in a while, but she knew the feeling, the drumming in her gut, the knocking that wouldn't stop.

The car turned left, and a chaotic scene of people and movement unfolded. She felt as if a heavy pressure crashed against her like a giant ocean wave, taking her breath away. She let out a quiet moan, clutching the handle on her right. She gasped and tried desperately to steady herself.

What's happening? She focused on her breath, the air coming in and out of her body. *This will pass.*

Finn was too absorbed with the scene outside to notice her discomfort. "What's going on here?"

Chris leaned forward to look. Up ahead, a mob had gathered on the left side of the street, spilling half way onto the road. Something was going on in the middle of it, with a fire burning, but it was hard to tell. Traffic slowly inched forward; some honked their horns impatiently.

The mob shouted incomprehensible words, and their movements spread like waves. A few ran away from the crowd with giddy faces and objects in their arms. Something dropped from the fourth-floor window of the adjacent building and crashed on the ground. Chairs, books, and lamps—one by one, they flew out the window to the middle of the crowd.

"What in the world?" Chris mumbled and then yelled, "Park the car."

Finn slowly turned the car around and stopped on the opposite side from the mob. A few police officers stood on the curb, hands across their chests and watching the scene. Chris got out, and Finn followed. Emmy hesitated.

Finn knocked on her window, his mouth saying, "Come on."

But she trembled as she looked out to the mob.

As he opened the car door, the sounds of people and yelling were deafening. "You shouldn't be alone. Hold my hand."

She reluctantly took his hand and got out of the car. The streets were filled with people.

"This way." He pulled her hand, following Chris, who was already disappearing into the crowd toward the mob's center. They walked quickly to not lose him.

Her body bumped and brushed against those of the mob, and each time, it hit her with a different feeling: anger, hatred, fear, and sadness. It was as if walking through a crowd and smelling the different smell of each person she bumped into, except that it was their emotions she felt. It was a hot, boiling place, and she couldn't think straight. Her fingers held tightly around Finn's as they squeezed through the undulating bodies.

When they finally reached the center, a bon fire burned high on one side. Next to it, an older couple and a young woman knelt with their hands tied behind their backs. Wooden signs around their necks said "Hindu." Their faces were smudged with dirt, blood, and tears.

Emmy was struck by the young woman's face, which was completely devoid of any emotion. Her eyes were open, but she didn't seem to see. Blood oozed from her arm and leg where her dress was torn. The crowd taunted with angry shouts.

A rock hit the old lady in the head with a pop, and she fell to the ground. The old man gasped and moved toward her, but there was nothing he could do. Another rock flew and rolled on the ground.

Emmy buried her face on Finn's shoulder, and he put his arms around her.

Breathe, just breathe, she told herself. No matter, tears streamed down her face.

"Let's get out of here." Chris turned.

Finn and Emmy firmly held hands and followed to painfully make their way back to the car. She felt waves of emotions from the crowd near her, and this time, it was more singular: fear. They were afraid more than they hated. But of what?

"I'll drive," Chris said. Finn handed him the keys and got into the back seat with Emmy, who had crawled up into a ball with her head between her knees, sobbing.

"Shit," he said, his hands on his head.

Chris started the car and slowly drove the car through the crowd.

"Shouldn't we do something? Are we just going to leave?" Finn yelled, his voice sharp. "Aren't you supposed to be a fighter?"

"What do you want me to do?" Chris answered coolly. "Our mission is to find the camp, remember? We can't compromise that right now, not to mention we don't have any backup."

Wiping her tears away, Emmy looked at Chris's face in the rearview mirror. His ashen but blank face reminded her of that young lady in the center of the crowd. She cried harder, holding both of their pain in her heart.

{ 26 }

December 4

The room was full of dark shadows and gray light from the window. Emmy's heart pounded, and her breath was short. She felt hot and sweaty.

The dream lingered with her. It was about those people yesterday, the Hindus. Her dream was no more than a repetition of all of the images she'd seen, all of the emotions she'd felt. She felt them still, even in wakefulness, stuck on her like a wet shirt that needed time to dry out. Sadness returned too, which was her own, and she lay with it, deep inside, not knowing what else to do.

She tossed and turned in all directions. The room was small and simple with white walls and ceiling. She stared at the window for a while, where the night sky hung in one corner with faintly glimmering stars, trying to distract herself. It was no use, though, because her thoughts ran wild and fast.

Everything about what she saw boggled her mind, as to the why and the how of it all. After a while, the faces of those three Hindus were replaced by those of her mom, dad, and sister, and fear and anxiety bubbled up with surprising speed from her gut. She told herself that they were safe and unharmed, but she didn't know that for sure. The only thing she could count on was what her grandmother had showed her on the other side.

But even that felt trivial at this point. What good was a memory when so much was at stake? But then again, what choice did she have?

At least now she was on her way to find out. She tried to calm her fears, rationalizing the arguments and voices until her mind was exhausted. She almost dozed off too, except a flash of thought woke her again.

Grandma Ethel had said that a way would be shown to find her family, and Emmy was, miraculously, on her way, with the help of her new friends. She had said that Emmy would find her seeing abilities, and something was happening, for sure. She'd felt Pablo's sickness and pain and felt the emotions and heard the thoughts of strangers, whether she wanted or not.

Everything was happening just like her grandmother had said. Chances were that her family was safe, at least until she could reach them. At least she liked to think so.

But how could she better control this ability? She couldn't be surprised and overwhelmed by others' feelings, especially the bad ones, whenever she had to face something. She had to learn to hold her ground and manage it. So she could feel her emotions and stay in her own skin. But how?

Emmy had not sensed her grandmother around her since she'd been back; she was supposed to be her guide. She remembered what her Grandma Ethel had said about meditation, that it was the closest thing she could do to connect with that place.

The idea hit her like a lightning rod, and she sat up immediately in bed. She stacked a couple of pillows together on top of the bed and sat, covering her lower body with a blanket. She put her hands gently together, palms facing upward on top of each other, in the hollow of her crossed legs. When she felt her spine straight and settled in the position, she took a deep breath and closed her eyes.

Please, show me how to control it.

She eased into it, following her breath coming in and out of her body. Thoughts came, and she let them go, one by one, and each time, she came back to her question and intention. It had become easier to get quiet inside.

Time passed, but she was oblivious. She was in that space where time disappeared and everything expanded. She breathed. A vision came.

Emmy found herself on a small wooden boat in the middle of the ocean. There was nothing around except for the calm, blue water that sparkled in in all direction. The sun was warm and tingly against her skin; a salty breeze caressed her cheeks and hair. The boat rose and fell with gentle waves, which chirped gingerly against the wooden planks.

She looked down to find her hands holding a giant fish net. The net looked strong and tightly woven, with small holes. *Would I be able to catch the big fish with this net?*

Before she had an answer, her arms threw the net out into the ocean. It spread wide and deep. She waited in anticipation, imagining the big fish that she wanted to catch. When she felt ready, she pulled it up. It was easy and light, as if everything was weightless.

There were about a dozen fish in the net, as big as she'd imagined, much bigger than the small holes of the net. Some of them were round and fat, others were long and lean. Their scales glistened against the sun with blue, silver, turquoise, and red. Each was distinct.

One by one, she freed them from the net and admired their beauty. They looked right at her in acknowledgment too, with a certain knowing in their beady eyes. When they were done, she gently released them back into the ocean. She sat in peace and contentment.

Coming back to her body and finding herself on the hotel bed again, she smiled. She had her answer.

* * *

Emmy turned her head away from the bright window, covering her eyes. It was going to be a sunny day. She picked up the hot tea and sniffed its fragrance before taking a sip. The hotel's cafe next to the lobby was small. Sitting at one of the tables with breakfast, she watched the clerk at the front desk—a red-haired lady with heavy, foreign accent—interact with her customers. Her voice rose in volume whenever someone didn't understand her, causing her to repeat the same sentence over and over. She seemed focused and friendly though, and this made Emmy smile.

"How long have you been here?" Finn said.

She turned, and he was at the breakfast bar pouring himself a cup of coffee. His eyes were sunken with dark circles, although he was clean and showered.

"Not long. You look tired." She looked at him with a question in her eyes.

"I couldn't sleep at all last night." He frowned, took a piece of toast, and pulled up a chair next to her. He sipped the coffee, savoring its aroma, and bit into his breakfast.

"Are you going to be all right to drive?"

"I'll nap in the car. Chris didn't seem bothered, so he should be all set." He was clearly annoyed.

"Is that bad?" Emmy smiled.

"No, it's not bad." He chewed. "What about you?"

"Nightmares." She took a sip of tea. "But I'm okay. Feel better this morning."

"About what happened yesterday?"

"A little." Emmy was about to say something else when Chris's heavy footsteps approached.

"Good morning." He dropped his bags on the floor and proceeded to the breakfast bar.

Finn continued to eat in silence, full of emotion. Chris came back with a large cup of black coffee and a plate full of bread, eggs, and toast. He sat down and ate.

"So what are the rebels doing, anyway?" Finn asked. "Is there like, a plan?"

Chris stopped to look around and gave him a sharp look. There was no one nearby.

"If there was, I don't think this is the time or place to discuss it." He took a bit of the egg. "Is this still about yesterday?"

"Just wish we could've done something. Not sure if my grandmother would have approved."

"She passed away years ago," Emmy explained to Chris and then whispered, "She was Catholic."

Finn burst into laughter. "Yes, she was. She was Catholic."

Some people from the lobby looked over briefly before getting back to their business. Chris continued to eat.

Emmy placed her hand on Finn's arm. "There was nothing we could do, you know. It was just three of us—"

"I know. I'm sorry." He struggled to smile. "I just hate them so much, all of them."

Chris put down his fork, looked at him and sighed. He picked up his coffee and said in a softer voice, "I felt like you once. That's why I joined the group. But if you want my advice, I'd channel that energy into something more constructive. What I mean is, what you feel now, the hate for the Party and all those people, turn that into support for the opposite. Does that make sense?"

"You mean, to fight with the rebels?"

"Sure. But it's more like, use that energy *for* something, like a fight for justice, as opposed to *against* the Party and the people you hate." Chris sipped his coffee. "The difference is that, if you're driven by hate and resistance, you might end up doing the same things that you hated in the first place."

Finn looked at him curiously. "That happened to you?"

"I didn't like what I became." After a long pause he said, "But now I just follow orders and babysit teenagers."

He chuckled.

Did he just make a joke? Emmy laughed. Finn smiled too, as he looked out the window with a thoughtful face.

"You all packed? It'll be another long day in the car." Chris looked at his watch. "If we hurry, we should get there before sundown."

Finn got up and grabbed his bags. "You drive first."

{ 27 }

"Where are we?" Emmy asked.

"Almost at the bridge. There's traffic, though. An accident up there." Finn tapped his fingers rhythmically on the steering wheel. "You slept for a long time. Did you know that you snore?"

"I do not." She gave him a sharp, disapproving look.

"I swear. Like this." He made a guttural, gurgling noise, as if he was choking, laughing under his breath. "

"Stop lying."

"He heard it too." He motioned toward Chris.

"Oh, yeah? So what? I was tired."

But he continued the noise, even louder. Emmy reached over and pinched the skin of his upper arm, and squeezed.

"Ouch!" He twisted away from her hand and rubbed his arm. "That hurts."

"Serves you right." She smirked.

"All right, kids." Chris took a sip of water and looked out at the traffic. "Settle down."

Outside the sky was full of gray clouds. Up ahead, the road was lined with red brake lights of slow-moving cars. Emmy rolled down the window, and a gush of cold air hit her face.

She breathed it all in, enjoying the tingling sensations on her face and lungs. The air felt wet and smelled like salt. They were near the ocean.

The car slowly moved forward in the traffic. Ahead on the left, two police cars had blocked the road around a couple of damaged cars. The entire front half of the second car was wrecked, with broken parts scattered on the road. A couple of officers directed traffic, but there was no one else.

"Hope no one died." Finn looked over at the scene as they drove past.

"There's the bridge." Chris pointed ahead as the car gained in speed. "Let me know if you want to switch," he told Finn, "It's known to make people nervous."

"No. Piece of cake."

The car sped forward. The heavy steel bridge stretched for more than a mile. On the other side was Catalan Island, shrouded in high fog, rocky cliffs, and tall trees. The ocean was greenish-gray under the bridge, reflecting the color of the cloudy sky. Several boats looked like tiny dots in the distance.

Is this what I saw? Emmy tried to remember, but it was hard to tell. With her grandmother, she had closed in from the above. She sighed, frustrated that she couldn't more readily decipher her whereabouts.

Finn sat up straight with both hands tightly on the wheel, looking forward. Only two lanes headed in each direction, and there wasn't much room to waver on either side of the car.

"Is there a way that we can look at it from the sky?" Emmy asked.

"What do you mean?" Chris asked.

"The islands. I came down from the sky. I mean, that's how I saw it. I'll be able to recognize it better."

"I don't think that's a good idea. Especially if there really is something out here, in which case the Party probably has their fingers on everything. This isn't exactly the tourist season." He looked at her for a moment. "Are you getting nervous?"

"Well, I didn't come in by car the last time I was here." She looked out the window. She wasn't ready to answer any questions yet.

"So you don't think you'll find it?" Chris probed.

Emmy took a deep breath. "I'd like to think I will."

"We'll find it," Finn said, his eyes still on the road. "I think we will."

"We have two days. The island is about five hours' drive at length. Two days should be enough time to look through."

They rode in silence until the car reached the end of the bridge and its tires hit solid ground.

Finn breathed deeply and cracked his window open to let in fresh air. He stretched his neck in his seat, his hands still on the wheel. "I think the question is what do we do when we find it?"

* * *

"No?" Chris studied Emmy's face.

She took her time before answering, studying the contours of the small island across the water. She felt frustrated. It seemed like a hopeless task. She couldn't be sure if any of these were it. Nothing looked the same from this angle, and there were many islands. "No, not it."

"Back in the car." Chris said, walking back.

Finn and Emmy slowly followed. Everyone was tired and a little anxious. They had been in the car for almost four days straight now, sitting, except for the occasional stops to get closer looks at the islands. They were now nearing the end of their two days. They'd covered most main roads that ran along the coastline and even been to the neighboring Tisch Island by boat, just in case. They'd looked at almost a hundred islands at this point. All the while, as Emmy took her time to look, Chris and Finn had looked at her, expectantly.

She was desperate to find it. She'd come so far. It felt close—almost at the tip of her fingers—but also elusive. Chris's increasing impatience didn't help. Finn kept up a bright face, but she could tell that he was also getting tired.

A part of her wanted this to be over with too. They could go back at the end of the two days but she intended to stay. She'd find it on her own if she had to.

Back in the car, Emmy sat in the front next to Chris. No one spoke, and she appreciated the silence. Outside the window, the scenery changed between the sea and the trees, back and forth, as the road swerved in gentle curves along the coastline. She tried to breathe into her heart, to feel centered and make some room inside. She closed her eyes.

Where are you? Come. Show yourself. I know you're close.
I feel you here. Come, show me where you are.

She breathed deeply and opened her eyes. The sun lowered over the ocean in a bright glow of light, and its reflection—a second sun—also glowed on the surface of the water, dancing with sparkling ripples. The intense light hurt her eyes, and she looked away.

"Can you pull in there?" She pointed an exit sign for a scenic overlook.

"What for?"

"It's worth a look."

"I say yes," Finn said lazily from the back, holding on to the last of his enthusiasm.

Chris took the exit without another word. The road took them through a short patch of woods and into a small, open area on the edge of land. He parked the car, and they all get out.

A tall fence, bigger than Emmy's height, separated a high cliff from the water. Heavy wind blew in from the sea, messing up her hair. The sound of breaking waves underneath was loud and powerful, vibrating the ground underneath.

She stood right up against the steel fence and looked out, feeling the sun on her face. There were no islands in view. But from there, the sun seemed even bigger and brighter over the sea line, and beautiful. Every ripple of the ocean glistened in its dance with the wind and the light. Finn came to her, also mesmerized by the view. They looked at each other and smiled. This made her feel better—lighter—somehow. The sun rose and fell, every day. The wind constantly moved. She would be here tomorrow, just like the sun.

"You see anything?" Chris asked, standing near the car.

"No. We can go. Thanks for stopping." Emmy smiled and walked back. She got in the front and closed the door. The car moved.

"So we can look until it gets dark, but I think we've given it a good try." He glanced at her before turning his eyes back on the road. "This doesn't mean you were wrong, but we agreed on two days."

She nodded. She couldn't blame him for wanting to be done. She just wished she had something to prove to him that his efforts weren't for nothing. Still, it wasn't really over. She'd look for the camp until she found it, she knew, whether that'd be tomorrow or a year from now. The thought made her feel better, closer.

The car merged onto the main road, the same they were on before. It was pretty empty. A small, white car passed them in the next lane, a yellow Labrador's face out the window in the backseat. Its nose pointed up in the air, and its ears flapped in the wind.

"There are many side roads that we haven't covered yet," Finn said cautiously, "and islands we didn't see. We could stay longer in theory."

"We could stay indefinitely, but doesn't mean we should." Chris looked through the rearview mirror.

Emmy didn't say anything. As far as she was concerned, she was sneaking off in the morning before they got up to continue looking. She kept this to herself because she knew that Finn would object and possibly insist on staying too. She didn't want to trouble him any further. She wanted to return him to his family, to Bree, Pablo, and Chester.

"What's that?" Chris's eyes were still fixed in the rearview mirror.

Emmy looked through the side mirror, which showed a convoy of cars and trucks speeding behind them.

Finn turned to look. "Are those military trucks?"

"Looks like it. Sit back," Chris answered, his eyes going back and forth between the mirrors and the road ahead of him. Finn quickly turned around, just as the convoy passed their car in the next lane. The first car was a black, luxury sedan with tinted windows. There was no way to tell who or what was inside.

The last time Emmy saw a car like that had been back in Bath, when Stryker had given her a ride to school. The memory gave her goosebumps all over her body.

Next, three identical trucks, camouflaged with green and brown and plastic sheets covering their cargo, sped past them. Emmy could feel the heavy vibration of the trucks' movement through her bones.

"We'll have to see where this goes." Chris accelerated the car just enough to keep up, keeping distance with the convoy. "As far as I know, there's no military base here. Wherever they are going, it could be what we've been looking for."

{ 28 }

They followed the convoy all the way to the northernmost tip of the island, until the trucks turned on to a side road that led to a military checkpoint. Chris continued on the main road until the next exit and made that turn. A couple of minutes of driving led them to a fishing dock, where boats came in and fishermen unloaded their catch from the day. Men wearing rubber pants with suspenders took crates of fish into a big warehouse near the water; next to it, tired workers rested on the porch of a wide log cabin, sipping tea and beer.

Chris parked the car and grabbed his binoculars, moving quickly and lightly. "Let's check this out."

Finn was right behind him, also moving quickly, and Emmy followed. Chris looked around for a way to get to the water, to get a better look at the shoreline in the direction of where the trucks had stopped. They walked through the woods behind the fishing warehouse, where a narrow path led them down to the water. A small fire pit and empty liquor bottles laid around a rocky beach.

"Look," Chris said, looking east.

In short distance, where the trucks had turned, a bridge connected Catalan Island to a smaller one, about half a mile over the water. It was a new, single-lane bridge.

Chris looked at Emmy. "What do you think?"

"I don't know. I don't remember seeing a bridge, but that doesn't mean it wasn't there. The size and location seem about right. But I'm not sure."

He studied the island through his binoculars. All they could see from there were the ocean waves, rocks, and trees. He turned abruptly and walked back, moving faster than before. He handed his binoculars to Finn and headed toward the fishermen's log cabin.

"Go wait in the car."

Finn and Emmy looked at each other for a moment in hesitation but slowly walked to the car.

They waited in silence. She watched the seagulls as they flew low above the boats, looking for any throw-away fish, and the setting sun over the horizon. It got darker by the minute now. The warehouse finished its business and closed its doors; men got into their cars and drove off for another day.

Chris came back about half an hour later with a brown, paper bag in his hand. He got into the driver's seat, and a smell of something delicious, fried and fishy, filled the small space inside the car. "Hungry?"

She put the bag on her lap and opened its contents. Finn popped his head to the front, curious. Out came two newspaper-wrapped bundles of fried fish and potatoes, their grease seeping through the paper.

"Dig in," Chris said.

Emmy handed one to Finn and ate. The fish had a light and crispy coat of breading and fresh and flaky filet on the inside. The fried potatoes were seasoned perfectly with salt and garlic, a little crispy and dark around the edges. Emmy went back and forth between chewing and licking her greasy fingers.

"Eat up. We're in for a rough night." Chris watched the two eat, seemingly pleased.

"What do you mean?" Finn put a potato in his mouth.

"They were eager to talk," Chris started, clearly excited and looking in the direction of the island. "They messed up a lot with the locals. That's called Wick Island. The Party took it over a few years ago and kicked off the residents. There weren't a lot, but they'd lived there for generations. Then that bridge went up, and lots of trucks went back and forth. The locals don't know what else is going on, but the fishing boats aren't allowed to go near. So everyone has to go around it, which makes it difficult for them to fish like they used to." He chuckled. "Some of the old geezers in there were mad."

"So what now?" Emmy asked.

"Someone will take us to the island tonight. We'll have to be real careful. I'll pack some camping gear. Take a nap after you eat."

* * *

Emmy tried to sleep after finishing her meal. But she was too excited and nervous, and no matter what position she tried in the car, she couldn't bring herself to fall asleep. Once or twice she dozed off, only to be awakened by the cold and unfamiliar sounds of the waves. Finn and Chris seemed not to have any problems sleeping, however, and only turned occasionally. Time passed slowly as Emmy went back and forth between trying to sleep and watching the bright stars in the night sky.

An abrupt knocking on the car window startled everyone awake a few minutes past midnight. Chris got out of the car and greeted the man, who had a flashlight. She couldn't see his face in the dark; only his shape moved in the shadows.

The men shook hands and exchanged a few words. She sat up and straightened out her hair, and stretched the parts of her body that were sore from sitting for so long. Chris opened the back of the car and picked out what to bring with them, giving Emmy and Finn each a tightly packed bag to carry. When they were done, they followed the man toward the docks in complete darkness. The only thing she could make out was the strange man's voice, occasionally talking with Chris, and that he had an accent she'd never heard before.

Her eyes soon adjusted to darkness, and there was more light near the water, which reflected the night's bright, full moon. The man quietly led them to a small row boat and helped them into it. He rowed, carefully moving the boat out of the docks and then toward the water. Once they were out, the boat headed in the opposite direction from the island.

"Where are we going?" Emmy whispered to Chris.

"We're going around," the man answered in a low voice. The rough outline of his face was visible in the moonlight. He looked to be in his late 40s or early 50s, and a salt-and-pepper beard covered most of his face. He moved as if the boat was an extension of his body and made rowing look as easy as walking.

Everyone was quiet. Only the squeaky rhythm of the man's moving oars and water breaking against the boat continued. It moved forward at a steady pace; the wind chilled through every open crevice of her clothes. Slowly they approached Wick Island, not too far from the bridge that connected the two bodies of land.

She felt incredibly alive and alert. Her body tingled as she looked forward, watching the island get bigger and bigger.

{ 29 }

December 5

Chris, Finn, and Emmy moved as soon as the sun appeared over the horizon. Wick Island had a small mountain on its southern half, effectively providing a wall between the bridge and the north. They climbed this mountain from the west, from where they were dropped off the night before, headed for the highest point possible. They would be able to survey the land from there.

They had hiked for a couple of hours in slow progress. The mountain had a steep incline, requiring her to fall behind and take breaks. They were also trying to keep as quiet as possible and be on the lookout for possible Party soldiers.

Chris was clearly in his element. It was as if this mission, the forward movement, made him stronger. Finn seemed as tired as she was, but his steady presence helped calm and reassure her.

"What's that?" Finn said suddenly, looking around.

Something bristled nearby, and Chris quickly grabbed his pistol from a holster on his thigh. They stopped in their tracks and stood perfectly still, all of their attention focused on the noise. It bristled again, and twigs snapped. Emmy's heart began to beat fast and hard, its sound almost loud enough, she thought, for everyone to hear.

The bristling got closer. Chris slowly cocked his gun.

Out from behind the bushes appeared the head of a white goat with black horns. Immediately it saw the humans and let out a big, rough huff, a thin strand of steam rising from its nose and mouth.

Chris put his gun back on his thigh. "A mountain goat."

Finn and Emmy also let out a breath and laughed. The goat continued to walk down a few steps, watching them closely and occasionally thrusting its horns in their direction for a warning. It looked magnificent, with long, heavy, white hair and wise, brown eyes.

"Come on," Finn said, and they pushed on toward the top.

* * *

Her heart fluttered as she handed the binoculars to Finn, who took them eagerly. Chris knelt next to them, silently surveying the area through his own glasses.

"Shit," Finn said as he took in the view. "Holy shit!"

Emmy fell to the ground and covered her face with her hands.

There it was.

She was surprised, nervous, and exhausted, all at the same time—surprised that it was all real, even though she'd told herself it was; nervous that her family was near, but she didn't know what came next. She closed her eyes and breathed, trying to stay in the moment.

Chris put down his binoculars and tumbled next to her. He looked up at the sky, which was now darkening by the minute, and then at her with an expression she didn't understand, about to say something, but stopped.

"What?" She thought she knew—she was in shock too.

His mouth was open but no words came out. On their way here, on the boat and coming over these hills, nothing had been proven yet. Whatever they thought they'd find there, could have turned out to be something else.

But from where they now stood, high up on the hills, they could actually see the barbed wire over huge walls, soldiers on the ground, and the barracks with rows and rows of windows where countless prisoners—outlaws of thought and belief, young and old—were held against their will. Rational Party signs were plastered all over the place.

"You don't have to say anything. Besides, it was you who brought us here." She was grateful that he'd obeyed the Council and come here with her. Without him and Finn, she wasn't sure if she could have found it.

He looked back quietly, his eyes softer. "Is this really what you saw? But how…"

She shrugged. "I don't know. I already told you everything I know."

"It's huge." Finn put down the binoculars, sat, and looked at Emmy. "But I'm surprised it's not bigger. A lot of people disappeared. This can't be the only one there is."

"I don't know." She shrugged. "But this is the one I saw."

"You did it. You weren't lying!" He broke into a huge smile and leaned over her, putting his arm around her neck and shaking her back and forth, horsing around. "Or crazy."

"Crazy?" Emmy laughed. "Okay, that's enough." She tried to break away, but his arm was strong and tight around her. "Let me go."

"Good job," he whispered in her ear before releasing her.

Her face was hot when she glanced at Chris, who watched quietly with a grin. His thoughts were somewhere else, though.

"What now?" Finn grabbed the binoculars again and turned toward the camp.

"We go back to Innisfree," Chris answered, getting up. "We inform the Council and figure out what to do. We could be there late tomorrow night if we hurry."

"Sure," Finn said, his eyes still on the camp.

Emmy looked up at them from where she sat. "I'm not going. I'll wait here until you get back."

{ 30 }

Stars sparkled in a rainbow of colors across the velvety night sky. The moon was perfectly round and bright, just above the sea line and near. All was quiet except for the wind and the occasional noise of engines and shouts coming from the camp below.

Emmy sat on a fallen tree trunk and watched. Wrapped up in a blanket in the cold December night, she bounced her knees and wiggled her toes to keep them from freezing. Bright spotlights illuminated the dirt grounds inside long walls topped with barbed wires. Soldiers with rifles across their chests kept watch from tall posts. All lights were out at the prisoner barracks—countless windows now dark—except for a few on the ground level.

What was it like for them in there? Her heart ached for her family. She wanted to run over there and shout their names, let them know she was there. But the thought only whimpered in her head.

She took out her silver locket, still safely tucked under her sweater, and brought it under her nose. The metal was warm from staying close to her skin; the smell of lavender still exuded from it. She closed her eyes, inhaling the scent and listening to the constant rhythm of her heart. Slowly the space inside her became bigger, clearer, and quieter. Time passed without notice. She now felt ready to try something, to use her intuition in a way that she intended.

Soon her mind became clear and she pictured a big, woven net—like the one in her vision with the fish and the ocean—and imagined it spreading out from her heart and into the world around her. She asked it to bring her only what she wanted to know, only what she needed to know.

What Emmy wanted was her mother. She was near, practically right in front of her, and she wanted to reach her. Calling her forth, she imagined what her mother felt like: her smells, her smile, and her essence—the signature of her energy imprint. She imagined being held in her mom's arms, like she used to when she was little, and began to feel warm and safe.

A smile spread on her face. Her heart was full of love, an energy that overflowed and extended out from her center. Goosebumps broke out all over her skin, from back to front, then out through the top of her head. Sensations tingled all over. She let out a deep breath.

"Emmy?"

Her eyes opened, and she was back on the tree trunk, sitting in the dark. She looked around, but there was no one else. She listened for a minute. Before her, the camp grounds were still brightly lit and quiet; behind her stood dark and empty woods. Moments passed quietly. Was it her imagination?

She closed her eyes again and breathed, trying to get back to where she was. The scent of lavender was stronger now, even though she'd dropped the locket back under her shirt.

Then she heard it again.

"It's me, sweetie." It was like a whisper in her ear and a wringing in her heart. "Don't be afraid."

She'd definitely heard it this time.

"Mom, Is that you?" she asked in her thoughts, her eyes still closed.

"Yes. I've felt you coming for a while."

Tears flowed down Emmy's face. "I've missed you so much. And I'm sorry, I am sorry. I didn't know. I didn't think they'd take you away. I was stupid. I'm sorry…"

"Oh, my dear girl, it's okay. It really is. I know you didn't know. We always knew."

She felt her mother's energy all around her, like the unmistakable scent of lavender in the air. It was as if she was embracing and keeping her warm. She wanted to lean in more, to get closer. She couldn't believe it was really happening.

"There's no one to blame, especially not you," Leona continued. "You have a huge heart, and you're a good person. Look how far you've come all on your own. I'm proud of you. I hope you know that."

The communication was like soft and beautiful music. Emmy didn't know what to say, but her tears continued.

"Cry as much as you want, until you feel better," her mother said.

She did. She cried until every last knot in her gut was released and she felt lighter inside. All the while, Leona's essence remained with her, embracing and supporting her. After a while Emmy managed to ask, "How are Dad and Nora? Do you see them?"

"Sometimes. Just glimpses. But I visit them without their knowing or in their dreams." Leona giggled.

"Are they all right?"

"Mostly. But they miss us and miss home, very much. Life here is starting to wear them down."

Emmy sighed. That much was expected, and she wanted to give some good news. "Help is coming. Something will happen. I don't know exactly what but something."

"I know. We'll see each other again soon. I know it."

"Do you talk to Grandma? Do you ever see her?" She had many questions for her mom that she didn't know what to ask first.

Leona laughed. "You know I've always—"

"Are you okay?" Finn's worried voice yanked Emmy out of her trance, opening her eyes. He stood near the tent with arms full of tree branches and twigs. She quickly closed her eyes and felt around her, but Leona's presence had already disappeared. Giving up, she opened her eyes and smiled, wiping her eyes and nose.

He dropped everything to the ground, came to kneel in front of her, and studied her face. His eyes were full of concern. "What's wrong?"

"I'm sorry. It's just that, they're right there, you know? My family. I miss them so much." Tears started again, and she covered her face in her hands.

"It's cold here." Finn sat down next to her. He smiled, rubbed his hands together, and pointed to her blanket. "Want to share?"

She nodded and unwrapped herself. He put it around both of their bodies, his arm gently moving around her back. His body brought in the cold, giving her a shiver.

"Too bad we can't light a fire," Finn said, settling in. "I didn't think I was ever going to say this, but I miss our cave." He laughed. "And hot stew. Delicious, hot, thick stew." He smacked his lips a couple of times. "I hope Pablo's better. They'd better be taking good care of Chester."

"I hope so too," Emmy said, sniffling. "You should've gone back."

"Like I could leave you here alone. It was my choice. You could just thank me, you know." He elbowed her lightly.

"Okay. Thank you." She smiled. It would have been definitely harder if she was alone.

"I just hope he'll be back soon." Finn looked up at the night sky. "He sure wasn't happy to leave us. But you're just as stubborn as he is." He laughed. "I know you miss your family, but think of how far you've come. They're right there. You actually might get to see them again someday. That's a lot more than I could say."

"I know." Looking at him, so close by, she was glad that he was here, saying these things. It was funny to realize just then, that somewhere along the way, she'd made friends she could really depend on. He'd given her so much without expecting anything in return. That seemed to her a miracle in itself. She smiled.

Down at the camp, a big military truck like the ones they'd seen the day before entered through the gate and drove to the main building.

"Here." Finn picked up the binoculars and handed one to Emmy.

As they looked, a few soldiers ran out from the buildings and unloaded the truck, banging on the canopy. A throng of people stepped down from the back, some falling over the others, disheveled and confused. Some desperately held on to their children as they looked around the massive compound.

{ 31 }

December 6

Emmy and Finn had slept side by side, each in a
sleeping bag. She'd felt a little nervous about it
earlier in the evening, but the two were both tired by
the time they lay down that they'd fallen asleep as soon as
their heads had hit the ground. She'd slept soundly through
the night, despite the cold, and was now feeling refreshed and
determined to make the most of her day.

She stepped out of the tent and stretched her arms, looking
around for Finn. The sun was bright, but she felt the chill
against her skin. She quickly put on her coat and shoes,
suddenly excited for the day.

In daylight, her surroundings looked much different than
the night before. She now saw how well Finn had built the
tent and hidden it under a layer of thick leaves and branches,
in a small nook under a hill. They'd picked this location in the
dark the night before, and it was as if she was looking at it for
the first time.

A small pot of coffee still steamed over an unlit gas
burner. She poured herself a cup and sat down on the tree

trunk, like the night before, and savored the smell. She slowly took a sip, careful not to burn her mouth. Its warmth spread from the tip of her tongue down to her stomach.

Emmy looked into the contents of their food bag. Their entire inventory included a few cans of packaged meats, a couple of boxes of biscuits, and a few bottles of water. They needed to find fresh water and set some traps if they didn't want to starve.

She took out a biscuit and bit into it. It was hard and crumbly between her teeth, soaking up the moisture in her mouth until it became a sandy paste. She passed it down with some coffee. This was the result of Chris packing their food, although, he'd confessed, he had never expected to actually use them.

Far ahead, the wide ocean met the sky in a single, flat line, and heavy clouds made everything seem a little gray. The day had started down at the camp too. Countless strands of white smoke rose from the chimneys; trucks came and went, transporting mysterious cargo.

She took another bite of the biscuit and spied through the binoculars. From one of the barracks a group of male prisoners stumbled out, herded like animals by the armed soldiers. The prisoners seemed cold without their coats and moved quickly, if chaotically, to follow the guards across the dirt grounds.

Emmy peered at the men's faces, looking for her dad. Face by face, she scanned, but it wasn't easy to tell. They were all dirty, tired, unshaven—and sad. There was no sign of Sohan, but would she even be able to recognize him in that condition?

"Shit," she said to herself as she watched the last of the prisoners enter a building and disappear from her view. Putting down the binoculars, she cracked her knuckles. The entire scene made her a little anxious.

Additional prisoners come out of the buildings, in groups of fifty or so, and were moved to different places. There were men, women, and children. Some groups got time just to be outside in the sun, if only under the constant watch of the guards, but were never allowed to mingle. Emmy plunged herself into the binoculars every time a new group came into view, eager to get through as many as possible, but there were thousands.

Taking a break, she turned on the gas burner to heat up leftover coffee. She got up and moved around. *One, two, one two*, she counted in her head as she lifted her knee to her elbow, periodically switching sides. She did some jumping jacks and lifted her knees some more.

"What are you doing?" Finn approached, laughing and carrying something over his shoulder on a stick.

"Don't make fun. It's my beauty routine. Can't you tell?" She continued to move.

"That's what you do?" He shook his head. "Maybe you should try making yourself useful sometimes; then you wouldn't need to move on purpose." He swung around the stick from his shoulder and showed off a rabbit tied at the end, already dressed and cleaned.

"You caught that this morning?" She stopped moving in surprise. That was, impressive.

"I've been industrious." He smirked, sat by the tree trunk, and cut it up with a knife, putting the pieces into an empty pot.

"I would've gone out, but didn't know where you were." She smiled.

The coffee boiled. She poured the last of it into a cup and held it out to him. He placed the pot of rabbit on the burner, added some water and seasonings, and took the coffee, sitting back and taking a sip.

"Well, I didn't go far. And we should still be careful. So what you been doing?"

"Watching the camp."

"Anything interesting?" Finn looked at the camp curiously, savoring his coffee.

"I looked for my family, but there are so many of them." Emmy sighed. No one said it would be easy.

"I can imagine." He grabbed the binoculars and looked down at the camp. "We should try to identify the buildings. Keep track of everything."

"Do you see that big one with a Rational Party sign at the entrance, the one with double doors and white awning?"

He redirected his glasses. "Yeah."

"I think that's where they eat. Prisoners have been going in and out all morning. They go in, and about half an hour later, they come out. Then the two long buildings next to it are where they sleep, because that's where people have been coming out from." She paused. "The smaller building on the far left with the barbed wire fence around it, I've only seen soldiers going in and out."

"Someone seems headed there now."

"Where?"

"Look." He passed on the binoculars.

Emmy saw two soldiers pushing a man with the muzzle of their rifles, in the direction of that smaller building. The man limped slowly forward, hunched forward, and bled from the head. He held his left elbow with his right hand, a pained expression on his face. She quietly watched, her eyes nervously following the man's every move.

After about ten steps, he fell to the ground. He squirmed to stand up again, but one of the soldiers kicked him in the stomach. The man cowered and begged for mercy, holding up his hands. But the other soldier thrashed him over his head with a baton, yelling something.

Her heart shrank, and a ball formed in her throat. Giving the glasses back, she closed her eyes and breathed deeply, waiting for it to end.

"They're gone." Finn slowly put down his glasses and looked at her. "You okay?"

"What happened?"

"They took him into that building. That must be a bad place." He got up, walked over to their bag of supplies, and took out a small notepad and a pen. "We're going to write down everything we see. We have to."

* * *

For two days straight, they watched the camp and got to know it pretty well, as much as possible from the distance. Six barracks, one commissary, two command posts—one of which seemed to be a police station of sort—two armories, and one that they were still trying to figure out. A brand-new building was being constructed east of the commissary, where hundreds of prisoners conducted daily manual labor. Trucks came in a couple of times a day from the outside, and even though most of them were cargo, two had been prisoner transports.

Thick walls around the camp were about twenty feet high. In the north, the camp directly faced the ocean and had a dock and a medium-sized boat, heavily guarded by the soldiers. They had seen the boat operate just once, the day before. Soldiers had loaded it up with prisoners at the break of dawn; when it came back in the late afternoon, it was empty.

Emmy and Finn came up with three possibilities for where they'd taken the prisoners: one, they were transferred to a different camp; two, they were expelled to the neighboring country, Surian, which was close; and three, as much as the two doubted, they were dumped in the middle of the ocean. It couldn't be the last, they figured, since that would have been a lot of people thrown overboard—and wouldn't the bodies float back to land, at least some of them?

They wrote everything down in the small notebook, which they planned to give to Chris when he came back. He had said that he'd try to be back as soon as possible. As to what would happen, he couldn't promise, because he had no idea what the Council would decide. There were different opinions and personalities within the Council, he'd explained, and sometimes it could take a while to make a decision. But his recommendation would be for an attack—if only to take advantage of the element of surprise—for which he believed the rebel forces were ready.

So they could be on their own for a while. But Emmy was starting to feel restless. What if it took weeks, or even months? She didn't regret staying behind, but it had also felt, at the time, as if she didn't have a choice but to stay. She would have never been able to forgive herself if she had left and was not able to come back, for whatever reason. Besides, the restless inside of her said that something would happen, although she didn't know exactly what.

For his part, Finn tried to keep busy. He'd found a small, freshwater stream in a manageable distance while he was out setting traps. He'd also caught at least an animal a day, thus far, which he attributed to the fact that the animals were not used to his traps. In any case, he had kept them both well-fed and enjoyed the activities.

It was about midmorning, and her eyes were glued to the binoculars. She'd given up finding the faces of her family and instead had been watching the activities at the command post. Something had been bugging her since the previous day because—although she was sure she was mistaken, as chances were extremely small if not impossible—she thought she saw Stryker down there.

All she saw was the profile of a tall, light-skinned man with gray hair in a suit. Anyone could look like that, especially from that distance, but something in the way the man moved had alarmed her. She wanted to make sure she was wrong; she certainly hoped, with all of her heart, that she was.

So she watched incessantly, obsessed with finding this man.

It had been a relatively quiet day at the camp. No beatings or bloodshed had yet taken place, but the day was young. Soldiers busily moved about, some on patrol and some on watch. She lost the track of time until a snowflake landed on her cheek. It was the first snow of the year.

Looking up at the sky, she was suddenly aware of her surroundings. Finn had been gone a long time. She stood up and looked around. Everything was quiet and still, except for the heavy snowflakes. Where had he gone? Since they'd been here, he'd developed the habit of disappearing without letting her know where he was going.

Emmy gathered the empty water bottles, put them in a bag, and headed toward the stream. She could use the exercise and figured she might find him on the way. As she walked, everything was quiet except for the wind and the sound of her footsteps.

Snow fell heavily now and accumulate on the ground. Covered with a thin layer of white, everything looked magnificent—the sinewy lines of dark tree branches and the soft curves of the hills, all covered in soft, white snow. Far away, the line between the sea and the sky had disappeared into a smoky mesh of gray and white. She couldn't remember if she'd ever seen snow on the ocean before. These were breathtaking views.

When she finally reached the stream, the water sounded like a thousand little flutes playing a mysterious tune. Tiny icicles sparkled like little crystals poking out of the water; patches of green moss on black rocks peaked out from under the cover of white snow.

Being careful not to slip, Emmy knelt down and dipped her hand into the cold water and wet her mouth. The air was sharp, and steam rose out of her mouth. She saw beauty in everything around her; everywhere she looked, there was life and movement. She giggled and blew on her fingers as she filled the empty bottles with cold spring water, one by one. By the time she turned back, her tracks were already covered by a fresh layer of white.

As she walked back toward the tent, everything looked different under the thick layer of snow. The trail between the two places had disappeared, and many of the little posts she'd remembered as path markers were also hidden. She tried to stay sharp and pay attention, but confusion stopped her multiple times and slowed her down.

Just as she realized she'd taken another wrong turn and was about to go back, something caught her eye. A white rabbit—she'd almost missed it entirely—was caught in a snare and looking at her with two red eyes. It was small and had fluffy fur. It was Finn's handiwork. There were no footsteps nearby; he must have set it before it had started snowing.

She imagined the look on his face when she brought this back to the tent. She could pretend that she caught it herself, and he wouldn't be able to tease her for not being useful any more. The thought made her laugh.

But she had no idea how to get it out and carry it back. Finn and Bree had always done that. Emmy didn't want to kill it or lose it. She held out her hand near the rabbit's head and it jerked hard, trying to get away, making the snare close in even tighter around its neck. Startled, she backed off.

Something bristled and clicked behind her. A chill spread on the back of her neck. When she slowly turned around to see what it was, she knew exactly how the rabbit felt.

"Hands up over your head."

The black tip of a rifle pointed at her head. Behind it, two soldiers in heavy uniforms glared at her.

{ 32 }

December 9

Every surface of the empty room was covered with gray cement. Emmy felt the cold inside her bones as she sat on the floor, from where it rose like heat. She rubbed her hands together to keep her fingers warm and watched the steam from her breath.

She looked around her surroundings, but there was nothing to see. No furniture and nothing but the walls, except herself sitting in the corner. The room was lit by a small bulb in the center of the ceiling; the only other distraction was the small window—maybe a square foot—high up on a wall.

But she knew exactly where she was. This was what she and Finn had jokingly called the police station of the camp.

She'd been there a couple of hours, although she couldn't be sure. Now she knew what it felt like to be inside these walls.

What would they do to her? What would she say? She could pretend that she was hiking and had no idea that the island was restricted. Brilliant—she could play ignorance and tell them that she'd already taken the Oath and had joined the

Student Brigade. She frantically searched her coat pocket for the Brigade pin. She still had it on her somewhere, she thought—but her pockets were empty. *Shit.*

Emmy nervously shook her knees in front of her. She should have been more careful, but there was nothing she could have done differently.

Where was Finn? If he'd also been caught, and that was why she couldn't find him earlier, or if he was hurt in any way, all of this was on her. She'd brought him there and had insisted on staying behind. She should have left with Chris; then Finn would be with her, and they'd both be safe. She buried her head between her knees and tried to suppress the anxiety that formed in her gut.

She breathed deeply and tried to feel him out through her senses, like she did with her mother. But it was no use. Maybe it was the shock or fear, she didn't know, but she found it impossible to quiet her mind and get to that calm, clear place. Anxiety was funny, how it fluttered like butterflies in your body and made you useless.

Her eyes still closed, the image of Finn hurt and being beaten by the soldiers filled her head. *Shit, shit, shit, and shit.*

This was wrong. It was terribly wrong. She needed to do something, be in control or at least try, but there was nothing she could do. Everything raced inside her, and she didn't know how to calm down. The last time she'd felt like this was before she tried to kill herself, up on that mountain and before she ever knew Finn. She hated feeling that way then, and she hated it now. She buried her head even deeper.

But you survived, said a voice in her head. *You chose to come back. Remember, there's a reason for this. Stay awake. Pay attention.*

The words reverberated through her. Sitting with it for a while, she remained balled up until it became quieter inside. Then, after a moment of stillness, something tugged at her to lift her head and get up.

She walked around the room, lifting her arms and knees high, as if she was marching. Right up along the four square walls she went, turning mechanically in every corner. In a few turns she even mumbled, "Peter Piper picked a peck of pickled peppers. A peck of pickled peppers Peter Piper picked. If Peter Piper pick, pickle, picked a peck of pickled peppers—"

The door opened with a loud, screeching creak, and a guard entered the room. Behind him was a tall man in a suit whose face she could not see at first. When he stepped forward, a shiver went up her spine. It couldn't be—

"Well, well, Miss Emmy Sukar," Stryker said.

She froze in her track. Her knees gave out a moment, and she had to lift her hand to lean against the wall to not lose balance. Her heart thumped against her chest. She had, in fact, seen his terrible face the other day.

The guard brought in a wooden chair and placed it in the center of the room. Stryker sat and got comfortable, his eyes fixed on her.

How could this be? She wanted to scream, but she held herself very still, very tight.

"Nice to see you," Stryker said, "I thought that we'd never cross paths again. You look quite different. I'm not sure I would've recognized you." His eyes studied every inch of her body and face. "You've lost some weight. Was it hard on the road?"

Emmy looked back coolly. *Not again. Please.*

"What, the cat got your tongue? I thought we were friends."

She looked away, clenching her fists until her fingernails pierced into her skin.

"I was rather fond of you, Miss Sukar. You see, after you disappeared, I questioned myself for letting you stay and came to the conclusion that it was a regrettable mistake. And I hate to make mistakes." He paused. "So I've made it my responsibility to look for you, although you were very good at hiding. Where *have* you been?"

Her eyes were fixed on the floor. She'd seen his face and heard his voice, but it still felt surreal. Not only that, she didn't know what to say—her mind was like a white cloud full of fuzz, and it was impossible to grasp a single thought.

Stryker took a breath. "In fact, your entire family has been a pain. For reasons beyond my comprehension, the leadership is paying special attention to your mother. Can you tell me why?" He briefly waited for her answer and slowly stood up to walk over to her. He leaned his face close to hers. "No? Well, that's too bad."

She felt his moist, warm breath on her cheek and winced. Emmy turned her face away and closed her eyes, wanting to puke. She wanted him—and all of this—to go away.

"But what I don't understand—and I think if we can answer this, it would make up for a lot—is how you found this place and got here." He stared at her expectantly. She did not move. "Really not going to talk?"

He waited.

"As you wish. I hope you'll be more cooperative when I come back. It bothers me, Miss Sukar, that you never seem to appreciate my generosity. But I promise you, I do not make the same mistake twice." He walked out and glanced over to the guard, giving him a nod.

The door closed with another loud, creaking sound. Someone grabbed her arm and pulled. When she opened her eyes, the guard had his baton raised over his head, towering over her. She cowered instinctively. The next thing she knew, she was on the floor clutching her head, feeling the blows on her back and listening to the sound of her own screams.

{ 33 }

Pain screamed at Emmy from all over her body as she regained consciousness. Her face was on the ground, her right cheek numb and frozen against the rough cement floor. She opened her eyes, but it was completely dark in the room; only a faint sliver of moonlight entered through the small window on the wall. As she tried to sit up, her limbs burned, even as the rest her violently shivered. Her head throbbed, and she was parched, even as she tasted blood and salt on her lips.

She slowly managed to sit up and leaned against the wall. Tears flowed down her cheeks. She wasn't even sure what she was feeling. Was it the pain? Anger? Fear? Maybe all of the above.

It had been sheer relief to lose consciousness, and she didn't know how long she'd been out. She looked down at her hands, which were dirty and bloody, and rubbed them against her pants. She didn't want this to be the end. It couldn't be.

Emmy tried to control her breath, counting *one-two-three* on the inhale and *one-two-three-four* on the exhale, even as her body continued to send shooting pains all over. Trying to collect her thoughts, she realized that Finn must have been okay. Stryker would have mentioned him if they had him. She let out a sigh of relief.

Thank you, thank you, thank you. She wasn't sure who she was thanking, but it sure was something to hold on to. She wiped the tears from her face. At least he was okay.

The wooden chair that Stryker brought in still stood in the middle of the room. She got up slowly, leaning and balancing herself carefully against the wall, and limped over. Just as she extended her arm out and let go of the wall, the tip of her fingers almost reaching the back of the chair, she lost her balance and fell to the ground. The chair fell with her, making a loud noise. She grunted, lifting herself up and rubbing her elbow.

The slit in the metal door opened, and a guard looked in from the hallway; it closed just as quickly as it had opened. Soon footsteps echoed outside.

Shit. Now they knew she was awake. She'd have to hurry.

She managed to get up, set the chair straight, and sit. She took a deep breath once she settled, feeling the relief on her joints. Closing her eyes, she tried to focus and get quiet inside. It was easier to calm herself now, knowing that Finn was still safe. A couple of minutes passed.

The door opened with a loud screech, and Stryker walked in, this time alone. As the door closed behind him, he shook his head and clicked his tongue, looking down at her. "This is a sad sight."

"Thanks to you." Her voice cracked. She wouldn't let him have the best of her, not again. The shock of seeing him again had worn off, and she knew that she'd have to deal with him somehow. Besides, now that she'd already been beaten, she strangely felt less afraid.

"Ah, you found your voice. I knew we'd be talking in no time." A grin slowly spread on his face. He stepped forward until he was just a couple of feet in front of her. She looked straight back at him, and he looked back at her curiously. "I hope this means you're ready to talk?"

"Depends on what you want to know."

"How did you find this place?"

"Saw it in a dream." She chuckled. It amused her to tell the truth knowing full well he wouldn't believe her.

"A dream?" He clicked his heel.

"Yep."

A hint of anger flashed on his face before he forced a smile. "Let me remind you that I'm not limited in my ability, or intention for that matter, to put in a little more effort to get to the truth."

"I'm not lying." Emmy shook her head. She let out a deep breath, shifting her aching body in the chair.

"What happened in this dream, then?"

"My dead grandmother showed me this place, where my family was. And when I woke up, I was able to find it." She tried to hide her amusement; maybe he'd think she had lost her mind.

"Did you come alone? You didn't swim across the ocean, for example." He slowly walked around the room with a stern face, his hands behind his back and his eyes on the ground.

"I came alone."

"You can't possibly expect me to believe that." Stryker became louder. Bit by bit, he was revealing his anger. "You mean to say you flew here? Or walked across the bridge crawling with soldiers? You had help, someone with a boat and possibly more. I need to know who that was."

She looked back at him in silence.

"I don't think you understand. They're already scouring the island. Your silence only delays the inevitable. We'll find whatever is out there." He looked at her coolly.

"There was…someone." Emmy sighed in hesitation. A spark of curiosity on his face, and she grinned. "It was you. It was your car and your trucks. I followed you here. Alone."

He slapped her across the face, and she flew off her chair to the ground. Her cheek throbbed like the angry siren of a firetruck, until the hard edge of his leather shoe kicked into her gut. Instinctively she crawled into a ball, and the kicking continued. She screamed, although it was more of an animal's roar.

Stryker stopped kicking, caught his breath, and straightened himself out. She remained completely still on the floor as he stood over her, anger still fuming from his body.

"Sit up." He ordered, picking up the chair and setting it in front of him.

Clenching her jaw, she struggled to get up and sit.

He grabbed her face and held it right in front of his. "Listen carefully, bitch. You think this is a joke. But remember that I can always bring in your mother, father, and even your tiny little sister here to shed some blood. I can cut some skin right in front of you. Is that what you want?"

"No." She whimpered and looked down at the floor. She hadn't thought of that possibility. What did she expect— fairness or mercy? From *him*?

"Then think about what you want to tell me next time. If you don't, someone's going to get real hurt." He walked over to the door and knocked on the metal. It opened and closed behind him. The sudden emptiness and silence of the room engulfed her like a heavy ocean wave about to suck her under.

What do I do? Shit, shit, shit. I need to figure this out. My family doesn't have a chance in here. They'll die.

But they'll hurt Finn. I can't betray him. Remember what happened last time when you told him things?

But what choice do I have? Let my family get hurt right in front of my eyes?

I can't. I can't.

Her thoughts circled over and over for a long time, until eventually there was no coherent thread. Her body ached all over, and she was exhausted, emotionally and physically—her mind was shutting down, and she desperately wanted to rest, even as she tried to keep awake and figure this out. Stryker could be back any minute.

What do I do?

She fought sleep like trying to block a waterfall through her fingers. She shook her head and slapped her face, trying to hold on.

Mom, she called out in her mind. *Grandma, you said you'd help. You said you'd guide me if I came back. But where are you? I need your help, now. I don't know what to do...*

Little by little, consciousness drifted away.

{ 34 }

The sun tickled Emmy's face like a feather. All around, light sparkled through green leaves and in between the tall tree branches; the sky glowed in the purest of blue. A warm, soft breeze stroked her cheeks and hair; the sweet grass scented the air. She walked along a tree-lined path in the woods, just like the ones in the mountains of Bath. Birds sang and chirped overhead. Nearby, a narrow stream gently gurgled in delight.

There was something magical in the air. Everything flowed in this wonderful harmony of existence. Every single blade of grass danced softly with the wind, to a particular life-song that only they knew.

Emmy let out a giggle. Up ahead in the path, a bright light beckoned her forth. She walked, but when she moved it felt more like she was floating forward in the air, smooth and steady. It was beautiful and warm, and it felt good to be there.

As she neared the bright light, it softened to reveal an open field of grass. There, in the middle of it, was a giant tree that shot up from the earth but twisted parallel to the ground before it shot up again like a magnificent statue. It looked strong and sturdy, and near the ground, moss blanketed its black bark in a plush layer of bright green. The tree was an invitation, and as she hopped on it, she could see the path that she'd just been on. A beautiful, white horse with a long mane now watched her from there. As she met its dark, gentle eyes, she instantly felt drawn to it.

Suddenly the scene changed, and Emmy found herself walking up the path toward her house in Bath. It was summer, and as she neared the house, her mother's kitchen garden was in full bloom with flowers of purple, pink, and yellow. Bees buzzed by, and butterflies fluttered about; the air smelled like sweet lavender.

She hurried to turn the knob of her kitchen door, yelling, "Mom, I'm home."

A gentle smile greeted her from the dining table. Grandma Ethel sat there, a cup of tea in her hand. The giant hearth on the wall crackled with a fire. Dried herbs and small potion bottles waited in the cabinet, just like she had last seen them. It was warm and cozy—it was home.

"Emmy," her grandmother called.

"Hi, Grandma." Emmy walked over and kissed her gently on the cheek. She sat next to her, holding her warm hand.

"You made it. I'm proud of you." Ethel embraced her with a big smile.

Suddenly the reality back at the camp—its terrible feelings—flooded back to her like a faucet had turned on. She retracted and let out a small cry, shaking her head. "No, Grandma. It's terrible. Everything's messed up, and I don't know what to do. I'm captured."

"No." She gently rubbed Emmy's hand. "Things happened the way they should. It's not the end."

"What do you mean?"

"You're still on your journey. You'll see when time comes. You know it now, somewhere deep inside, but can't see it."

"I'm not sure about that." Emmy chuckled. "Are you telling me that something's going to change dramatically? Soon?"

"If you want it to. You're not as helpless as you think." Ethel winked, with a slight smile, and let go of Emmy's hand to sip her tea.

"Doesn't feel that way." She out a big sigh and put her face on the table. *If you only knew!*

"I do know, and that's why I'm here—to remind you." Her grandma could listen to her thoughts, even here.

Emmy lifted her head back up. "Remind me what?"

"Listen carefully and remember." Ethel leaned in. "Every moment is a new opportunity. What you give your attention to grows. When you focus on something, you're giving it energy, your power. If you give your energy to love, that grows inside you and around you. If you give your energy to hate or feeling like a victim, that grows in and around you. Giving your attention to something is like feeding a fire, every single moment. It will only burn bigger and brighter because you're giving it fuel. Does that make sense?"

"I think so." She pondered the concept.

"That's why quieting your mind, which is what I asked you to practice, is important. It lets you distinguish and be aware of what you're thinking and feeling. When you're in it, thick and deep, it's hard to see. When you give it distance, you can see more clearly. This allows you to make choices in your inner world. Then the outer world reflects." Ethel looked at her with focus.

"Okay, but how does that help me now? They're about to hurt Mom, Dad, and Nora if I don't give them Finn." This seemed like no time to talk philosophy. "And even if I tell him everything there's no guarantee—"

"If you believe—trust—that there is a way out, a path will be shown to you. You'll have to be wide awake and act accordingly, moment by moment, but it will. Focus on the thoughts and feelings of a solution, of ease and clarity. Feelings are the language of the Universe, like a path on which energy travels." Ethel smiled, pausing for emphasis. "Then follow your intuition. Listen to your heart and do something. The nudges you get, they're your spirit guiding you. Use it to your advantage. It's something they certainly don't have."

"I tried to get there—I really did—but couldn't focus. I couldn't empty my mind or my feelings." Emmy lowered her eyes. Had she done it wrong?

"Sure, the challenge is bigger. And I'm not saying this is easy. But listen to yourself now. What are you giving your attention to?"

She thought for a moment. "That I couldn't do it?"

"That's right. As long as you hold on to that, that's what'll continue to show up. If you can let that go and open yourself up to the possibility that you still can, then you will."

"Is this a test?"

Ethel laughed. "No, it's not a test. But you're growing, and this is a part of your expansion. This was a possibility when you chose to come back, right? You knew it would be challenging."

"I'm not sure if I understand clearly." Emmy frowned.

"That's okay. It'll make sense someday." Ethel gently rubbed her granddaughter's back.

"But you're telling me that I can do this. If I can center and get to that place inside…my intuition will come back?"

"That's right. You have your spirit, intention, and intuition. That is all you need. Isn't that how you got there in the first place?"

"True. But…what else can I do?" She wanted to know the extent of her abilities. It would be easier if it was more clearly defined, what she could or could not do. Who knew? Maybe she could fly someday. Now *that* would be fun.

"I doubt that, although not impossible." Ethel laughed. "Your powers are, as you already know, of empathy—you can feel what others feel, read what they're thinking. But as you grow and develop yourself, your powers can change and expand too. To what, I couldn't tell you."

Emmy lit up. She liked the idea of seeing what else was possible for herself; she couldn't wait to find out. But first things first. "Still, you're not going to give me a gun or something?"

Her grandmother laughed again. "No, sweetie. Would you use it if I did?"

"Probably. Why not?" She laughed too. She imagined shooting Stryker. She thought it'd feel good, but she flinched instead. "But I'd feel better going back, if I had one."

"You'll need more than just a gun on this one."

Emmy sighed. "Do you promise you'll stay with me?"

"What am I doing now?" She brushed Emmy's hair warmly and squeezed her hand. "Remember: what you give your attention to grows. Every moment is an opportunity. Choose your thoughts and feelings carefully and listen to yourself. You'll know what to do."

Part IV.

{ 35 }

December 10

The metal door shrieked loudly—she had really come to hate this sound—and a guard stepped in, dropping a metal plate on the floor. He exited just as quickly, not noticing the prisoner inside. Thick steam rose from the plate and drew her attention—rice and vegetable stew.

She slowly got up, bracing the pain all over her body, and sat in front of the plate. With no utensils, she gathered some with her fingers and put it in her mouth. It wasn't much for taste, but it wet her mouth and warmed her body, making her feel better. Sunlight peeked through the small window on top of the wall. She didn't know what time it was, but it felt like morning.

Emmy tried to think as she chewed. She needed a plan. Stryker could be back any minute. She licked the last grain of rice and sauce on the plate, already feeling more energized, placed the empty plate near the door, and moved the chair to face the wall with the window on top. She sat, tried to relax her aching body, and closed her eyes.

Breathing, she watched the air enter her body through the nose and down to her lungs.

Excruciating pain screamed from her right hip and lower back. She breathed into those areas of her body and talked to them in her thoughts. *Hey, I hear you. I'm listening, and I care. There isn't much I can do, but I'm doing the best I can.*

The pain quieted after a while and disappeared into the background. She watched her thoughts arise and let them go, one by one. The voice of her grandmother echoed inside. *What you give your attention to grows. Every moment is an opportunity. Choose your thoughts and feelings carefully, and listen to yourself. You'll know what to do.*

The constant rhythm of her breath carried her like a wave to that quiet, spacious place where everything was calm and expansive. She felt relief throughout her body as if a layer of tension—that had been holding her hostage like a rope—released. Feelings of recognition and pleasure also came and gently passed through her body.

What do I need to know? Show me. Show me what I need to know.

She breathed into her heart. Only silence followed, but she stayed there and held the space with the single intention: *Show me what I need to know.*

Moments passed, and she slowly felt herself lifting from the chair. It was her perspective—the point of awareness that observes—disconnecting with her body and rising up into the air.

Emmy looked down when she felt completely out from her body, feeling weightless. And there she was, her poor, damaged, dirty body still sitting in the chair. But the expression on her face said peace, curiosity, and confidence.

So that's what I look like. She liked what she saw. But before she could linger, she continued to float as if someone other than herself led her away. It was gentle and reassuring, though, even through the shock of whooshing through the cement wall and seeing the guard outside her door biting his nails. He looked bored and thoughtless, which surprised her. She'd just pictured them all angry and rough.

She continued down the hallway and passed through more walls, until she found herself in a sunny office where Stryker sat behind a desk. It was a classy room, with luxurious, thick curtains and big furniture made of dark wood. A tall, wide bookcase stood against the wall, filled with countless volumes of Rational philosophy and critical treaties on religious thought. Piles of paper and folders sat on top of the ornate, wooden desk, as he hunched over and peered at some document. Emmy secretly watched from a corner of the room.

The phone rang in a loud, breaking shrill. He didn't move until the third ring.

"Hello." His eyes remained on the papers. Recognizing the voice on the other end, though, he sat up and straightened his body. "Yes, sir... Yes, I'm on it, sir. I've just started the process, and it's still early to tell. We're searching all over the island, and I'm confident that we'll get to the bottom of it."

He looked out the window, which showed dirt grounds and high walls.

"That's probable. Her dad was one of the early operatives before going underground. She must have known some of his connections and made contact, which explains why we couldn't find her... Yes, I understand. But it's highly unlikely she could have made it without the help of a highly organized cell. It could be the same group."

A tiny voice mumbled from the phone like a squeaking mouse.

"We have a theory, and it's possible the girl can tell us where." Stryker's eyes wandered from the window to the file in front of him.

Curious, Emmy's awareness floated around the room to the space right above his shoulder. A map of the New Republic laid before him, with a red star marking a city named Blacksburg.

There were two mountain ranges in the country. One ran long along the western part of the country and divided into two strands about half way up. Bath was located near its northern end; Innisfree hid near the fork in the middle, where the ridge divided in two. The other included a short line of mountains at the southern border of the New Republic. Blacksburg sat near there, according to the map.

Stryker, apparently, believed that the rebels were hiding out in Blacksburg.

"No, nothing so far," he continued, looking up from the map. "But that's why I wanted to speak with you. We can leverage her family. Using her mother would be the most effective... As you wish. Of course I'll follow the orders. I'm certainly curious as to his reasons, but the others will be sufficient for now."

Something pleased him.

"Yes, that's good to know. And what about the youngest? ... Of course it'll be quiet. None of this will ever get out, I promise you that... Yes... Understood, except for the mother. Clean enough." He tapped his fingers on the table rhythmically. "Sure, I'll report immediately. Thank you."

He put down the phone and sat for a moment, looking out the window. before he pushed a button on his desk. A soldier entered the room, who saluted and stood at attention.

"Bring the girl's dad and sister. Have them ready," Stryker said.

{ 36 }

What is he about to do? And what was that about Mom?

Frustration rattled Emmy when she found herself back in her body in the cold room. It was as if she had more questions than answers, and she still didn't have a plan.

Stryker knew of the rebels and that they were looking for the camp. Was that what she needed to know? No wonder the Party had been good at keeping them away; they knew. But how much did they know, and what did it mean for her, now? Her mind raced as she stared at the wall, until noises in the hallway snapped her out of her trance.

"No," a young girl cried.

Emmy jumped out of her chair and ran to the door, pressing her ear against the cold metal.

"Come," a man said, sounding tired and sad.

She banged on the door as hard as she could and called out for them. "Dad? Nora? It's Emmy. I'm in here."

"Emmy?" her dad shouted back, but his voice muffled and disappeared, followed by a loud shriek next door.

She followed the sound to the wall on her right and stood against it, pressing her body. They were just on the other side, although she'd put them in more danger than ever before. This wasn't how it was supposed to be.

What was she supposed to do?

Emmy banged on the wall with her fist, but it didn't even make any noise. The cement was too thick and massive. She felt desperate and trapped. Letting out a deep breath, she tried to release the heaviness inside. Instead, she asked, *Are you there, Grandma?*

Quietly and gently, Ethel's voice echoed in her head. *What you give your attention to grows. Choose your thoughts and feelings carefully and listen to yourself. You'll know what to do.*

She didn't know what to do, but maybe it was time to trust. She sat on the chair, shook her head a little, and took a deep breath, trying to relax and let go of her worries, frustration, and fear.

Help me. She closed her eyes and focused. *This could be okay. There's a way out, I just have to find it. There's a way out—what I focus on will grow... There is always a way.*

Her mind wandered, leading her into a daydream. She saw herself holding hands with her mom, dad, and Nora and walking out from these prison walls. They were all smiling at the ease and inevitability of their exit. There was no one else to stop them, no guards, and no Stryker. They walked outside, looked up at the clear blue sky, and hugged each other. It felt good to be free. A tremendous sense of relief assured Emmy that it was finally over.

She smiled as her mind came back to the room. *Only if it was that easy.* Still, the feelings lingered over her, real and immediate, sustaining her smile.

The door clanked and opened, followed by footsteps.

"Good morning," Stryker said.

Emmy stood and faced him. He wore the same outfit—a gray suit with a red bowtie—that she'd seen earlier. This amused her. She still couldn't believe that she was doing these things and that it had any basis in reality—that her abilities were real.

"You seem well this morning." He looked at her curiously; he hadn't expected her to be smiling, she thought. He took a few steps closer to her. "I intend to make some progress today." He glanced over to one of the guards and nodded. "Bring them in."

The guard walked in with Sohan and Nora, each with their hands tied in front. Their eyes widened as they saw her. Her sister's face was dirty and swollen from crying, and she as much skinnier than before. Sohan tried to get closer to his daughter, but a guard blocked him. His eyes teared up quietly, and he suppressed something he wanted to say. Emmy smiled at them, her eyes also tearing up.

"Sorry to interrupt this reunion," Stryker said, "but we have more pressing issues at hand. Miss Sukar, I'm going to ask you some questions today. If you don't tell me what I want to know, with every ten minutes that passes," he pointed to Sohan and Nora, "we'll cut off one of their fingers."

Sohan's face dropped. Nora looked at her with desperate, pleading eyes, her face full of terror. "

Emmy yelled in panic, her fists clenched on her side, "But what if I don't know what you want to know?"

"Please don't waste my time. There's no way that your dead grandmother showed you how to get here or carried you across the sea. You got help from someone, and we just want to know who, what, and when." He nodded to the guards again.

Two of them brought in a table and a chair and placed them, side by side, in the center of the room. A third brought in a tray full of shiny, metal things—sharp knives, scissors with interesting shapes she'd never seen before, and a hammer—and placed them on top of the table. One of them grabbed Nora, dragged her to the chair, made her sit, and untied her hands.

"No!" Sohan yelled and jumped forward. But the other guards held him back and beat him down to the ground.

The little girl's petrified face looked around the room, hard with confusion and fear. She was unable to say anything. The guard caught her wildly shaking hand and fixed it firmly on the table. Emmy trembled, and her fingernails cut into her palms as she stood there watching. She would have rather it be her fingers, her body. She would give anything to not see Nora suffer.

There is a solution, echoed a voice in her head. She realized then, there was only one thing she could do, whether she liked it or not.

Making a choice and following through moved her through stagnation. Made her unstuck. Even if she didn't like what she had to do and knew that, under different circumstances, she would've never gone this way. It was a door she opened, to see what waited on the other side. It set her on a new path until another door was shown. When she moved forward, at least she was getting somewhere, doing something, rather than letting it be done to her.

Stryker waited, studying her face for any clues that would contend with her words. But there was nothing else. Everything was clear now. Even all her mental chatter had disappeared.

I better not regret this, Emmy thought before she opened her mouth.

"I will. I'll tell you everything. But you have to promise— I want you to let us go once you get what you want. Including my mother."

He looked amused, perhaps slightly annoyed.

"What makes you think that I need to do anything? Why don't I just cut off a finger now," he said, tilting his head toward Nora, "and see how you feel after?"

"Because what I'm about to tell you is big," she said. "So big you need every last detail there is. I know where the rebels are."

A hint of surprise passed his face. He was playing coy. "You expect me to believe you? How would you even know the rebels?"

"Through my dad's old contacts." It was what he wanted and expected to hear. "Before I left Bath, I found his old address book. I needed help and went looking for it. I didn't know they were connected to the rebels, at first."

"Emmy, no." Sohan shook his head with a miserable face.

"What should I do, Dad? Let them cut her fingers?" she yelled sharply.

Nora vigorously shook her head, about to cry, and between her sister and father.

"But this isn't right. We can't—" he tried to say, but a guard punched him, and he fell to his knees.

Emmy turned to Stryker. "If you want to hear more, you'll have to trust me and give me my family. Otherwise, I can't promise I'll tell you everything and truthfully. You know it's true."

Stryker looked at her, his eyes narrow and calculating. He took a few steps around the room with his hands behind his back and stopped as he reached the wall with the window. He looked up with a grin on his face.

Everyone was quiet in the room, watching him. Nora still shook, and her fearful eyes jumped nervously around the room.

"I don't enter into any losing contracts, Miss Sukar, especially not with you. You can have your family, but you'll stay until I make sure what you tell me is true."

It was working. Emmy felt a sliver of relief inside. "How do I know that you won't hurt us after you get what you want?"

"You don't. Just like I won't know what you tell me is true, until I find out." He smiled. There was a challenge, a dare, in his eyes.

"Fine." Emmy didn't want him to change his mind. "But first, untie them and bring some food. And bring my mother."

{ 37 }

"What do you have to tell them?" Nora dug her head into Emmy's shoulder and squeezed her arms around her.

They're really here. Emmy embraced her sister's bony, little body and kissed her head. She felt as though her entire being reached out for this person, who she still couldn't believe was actually in her arms.

They sat on a bed with their backs against the wall, huddled together under a blanket. Sohan watched from across the room, on a second bed that faced theirs, his face happy and sad.

"Don't you worry about that. I told them what I had to." Emmy hushed her sister. Sohan looked away, trying to hide his emotions. "Dad."

He didn't respond.

"Dad," she called. He looked back. It was hard for him. So many emotions were going through him. "It's not what you think. Please trust me."

"It's not you. It's me. I'm responsible. If I wasn't stubborn and self-righteous, we wouldn't be here in the first place. I'm mad at myself. I mean, look at you. Look at all of us." He looked down at his hands, clenching the edge of the bed. "This is my fault."

"No, Dad, it's not like that. This is not your fault. If anyone's at fault, that'd be me." She smiled. "If I'd listened to you in Bath, if I knew better then… I'm sorry."

"You didn't know. We should have told you everything, but we thought we were protecting you." Sohan looked at her tenderly.

"I know." She tried to smile to put him at ease.

"Besides," he said with a sigh, "it was just a matter of time anyway." After a pause he asked, "Do you trust these guys?"

"No." She wanted to tell him more, but they could be listening. She couldn't risk it. She turned to Nora. "Excited to see Mom?"

She stroked her sister's head gently, feeling a million years older than when she had in Bath. *I won't let go.*

"Yes," Nora beamed, as if this was the one thing that made everything better. They hadn't seen each other since they'd gotten here. They'd all been alone this entire time. Emmy's heart ached, and tears welled up in her eyes.

"Me too," she whispered, trying to drum up excitement. "But I saw Mom in my dreams. Did you?"

"Lots. She came and played with me. She also told me you were coming, but I didn't believe her." Nora giggled.

"Well, I'm here, aren't I?" Emmy whispered. "It was her magic."

Nora closed her eyes and smiled meekly, tired, pushing Emmy away. "Magic's not real, silly."

Emmy's heart broke into pieces, suddenly aware how lonely her sister must have been, how scared she must have been. She pulled her close and squeezed her tightly.

"Stop," she protested, in that baby voice that she used to make with mom. But in a few seconds, she held Emmy tightly too.

Emmy's throat tightened, and tears started down her face, even as she tried to hide it. Sohan sat next to Nora and wrapped his arms around his daughters. They were like a giant, heavy ball on the bed, which squeaked in protest underneath.

Their love—that warm feeling of connection and belonging—filled Emmy from the inside. Like a powerful energy that flowed from her gut, through her heart and the top of her head. It was impossible to be contained. She laughed, and Nora laughed with her. Soon Sohan was too. The cold, cement room was filled with the sound of laughter, if only for a minute.

* * *

They brought Leona in the middle of night, just as Emmy was getting nervous that Stryker had broken his promise. But she came, as they lay awake in the dark, waiting and listening to the sounds of each other breathing. Sohan was the most anxious and the first to jump when the door opened.

"Mom!" Nora yelled as she ran into her arms. Leona, who looked tired and smaller than ever before, picked her right up and embraced her tightly, devouring her cheeks with kisses and inhaling her hair. She then reached for Emmy with her free arm, and Emmy went to her. Emmy held both of them and felt their flesh, as certain as the earth, next to her body.

"Let me look at you." Leona put Nora down and held out her arms. Her eyes filled with tears as she hugged her again. "My baby, I've missed you so much." Then she put her hands on Emmy's cheeks and looked into her eyes. "My big girl. I am proud of you."

They laughed out of sheer joy.

Finally Leona turned to Sohan, who'd waited patiently on the side, and jumped into his arms. He squeezed her tightly, his face full of happiness and tears. They kissed passionately and laughed, as though something released from deep inside their cores. They looked at their daughters, arm in arm, with big smiles and tears, and hugged them again.

They settled on a bed after a while, with Leona and Sohan in the center—their hands held tightly together, as if they never meant to let go. Leona kept on looking at her daughters, one after the other, as if she wanted to drink them in through her eyes. She looked happy and radiant. Her eyes sparkled like morning dew in the sun; her smile spread like the ocean wave. It amazed Emmy, watching her mother, that one could exude such light and beauty even in a place like that.

Nora's breath soon became steady and soft. She'd fallen asleep still leaning on her mother. Leona and Sohan whispered to each other about old times, in places far away from there, and broke into occasional fits of suppressed giggles.

I hope this never ends.

Emmy fought sleep, even though her eyes wanted to close and her parent's whispers came in and out of her consciousness.

Tomorrow was an unknown. Was she ready? She wasn't sure.

{ 38 }

Emmy was panting; she knew she couldn't stop there. The break in the wall, through which people were jumping over by the dozens, was just ahead. Her hand tightly held Nora's as they ran, but she kept on stumbling and falling down. Her mom and dad were right beside them, their hands together, also desperately running. Her heart raced, and her mind was blank.

Explosions and screams were all around them, and bullets flew over their heads. Occasionally a bullet hit the ground next to her foot, popping and launching dirt and debris into the air. People around her fell and didn't get up. But they had to go, over that wall, where they'd be safe.

Nora fell again, and the two tumbled down to the ground. This time, Sohan took Nora in his arms and carried her, running, as Emmy and her mom followed. He slowed down, though, as Nora weighed on his already weakened body. No matter how hard they ran, it seemed that the walls were in the same distance as before, just right up there and out of reach. But there was nowhere else to go. Stryker was after them.

Emmy felt a pinch on her back right below her right shoulder blade, as if she was hit by a rock. It didn't hurt much at first, but after a few steps her legs gave out, dropping her to the ground. She looked down at herself, and a circle of bright, red blood had spread over her chest. Before she could make a sound, her throat filled with liquid, and she choked from her own blood.

"Emmy!" she heard her mom scream faintly in the background. Her mom's tormented face and those of her dad and Nora hovered over her, as light in her vision blinked in and out. Liquid flowed out of her lungs, and her mouth gurgled as her chest tightened in convulsions.

Mom, she wanted to say, but nothing came out.

* * *

The sound of her own mumbled screams woke Emmy from her dream. She was drenched in sweat, and her body felt like it was on fire; her breath was short and fast. It felt as though she'd really been running and dying, although she fumbled around her chest and found it to be in one piece. Nora slept soundly next to her on the narrow bed, one of her legs laid over Emmy's. Across the room in the dark, Sohan slept with his back against them, spooning Leona.

Emmy laid back and tried to calm down. *A nightmare.*

Taking deep and controlled breaths, she looked up at the ceiling. There was a small window on top of the wall in this room too, where faint light trickled in. It was quiet outside, as far as she could tell, and still.

They'll kill us when they find out. A heavy feeling balled up and grew in her gut, even as she shook her head and counted her breaths. *You think you have everything figured out, don't you? But you don't.*

An ugly voice in her head.

Slowly she got up, carefully untangling Nora's leg from hers. She sat at the foot of the bed with her elbows on her knees, staring into the dark corner of the room.

Still here.

I know. But you can go now. I don't need you.

Really? What are you going to do when they find out? Can you really watch them die? Look at this place. There is no way you can get out.

The voice sounded triumphant and mean, mocking and belittling. It had no mercy, and Emmy was familiar with its ways.

That's not true. You never know. Some people survive out of falling buildings. I'm not listening to you. I'm going to think possibility *and not miss it when it comes, even if I die trying. So go away.*

Just like that, with those words, the voice disappeared into silence. It was her grandmother's words that filled the void. *What you give your attention to grows. Choose your thoughts and feelings carefully and listen to yourself. You'll know what to do.*

But Emmy didn't have a plan. There was no telling what Stryker would do tomorrow or if they'd ever be able to leave this place together. But something good could happen tomorrow too. Maybe, possibly—hopefully.

"Are you okay?" Leona whispered from across the room, her head popping up behind Sohan.

Emmy smiled and nodded, waving her hand for her to go back to sleep. Leona carefully sat up and crawled on all fours out of the bed. She sat next to Emmy and put her arm around her daughter's shoulders.

"I had a nightmare," she explained in a low whisper, leaning her head on her mom's shoulder.

Leona cooed and rocked her back and forth, stroking her head. "That's understandable. You've been so brave."

She chuckled. "But I've no idea what I'm doing."

"I think you do, more than you give yourself credit for. There are certain things we have control over and others that we don't. For everyone. The most we can do is to hope for the best and do our best."

"What will happen to us?" Emmy sighed, feeling the weight of the world.

"Are you scared?" Her mother's voice was gentle.

She paused to think. "Only for you guys. I don't want to lose you again. I don't want you to be hurt."

It was true. Even more than death, which she now knew wouldn't be bad, she feared for her family.

"Well, whatever happens, we'll be together, right?" Leona was great at always finding the upside.

"Hope so." Even that wasn't a guarantee.

"I don't know what'll happen, but I love that we got this chance to be together again. I love you, Nora, and your dad so much." Leona kissed her head.

"Me too." Emmy squeezed her mother in her arms.

"You should get some sleep. Whatever happens tomorrow, you'll want to be rested."

"Wait, I want to show you something." Emmy reached down under her shirt and took out the silver locket. With everything that had happened, she'd forgotten she still had it. She held it out to show her mother.

"You still have it," Leona said, touching it gently with her finger.

"I've always worn it," she said proudly.

Her mom smiled brightly in appreciation and wonder. They'd come a long way, this necklace and Emmy. Through the mountains, rebel camps, across the country, and over the water.

Then she had an idea. Breaking away from Leona's arms, she asked, "Can you help? I need to reach someone."

Leona nodded and shifted her body to face her. They held hands. They already knew exactly what to do, together, because it was just like when Leona used to give birthday readings. They smiled.

"All right, Mom. Here we go, okay?" She smiled before closing her eyes.

Breathing deeply in and out, she felt her mom's presence. It was the warmth that she felt on her hands but also her essence—gentle but roaring at the same time, shaking like the thunder—that she felt in the air, in the field before her. Leona gave it willingly, her love and power.

Before they knew it, it was as if they were two church bells making the same sound, ringing together at the same frequency. It was as if they were one, and Emmy's awareness felt bigger and more expansive than she could have ever imagined.

She flew swiftly and easily, up into the air and across the sea. She was looking for Chris, Finn, and Madame Alande. She had to reach them before it was too late. She needed their help, and it was time to fight.

{ 39 }

December 11

Nora was the first to wake in the morning. Without making a sound she'd gone over to the other bed and inserted herself between her parents, before anyone could protest, pushing Leona against the wall and Sohan halfway to the floor. The three were happy, though, for the moment of pretend normalcy, as if it was a Sunday morning in their home in Bath. Lying on her side, Emmy watched from across the room at them kidding around and enjoying each other's closeness. It was a scene she never wanted to forget, beautiful and heartbreaking at the same time.

Everyone stopped when the metal door screeched and opened. Sohan immediately jumped to his feet but relaxed after seeing the trays of food—vegetable stew and rice, like the day before—the guard carried. The man fidgeted, trying to balance multiple trays and the big rifle hanging over his shoulder. He looked young, not much older than Emmy, and rather short and skinny. He had pale, white skin and curly light hair and looked somewhat familiar, although she didn't remember seeing him before. He seemed not to know exactly what to do with the trays, for he stood there a moment, without saying anything and staring at the prisoners.

Sohan took the trays from him. "Thank you."

The guard nodded and smiled awkwardly. He still hadn't said anything when he backed away sheepishly, as if he had something to say. Leona smiled at him, and he smiled back. At last he exited the room and shut the door behind him.

"That was weird." Emmy sneered. Sohan handed her a plate, and she ate.

"Seems like a nice boy," Leona said lightly, also taking a plate.

"How can you call any of them nice?"

"There are nice people in the world, you know."

Sohan sat next to Emmy with his plate.

"But he's one of *them*," Emmy insisted, louder this time. *Here we go again.*

"I know," her mother said, sadly. "I hate what they're doing here and what they're doing to all these people." She paused. "But every person is different. That one, he's just trying to do his best. He's young, like you. He has a good heart."

"Dad?" Emmy looked for an ally.

He shrugged, glancing over between his wife and daughter as if to say, *Keep me out of this.* Nora happily sat next to her mom, absorbed in eating.

Shaking her head, Emmy sighed. "Fine. Just don't try to give any excuses for Stryker."

"Oh, honey. He's a very sad case, that one." Leona looked completely devoid of any anger toward the man who was responsible for so much of their grief. Emmy stared at her in wonder.

A gentle knock on the door made all heads turn. It opened slowly, and the subject of their debate, the skinny guard, entered, just as fidgety as before. This time he spoke.

"Emmy Sukar?" He looked around, not knowing which.

"That's me," Emmy said.

"Come with me."

She put down the half-eaten plate and got up. Everyone's worried eyes were on her; Sohan's face hardened.

"I'll be back." She tried to sound as light as possible and smile, but it was no use.

She followed the guard. He locked the door behind them. Another guard, an older and bigger man, sat on a chair outside the door. He glanced over only briefly before returning to whatever he was reading.

"This way," the skinny guard said, lifting his hand to the left, as if this was a hotel and he was guiding Emmy to her room.

"Where are we going?"

He looked back. "The director wants to see you."

Quietly they walked through the cold corridors lined with rows of metal doors. She'd seen them before, when she visited Stryker's office in her awareness, which now felt like a long time ago. What she didn't see at that time, though, was what was going on in these rooms. It was still hard to tell, with the thick walls and metal doors. But from some came the sounds of people moaning, crying, or yelling. In one, it was clear that someone was getting a beating, like Emmy had the other day.

The energy of that place gave her the chills, and her body tensed, even as she tried to focus and follow the guard. The noises bothered him too, and he periodically glanced back with uneasy and nervous expressions on his face. His strange demeanor unsettled her even more, though.

She couldn't understand him. Was he being apologetic about all this? Without thinking, she even feigned a smile when he looked back, only to regret it a moment later.

Finally they came to a section of the building that was built more like a regular office space, with painted walls and windows that looked out onto the grounds. They stopped at a wooden door, and the guard knocked before entering. Inside were three desks, where two men and a woman in crisp military uniforms were busily working. A door on the right wall led to another office, with a tag that read, amusingly, "Director of Outreach."

Is that what they call it? Outreach? Emmy frowned at the irony.

"Prisoner Emmy Sukar, ma'am." The skinny guard saluted in attention.

The woman nodded. "Let her in."

The guard opened the door for Emmy to enter and closed it behind her. Stryker's office was just as she remembered it: a heavy bookcase, an ornate wooden desk, and a big window.

He looked up from behind the desk. "Come, Miss Sukar."

Emmy stepped forward, stopping a few feet before his desk.

"Like to sit down?" His eyes pointed to the empty chair, but she shook her head. "Very well." He leaned back in his chair and observed her. "Our agents are on their way as we speak. It'll take no more than twenty-four hours to find the rebels, provided that the information was accurate, and less than forty-eight hours to make arrests."

His eyes were fixed on her, looking for the slightest of reaction.

Shit. They were faster than I thought. It had been less than a day. Trying not to seem surprised, she stood still. After a moment she asked, "So you'll let us go then?"

"If all goes as planned, of course. We'll send you out of the country; you promise never to come back, as we discussed." He brushed his hands together in front of him.

"Then what do you want?"

"To give you one last chance, if you have anything to say. There'll be serious consequences if you've lied, I promise you."

"I told you everything I know." Her heart raced, so she spoke more slowly. "If you don't find them, it's not because I didn't tell you the truth."

"Then you better pray that we do." He motioned her to the door. She turned to walk away, feeling panicked as she opened the door.

* * *

"Why don't you sit down, honey?" Leona asked for the third time.

"Sorry. I'm trying to think." Emmy paused briefly before going back to pacing the room. Maybe two hours had passed since she came back from Stryker's office. That meant twenty-two hours, at maximum, until something happened, something bad.

Should she just tell him everything now? Would that spare her family? Looking at the faces in the room, her blood simmered with anxiety.

They'll die.

Her head spun. But there were no guarantees. She remembered exactly what happened when she trusted him and played his game the last time. There had to be another way.

"I wish you'd tell us what's going on," Sohan said in exasperation, watching his anxious daughter.

But Emmy didn't know where to begin or if she should even say it out loud. She shook her head and went to the three of them, who were sitting on the bed and holding each other. Kneeling before them, she held Nora's hand in hers and looked into their faces. "I'm sorry for everything. I love you so much. I want you to know that, okay? No matter what happens."

{ 40 }

The day passed slowly. After hours of worrying and pacing, even Emmy got tired of herself. With each passing moment of quiet in the small, cold room, whatever she was worried about seemed less and less real anyway. But the anxiety didn't go away. It just went into hiding, in the deep part of her gut, as she pretended that everything was okay. But she knew it was there when she looked.

Emmy didn't know what could happen that would make everything okay. Maybe nothing was going to happen, until Stryker showed himself again sometime the next day and began his end of the bargain. But as the idea sank in, more and more and she got used to the final possibility, a part of her also felt free. There was, after all, relief in accepting the inevitable.

So instead, they played. They sang old children's rhymes, the ones that Leona used to sing to the girls when they were small enough to sit on her lap; they played word games that they used to play on long car rides. Nora and Leona beamed with happiness, each being light of spirit as neither Sohan nor

Emmy could ever be. He smiled a lot, but it was obvious what lay underneath. He suspected what was coming, she could tell.

Still, they laughed. There wasn't much else they could do, and as Emmy figured, if these were going to be their last moments together, they ought to make the most of it—inhale the last drop of each other's being; love them up as much as she could.

Twice more the skinny guard came by to deliver the same exact meal—vegetable stew and boiled rice—and each time he relaxed a little more, seemingly curious about their activities and glad for their laughter. He was a strange one, the skinny guard, but Emmy supposed she'd take him over a mean one any day. So it was with mild fanfare—Nora had said, "Thank you," with such enthusiasm that he seemed embarrassed—that he dropped off their dinner and left their room with a grin on his face.

When night came, though, and everyone was tired, Emmy's anxiety stirred and awoke again inside. She lay in bed next to Nora—who had covered her face with a blanket and was whispering things to herself that Emmy couldn't understand—looking up at the ceiling and listening to the sound of her heart. She had to stay out of her head.

The rhythm of her heart became louder; its constant beating, knocking gently against her chest, became more palpable inside. This was where she wanted to stay, in the present. Not in the past and not in the future.

What you give your attention to grows. Every moment is an opportunity. Choose your thoughts and feelings carefully, and listen to yourself. You'll know what to do.

As Emmy continued to breath, an empty space opened inside, of lightness and expansiveness. And the longer she stayed there, present in the moment of now, the quieter her fear became. Whatever it was, it seemed to say: *Everything is okay. This is your true home. You are not alone.*

Slowly she relaxed into that feeling of calm and peace. Nora's hand gently grabbed hers. She turned to her side to put her arms around her sister and sang a lullaby.

Down in the valley, valley so low,
Hang your head over, hear the wind blow.
Hear the wind blow, dear, hear the wind blow,
Hang your head over, hear the wind blow.

Roses love sunshine; violets love dew.
Angels in heaven know I love you,
Know I love you, dear, know I love you,
Angels in heaven, know I love you.

Writing this letter, containing three lines.
Answer my question, "Will you be mine?"
"Will you be mine, dear, will you be mine?"
Answer my question, "Will you be mine?"

Slowly, they both drifted into sleep.

* * *

Emmy's eyes opened. Sohan stood on a chair, trying to look out the window. Leona sat on the bed, looking worriedly at her husband, a hand covering her mouth. Nora was still asleep next to Emmy, her arms spread above her head. The room was dark and outside too. Propping herself up, Emmy was about to say something when it came—an explosion in the distance, followed by gunshots. The walls of the room vibrated, and dust fell from the ceiling.

"What is it?" she yelled across the room, jumping out of the bed. Nora stirred and looked up in confusion.

"The camp's under attack," Sohan answered, his face fixed at the window. "I can't see it from here, but soldiers are on the move. It looks serious."

"It's the rebels," Emmy whispered excitedly. She looked at her parents. "What do we do?"

"There's nothing we can do for now. It started just a few minutes ago." He stepped down from the chair, sat on it, and covered his face with his hands, letting out a sigh. "We'll have to see who wins and if we survive through this."

Emmy embraced her mother. Nora, now awake and startled, also joined them on the bed. Quietly they listened to the explosions and gun fights outside. Hurried footsteps occasionally ran right outside their window, lights flickered in their prison room, and shouts were heard in the hallway. Eventually Sohan joined the girls on the bed. They remained huddled together, holding their breath and listening to the chaos around them. The rebels could be their saviors or executioners.

* * *

Fighting continued outside for a couple of hours. It had gotten quiet for a while but resumed again, the sounds getting even closer. The Sukars had been alert and listening the entire time, unable to fall asleep or do anything else.

Suddenly the door shrieked loudly and opened. Stryker's angry face burst in with three guards behind him. Sohan jumped from the bed, but a guard, who Emmy recognized as the big, older one who'd sat outside their door before, quickly pinned him back on the bed. The skinny guard stood back near the door, his face looking ashen and overwhelmed; another stood behind Stryker, with a black club in his hand, ready to strike any moment.

Stryker marched straight to Emmy. He grabbed her by the collar, lifting her out of bed, and threw her violently to the floor. She fell hard, hitting her back against the edge of the empty bed.

"Emmy!" Sohan and Leona screamed, both jumping forward but held back.

Her ears rang, and she felt dizzy.

"You lying bitch!" Stryker screamed. He kicked Emmy in the gut, over and over. "Blacksburg, huh?"

Feeling it deep in her organs, she shut her eyes and crawled into a ball on the floor. The sound of her family's screams echoed in the distance, somewhere far away. When he'd had his fill, he bent over and propped her up roughly. She turned her face away, but he grabbed her chin, forcing her to face him.

"You knew this would happen, didn't you? You knew everything." His breath was hot and rancid.

"You're not very quick." Emmy smiled obnoxiously. "A little late, perha—"

He slapped her across the face, and her head hit the concrete floor. Everything went dark for a moment, the cold rising from the ground to her cheek. Stryker's shoe was just a few inches from her nose, which felt wet with blood. The skinny guard still stood by the doorway, frozen.

"You underestimate me, again." Stryker slowly stood up and straightened out his clothes. "There's a price for everything. You'll see what you've done soon enough."

Emmy tried to get up, but her body didn't cooperate.

"Take her," he ordered the guard who held Leona.

"No—" All she could muster was a whisper. Leona screamed and resisted, but she was tiny against the man. Sohan desperately pushed against the big one, and he almost looked like he could break through. But the guard took out a knife and held it against his neck.

Sohan still pushed on, pressing his neck against the knife, until a red line of blood slowly formed on the blade. But Leona and the guard were already out the door. Her screams became increasingly distant as the man practically carried her away.

"You'll get your turn." Stryker looked at Emmy with a distorted smile on his face. He exited, and the door locked from the outside with a clank.

{ 41 }

December 12

Sohan helped Emmy up from the floor and onto the bed. Nora knelt over her sister, wiping the blood off her face and stroking her hair. Nora's mouth was clenched and her eyes wet, but she was trying to hold it together. Emmy reached out for her hand and held it gently.

Everything hurt, but the thing that filled her head was that her mother was gone...again. She didn't know what Stryker wanted to do with her mother, but she didn't want that to be the last time that they saw each other.

Feeling defeated and hopeless, all she managed to say was, "I'm sorry. I'm sorry," over and over. She'd tried her best, but it obviously hadn't been enough.

"For what?" Sohan said, smiling softly and holding her hand. "It's not your fault. It's not us. It's them."

"She'll be back, right, Daddy?" Nora asked, sniffling.

"I don't know, honey," he answered softly.

A ball formed in Emmy's throat, and tears rolled down her face, even as she realized that there was no time to be sad.

There has to be something I can do. Some way. She breathed deeply and closed her eyes, trying to get calm and clear inside. *Please help. Please show me the way. I know there's something...*

She waited, quietly, and watched the screen inside her head. Only the sound of Nora's sniffling filled the room, even as Sohan tried to comfort his youngest. Time passed; then something shifted.

Emmy felt herself outside her prison door, looking at the skinny guard sitting on a chair, anxiously cleaning the rifle on his lap. He was alone, rapidly shaking his right leg up and down, seemingly lost in his thoughts as he messed with the gun. Emmy moved closer and looked straight at him at his eyes, although he couldn't see her. She tried to connect with his heart.

Immediately she heard the rhythmic thumping and felt it beating—foreign to her own—and vibrate through her awareness. It felt warm, clear, and open. This was her chance.

Please help us. You know we're good people. We need your help, or we'll die. I know you have a good heart. Please. She spoke to him through her emotions, from her heart to his. Then, still connected to his energy, she sent the feelings of relief and of empathy.

Suddenly a big thump rocked the building—an explosion—and Emmy got sucked back into her own body as Sohan pulled her under his arm. Everything rattled for a while. Dust fell from the ceiling, and the lights flickered.

Another thump hit, even closer, splashing gravel onto their small window, and everything shook again.

Sohan held his daughters tightly and braced for something to fall, but all that came down was white cement dust, everywhere. Coughing convulsively from debris, they covered their faces with bed sheets.

A loud siren went off outside like the wail of a monster. Busy footsteps ran down outside their door; indistinguishable shouts came and went. Gunshots continued in multiple directions, popping in clusters, even as the dust eventually settled in their room.

Time slowly passed on, and after a while, things settled. Sohan ran to the window and checked outside as the girls shook dust from their hair and clothes. It became dead quiet for a minute, eerily so, and Emmy looked up, holding her breath to listen.

Then the metal door creaked and slowly opened. Her dad jumped away from the window pulled his daughters behind him, and picked up the chair to hold has a weapon. But only the skinny guard peeked his head through the door, his index finger pressed on his lips. He motioned for them to come out, slowly pushing the door open a little more.

Confused, Sohan didn't move. He didn't trust the guy.

"Come," the skinny guard whispered, motioning his hand again. "There's no one else. You should go now, before they come back."

Sohan remained still, but Emmy knew. She slowly stepped around her dad and toward the door. She looked outside in the hallway, checking both directions. It was empty. She looked back and nodded to her dad and Nora.

"Where's our mom?" Emmy asked the guard.

He shook his head. "I don't know. But you should go now. They'll be back."

"Come," Sohan said, already a couple of steps down the hallway. "We can look for Mom."

Emmy nodded and was about to turn when she said, "Come with us," to the skinny guard.

Everyone paused in surprise.

"You'll be punished if we're gone," she continued. "You're not right for this anyway. Come."

She waited as he stared back, confused.

"But..." he finally said. It was obvious that he hadn't thought much through before he decided to let them out. He glanced over to Sohan, who nodded slightly. He hesitated for another moment and shook his head. "Okay."

"All right, we stay together and check the building for Mom, okay? If we run into a guard, you pretend that you're moving us." Sohan looked to the skinny guard, who nodded.

"What's your name?" Emmy asked.

"Alex King."

They walked quickly down the hallway and checked every room for Leona. Explosions and gunshots continued outside, but they had work to do.

* * *

"Is that the last one?" Sohan asked, snapping the small slot on the door. They had looked through fifty or sixty jail cells, about half of which were empty.

"A few more upstairs in the east wing," Alex answered. "By the director's office. They take high-security ones there. But she could be somewhere else too."

"What do we do?" Emmy asked.

"If it's near Stryker's office, there will be more guards. And they might recognize us. We can't all go," Sohan said.

"I can go," Alex said, "and come back. It won't take long. Why don't you stay in here and wait." He walked to one of the empty rooms and opened its door.

Sohan paused, looking at him suspiciously. "In there?"

"You have to hide. You can't just be standing here. Here, I won't lock it."

He looked at Emmy in hesitation. She nodded, although she didn't know for sure—he could've changed his mind—but they didn't have many options. She chose to trust. She certainly didn't have any better ideas. Taking a deep breath, she quickly walked into the cell. Sohan and Nora slowly followed.

"I'll be back as soon as I can." Alex closed the door behind them. Something clanked outside, and Emmy didn't want to question what it was. For a moment it was completely silent in the room.

Sohan and Nora looked at her nervously. They were standing in the middle of the empty room, suddenly aware of the stillness. It felt strange, somehow, considering how fast they'd been moving in the last hour. It felt wrong, like they should have still been looking and going.

Nora walked into Emmy's arms, burying her head in her chest. She kissed her little sister's head. "It'll be okay."

Time passed, more slowly than Emmy had hoped. Nora sat next to her on the floor with her knees in her chest, and Sohan went back and forth, between looking out the window—this room gave a different view—and pacing the room.

Emmy kept her eyes closed and tried to stay centered in her heart and not in her head. It wasn't easy. But if she wasn't at least trying, intentionally and actively, her mind ran wild with various worst-case scenarios. Each time that happened, she drew a deeper breath and exhaled, imagining that the breath carried the ugly thoughts away.

It was hard to tell exactly how long it'd been since Alex left. Sohan was getting increasingly anxious, with each moment that passed. "How long can it take to check a few rooms?"

"I don't know," Emmy answered. "Maybe he got tied up with something." She paused. "You think something could have happened to him?"

Sohan shook his head and walked up to the door. They had not touched it, as that would have been a test on Alex's word, and Emmy supposed, it would have been too much to find out. But it had been a long time.

Her father reached for the door knob and turned it. Nora and Emmy watched, holding their breath, as the knob clicked and he pushed against it. The door squealed, beautifully, and opened. He looked back at his daughters, visibly relieved, and smiled. Emmy smiled back at him, happy, until the door swung widely open from the outside.

"What's going on here?" shouted a husky man's voice. A tall figure appeared in the doorway in full uniform, with glaring eyes.

Surprised, Sohan took a few steps back, and Nora and Emmy jumped to their feet.

The man marched into the room with two other soldiers. He looked up and down at Sohan and around the girls' frozen faces.

"Your door wasn't locked," he said, not like a question but not quite a statement either. "Who are you?"

They didn't know what to say as the man walked out into the hallway and came back inside.

"This is supposed to be empty." He looked at them for another moment. "Take them upstairs."

They were led into Stryker's office with their hands tied around the back. His face changed as he saw them.

"Matter of time," he talked into the phone, his eyes fixed on them as they walked closer to his desk. "We're handling it... Yes. They can't hold much longer. I promise you... No, that's not possible... Of course you'll be the first to know. Thank you, sir. It won't be long." He hung up the phone and rose from his chair, his face icy and blank. He asked the guard, "Where were they?"

"Cell B41, sir," the soldier answered robotically. "They were leaving it when Colonel Young found them."

Stryker cocked his head to one side, his eyes frowning. "How? What about their guard?"

"Can't find him, sir."

Emmy smiled. Alex hadn't betrayed them. Maybe he'd found Leona somewhere.

"Is this funny, Miss Sukar?" Stryker was clearly angry.

"What have you done with my mother?"

He walked forward, stopping just in front of Emmy and pulling her hair from the back of her head.

"Don't," Sohan yelled, stepping forward, his entire body tense and ready to spring.

Stryker looked at him in amusement. He shrugged and let go of Emmy. Taking out a handkerchief from his chest pocket, he wiped his hand and walked away. "You people have been a royal pain in the ass. But, alas, this is when we say goodbye for the last time."

He sat in his chair, almost giddy with anticipation.

"Where is my mother?" Emmy asked again.

"Do you expect an answer?" he asked, enjoying the moment. "I'll do what I want with anyone as I please. That's the beauty of being in charge." He turned to the guard. "Take them to Pine."

The soldier saluted and pushed them with the muzzle of his rifle toward the door.

{ 42 }

They walked through the corridors with two guards behind, the soldiers' rifles occasionally poking on their backs. Underground passageways connected the buildings, and Emmy had no idea where they were headed. It was a dark hallway of cold, cement walls, with no windows and bare light bulbs buzzing above their heads. It felt as though they were marching through a crypt to their graves. Explosions from above ground occasionally shook the ground; no one looked at each other or spoke.

At the end of the corridor stood a gray, metal door. One of the guards pushed it open and led them up a set of stairs, leading them into a different building. Soldiers ran down the hallways and shouted at each other.

It was an entirely different place from the dark, cold prison cells, not that it was warm and cozy—it spoke austerity in a different way. The walls were painted white, like the shade used in hospitals, with big windows covered with steel fences. The shiny, stone floors were hard and cold; everyone's footsteps echoed against the tall ceilings, like a mental institution.

Emmy took a deep breath, trying to shake off this eerie feeling, when the guard stopped in front of a room. He knocked and entered in an efficient, military manner, leaving the door slightly open.

A small man with dark hair and a mustache peered at a map on the wall, looking like he was in charge. Three others stood behind him, their eyes also at the map and in a heated discussion. The first man's eyes were bloodshot; he moved quickly and abruptly. Looking preoccupied and stressed when the guard spoke, the man grunted something with visible annoyance without even glancing at him. The guard saluted and led Emmy and her family down a short hallway.

They had just turned the corner when a high-pitched child's cry ripped the air. It sounded like a little boy, not far away, and gave Emmy a chill up her spine. She instinctively looked over to her dad and Nora, who looked back in alarm, for the first time since they'd left Stryker's office.

But what she saw there startled her even more. Nora's face showed her exhaustion and fear, devoid of any color; she looked especially small then, her annoying little sister. It pained Emmy's heart to see her this way.

The guard stopped in front of a double door manned by three soldiers. The sound of the child's cry screeched again, this time coming from just behind the doors. The guards exchanged a few words, and one of them pushed the door open, revealing a cafeteria full of kids. Before they could react, they were pushed in, immediately thrust into the huge, crowded room. The door promptly closed behind them.

The three stood and looked around for a minute, overwhelmed with the scene and trying to figure out what it meant for their fate. Three older adults sat in the corner, in a sea of children, looking tired and dejected. The children were as young as five or six years old, with runny noses and dirty faces. The crying boy was smaller than Emmy had imagined and was on the other side of the room sitting on the lap of an older girl.

They were the camp's young prisoners. Many had shaved heads and wore tattered clothes, with dark, sunken eyes; a small number looked more normal, although nervous and upset, like they'd come in recently. Everyone looked tired and scared. Some slouched forward on tables, and others were curled up on the floor, trying to sleep. They'd been there a while.

Emmy walked over to the closest kid, a boy of maybe thirteen, who sat at the end of a bench with his hands over his face.

"Hey," she said in a soft voice. He looked up, squinting. She turned around to show him her hands, still tied around her back. "Can you help?"

Without a word he reached for the rope.

"Do you know why you're in here?"

"They said it'd be safer here," he answered unconvincingly. His small fingers moved around her wrists.

"How long have you been here?" Sohan asked as he walked closer.

"Since last night, after the fighting got real loud." He used his teeth to pull on a stubborn knot, and they waited quietly until the rope finally loosened around her wrists.

"Thanks." She let out a sigh, rubbing her arms and loosening her shoulders. The boy nodded. Emmy worked on Sohan's arms first. "You think that's true?"

"No, unfortunately not." His arms were free.

As she worked on freeing Nora's hands, he squeezed through the crowded room to the three adults squatting in the corner. They were much older, with gray hair and wrinkled faces; they looked up at him as he spoke and soon shook their heads. When he came back, he also shook his head.

"They have no idea what they're doing here." He sighed and looked around again, but there were no clues. He got down on one knee and took his daughters' hands into his. "We have to stay real close, okay?"

Nora and Emmy nodded.

"No matter what happens, we stick together." He squeezed their hands and hugged them.

Emmy was about to say something when explosions and gunshots started again outside, this time with more intensity, making everyone's eyes and ears turn upward in attention. It was getting closer. The crying boy stopped his wailing, although now a couple of others whimpered in fear.

The double doors swung open, and soldiers barged in, shouting, "Everyone line up."

Confused, no one moved at first. About a dozen soldiers quickly entered and walked around the room, pushing and yelling at everyone to stand in lines. Nora and Emmy held hands and stayed close to their dad; Nora hooked the fingers of her free hand on the waist of his pants. Three lines eventually formed. Having been close to the door, Emmy and her family were in the front of one. When everyone was in formation, a soldier blew a whistle.

"Follow me," he shouted, "and stay in line, no fooling around." He waved his black club in the air. "That goes for you too," he said to Sohan.

Another soldier lifted his pistol in the air. Soon, they were all marching out of the room and into the white and long hallway.

{ 43 }

"Now," the soldier shouted, shoving Sohan forward.

Before them laid open dirt grounds, where an intense battle was taking place about fifty yards ahead. Emmy watched in awe as bullets splashed sand and debris and fires burned, with thick, black smoke rising up into the air.

"Go where?" Sohan asked. The soldier glared at him and grabbed his arm to push him forward. He shook him off. "What do you—"

The soldier fired his rifle into the air. Kids screamed and ducked onto the ground; some cried, and a few tried to run, instinctively, only to be stopped by additional bullets flying by their feet. Screams filled the air, and chaos ensued, with kids moving in all directions.

"They're just kids!" Sohan yelled in exasperation, half pleading.

The soldier threw the handle of his rifle across Sohan's face, thrusting him onto the ground.

"Dad!" Emmy jumped. A line of dark red seeped from his cheek as he tried to get up.

"Move or die," the soldier said, the muzzle of his rifle pointed at them. Slowly he moved his aim toward Nora's head. She froze where she knelt and squeezed her eyes shut, holding her breath. The soldier grinned, snidely, showing a shiny silver tooth in his mouth.

Sohan lifted himself up and raised his arms in the air. "Okay, we move."

The soldier cocked his head and fired into the air. Kids panicked and screamed again.

"We're going!" Sohan yelled, stepping toward Nora, who was now shaking.

The soldier lowered his rifle, watching Sohan. Emmy ran to her sister, who fell into her arms and broke into a sob; Sohan put his arms around his daughters.

"Now," the soldier commanded.

They marched forward, slowly, putting one foot in front of the other. The kids followed, cowering and unsure, holding on to each other. Those who hesitated met the boot of the soldiers; there was nowhere else to go.

Gunshots were still ahead of them. Every time something exploded, a wave of gasps, screams, and cries spread in the lines.

Did they see the kids marching forward? Would they stop firing?

Emmy squeezed her sister's hand as they walked, her heart tightening into a small, dense ball and jumping in all directions. Nora's hand shook violently, the sound of her breath heavy and irregular.

They were still inching closer when a boy screamed and ran toward the buildings. He ran fiercely, his chest thrust forward and hands in tight fists. But he'd only gone about ten steps when the soldier with the silver tooth brought the rifle to his face, aimed for him, and fired.

The boy fell forward in a strangely graceful and quiet tumble and soon lay motionless on the ground. The soldier fired another shot in Emmy's direction, and the bullet splashed the ground a few feet away.

"Come on," Sohan said, pulling his daughters.

They moved again. Emmy breathed deeply, intentionally, into her heart, to distract herself from this situation. How had she gotten here? Would she ever see her mother's beautiful face? She looked at Nora and pulled her closer.

In the distance, brown hills stretched over the camp's walls—now open and fallen into rubbles in places—behind the rebels' line. Gunfire continued as they moved forward; Sohan's grip on his daughters became tighter as they neared it. Another step, another breath—they moved slowly, in a pathetic march of the helpless.

The fighting felt far away, and everything became silent in Emmy's head. The sky was full of dark, gray clouds. She hadn't noticed before. The wind blew cold and snippy against her cheeks; she felt a quiet heaviness in the air. It was about to snow. She could almost smell it in the air. This could have been just another lazy snow day…back in Bath. She lowered her eyes and continued to walk, her hand tightly holding Nora's, who flinched every time a bullet flew past her.

A long, loud horn erupted from the hillside. The gunfire slowed down, in a scattered rhythm. Soon everything went quiet except for the sounds of their feet on the ground, still marching forward on sand and gravel, and the crackling and popping of fires nearby. Both sides had ceased fire.

The hills were eerily quiet. Nearby, rebel fighters hiding behind brick mounds and trucks remained tense and still. They were much closer than she had thought. Behind the long line of kids, Party soldiers peeked up and through the barriers of gray sandbags, trying to gauge the situation.

Emmy and Sohan looked at each other and stopped, frozen like trapped animals in a cage.

"What do we do now?" she whispered.

"I don't know, honey" he answered, looking back and forth between the rebels and the soldiers. Everything stayed quiet for a moment, except for the kids' sniffles and whimpering behind them.

Ta ta ta ta! The soldiers fired.

"Everybody down!" Sohan pulled his daughters to the ground.

They all dropped, with older kids helping the little ones, staying as low as possible. The soldiers continued to shoot over their heads in greater numbers, showering the hills and the rebel fighters with bullets. Emmy lay flat on the ground with her stomach down, staying low, as if she was about to dig through the dirt with her body. Her dad lay beside her, on his side and shielding Nora with his body.

Bullets pierced through the air just above their heads, with amazing speed and frequency, hissing as if they were flying insects. Small rockets also flew in the sky, rhythmically exploding near and far. The sounds were one-sided. Lifting her head a bit, Emmy saw that the rebels held back. Those closest to her were unmoving but watching, seemingly waiting for something.

It was because of them—hundreds of innocent kids lying on the ground in the middle of battle. They'd become human shields for the Party.

A rocket exploded on a truck near where the rebels hid, exploding the car's gas tank with a loud boom and enormous flames. Just as soon as Emmy noticed the heat on her cheeks, the burning figure of a man ran out from behind, screaming with pain. He rolled around on the ground as another figure ran over and covered his body with a coat, trying to put the fire out. But it had no intention of letting go.

Shit, shit, shit. Emmy watched as the man's screams disappeared and his body lay still on the ground, still in flames. The fighter who tried to help finally gave up and lifted his head, revealing his face.

It was Chris. He'd come back, after all, as promised.

The sight of him gave Emmy a strange feeling, as she watched him run back to the closest rubble for cover. He had not seen her.

But he'd come for her, to help her and her family, and everyone else in this miserable place. The rebels, including Chris and probably Finn, were risking their lives to help these people, who they barely knew. Suddenly Emmy felt the urge to be better, to do more—to do something to deserve their sacrifice. She felt ashamed that she was crawling on the ground on all fours.

Just then something cold and wet brushed her cheek and the tip of her nose. She looked up, and the sky was full of white dots of snow, falling slowly and gently down to the ground. It was good snow, like the kind that was fluffy but wet enough to stick together to make a snowball—the kind that they always wished for but rarely got. The flakes hit the ground and remained, sprinkling the surface with white, dot by dot.

The Party soldiers' firing continued with bullets and bombs. They were trying to drive the rebels out of the camp, and it was working. More had been killed and lay motionless on the ground, but they still weren't fighting back. If this continued, there was only one possible ending.

Emmy lowered her head and closed her eyes against the helplessness. Snow continued to fall and gave her cold and gentle kisses on the back of her neck, one after another. It was such a contrast from the anxiety she felt inside. But she focused on it, just like she used to focus on her breath, until the sensation slowly drew her out from her surroundings and led her into the quiet and expansive place of her heart. It was quiet and gentle there, full of clarity and ease that embodied all of nature.

Show me the way. I know there's a way. It doesn't have to be easy, but I'm here. I have always been here.

She breathed deeply. Goosebumps started at the core of her stomach and spread through her shoulders, arms, and legs, going up her neck and out through her head. It was like an electrical charge started from her gut, extending out from her body and into the air around her. All of her buzzed, inside and out, as if she was a part of a bigger current of energies all around her.

It was pleasure—like ecstasy. She let out a quiet moan. Then a voice echoed in her head, and she heard it as if she was receiving the words—their meaning—through her entire being.

What you give your attention to grows. Every moment is an opportunity. Choose your thoughts and feelings carefully and listen to yourself. You'll know what to do.

Her grandmother's reminder. She smiled.

Still feeling the electric current all through and around her, Emmy saw herself in her mind, standing tall, arms spread wide. She felt safe and powerful, with a knowing that there was something out there, an unseen force in partnership with her, that knew what to do to protect and guide her. The others—her dad and Nora, the kids and the rebels—were still around in the scene of her mind, but she saw them also standing up in relief, safety, and complete freedom.

It was over. The Party soldiers and their guns floated away behind them as if being washed off in a current of river, disappearing in the distance. Everything had already worked out beautifully, somehow, and they were all safe and free. They were all enveloped in bright light, in protection. Her face lit up with a smile, ear to ear, as she indulged in a deep sense of relief and gratitude, which pulsed from her gut and sent more goosebumps throughout her body.

Slowly the vision passed, and the sound of gunshots and explosions became louder around her. When she opened her eyes, her dad was tightly holding Nora's head against his chest. To her left, the rebels were starting to retreat back up the hills, judging by the way they moved. Fires still burned with black smoke; snow continued to fall, quietly blanketing the entire place.

Emmy searched for something. She had no idea what yet, but the knowing of an imminent shift—as strange as it sounded—was unquestionable. So she waited, as alert as she had ever been in her life, her eyes and ears wide open. The snowflakes got bigger as time went on, starting to cover the bodies of those on the ground. Everything was getting covered in a clean, soft layer of white.

Then a spark of color moving in a peculiar pattern caught Emmy's eye. What she saw in front of her was impossible, and she blinked a few times to make sure that it was real. But there it was, a giant and beautiful monarch butterfly, in all its golden and black glory, fluttering down from the sky and floating through the bullets and the snowflakes. It landed just a couple of feet away from Emmy's face, on the blanket of snow, and opened and closed its wings a couple of times.

How could this be? A butterfly in the middle of a winter snowstorm—was this her sign?

The butterfly launched into the air again, as swiftly as it had landed, away from her.

An explosion shook the ground. This one was very close. Something had hit the camp's wall, about forty feet away, close to where Emmy was. Dust and smoke flew in front of her and engulfed the butterfly in the air. She held her breath and waited for things to settle, hoping the butterfly was safe.

Gradually a silhouette of the broken wall began to take shape, and her eyes searched for the butterfly. To her relief, it sat on top of the still-standing edge of the wall, slowly fluttering its wings. It stayed there this time, not moving much, giving her a strange feeling that it was watching, beckoning her.

She broke into laughter. The situation felt unreal to her, as if in a dream. But this clearly was not one of her visions. She looked back at her dad and Nora, who had crawled into an even smaller position together after the last explosion. She looked at the line of Party soldiers, who were busy targeting the retreating rebels. Whatever it was that hit the wall, it must have been an accident, since it was nowhere near the direction of the rebels.

The wall gave her and the kids an exit—if they only dared.

Emmy studied the wall to gauge how far it was, considering that it would take longer for the littlest ones to run the distance. She also looked at where the bullets were flying and was glad to find out, as long as the Party soldiers did not decide to shoot at them, chances were low that they'd be caught in the crossfire along the way.

But the more she looked at the wall, the more she thought it looked familiar—the shape of its breaking, the color of the ocean behind, and arrangement of the fallen stones around it. How could she have seen it?

She tried to jog her memory, but there was no way that she could have seen it before. What was this feeling then? Her eyes wandered to the butterfly, still sitting on top of the wall and slowly moving its wings.

Then she remembered: she'd seen it in a nightmare. She'd been shot in the end.

{ 44 }

The golden butterfly fluttered more quickly now, as if urging Emmy to move. But she was frozen on the ground, desperately trying to remember. How had her dream ended? Had she died?

She couldn't remember. She knew that she woke up in screams and cold sweats. In the dream, she'd been crossing the wall with her mom, dad, and sister, when shots were fired and everything went dark. Was it a premonition?

Emmy looked at Nora and her dad. Her sister's face was smeared with tears and dirt, and her dad looked defeated. Violence and chaos ensued, even as the rebels had retreated almost out of the camp. Behind her, hundreds of kids lay in dirt, snow, and fear, their immediate future unknown and unprotected.

Whatever the dream had meant, there was no time to figure it out. She had to do this, now. She'd promised that she'd do anything for a way out. She'd have to get over her fear and the need for certainty.

The butterfly fluttered on the wall, watching her.

She took a deep breath and slowly lifted her body up from the ground.

"What are you... Get down!" Sohan yelled, his arm reaching up to pull her back down.

"Look." She pointed to the broken wall. "We can go."

"They'll shoot you!" He looked at the soldiers, still firing over their heads.

"But we can do this." She didn't really know if that was true. Standing tall, she turned to the kids behind her. For a second she didn't even know what to say. She tried to get their attention. "Hey!"

Only those near her looked up. The air was still loud with gunshots.

"We're going to run," Emmy yelled louder, pointing to the broken wall. "We go together." Half of the kids' eyes were on her now, even as they remained unmoving, cowering on the ground. "Now!"

There was no reaction; they just stared blankly.

She waited, looking for any sign of agreement, when Nora pushed her from behind.

"Just go." Nora looked ready. Sohan looked unsure but willing, nonetheless. Nora pushed Emmy again. Before they knew it, they were running toward the wall. In a few steps Emmy looked back for the kids. Like a herd of sheep they'd followed, fumbling and unsure.

She chuckled, going back to help speed them along. Some of the older kids were already helping the littlest ones and each other, but it helped to have someone point them to a direction. Soon, everyone was up and running or walking away from the gunshots and toward the wall.

Whatever euphoria there was about this turn of events didn't last long, though. Soldiers wasted no time firing in the kids' direction, and bullets hit near them, causing dirt and debris to ricochet all around. But there was no time to be afraid and nowhere to hide. They had to get over that wall, and it was right there, right in front of them. A couple of the last stragglers were shot—one in the head and another in the shoulder—and Emmy ran back to help the injured, a girl of about thirteen, get moving again.

Soon, things became even louder. The rebels had resumed their counterattack, and now explosions and bullets were landing on the soldiers' side too. The rebels were covering for the kids.

Emmy finally reached the foot of the wall and handed the injured girl to walk with another. Many of the kids had already crossed the beach and reached the ocean, hovering in an area full of big, black volcanic rocks, now covered in white snow. She helped the rest of the kids climb over. Several others had been injured along the way. A couple of small bodies lay motionless on the ground, far behind them. She looked up to the top of the wall—the butterfly was gone, nowhere to be found.

The soldiers were focused on fighting back the rebels, who had stepped up their attack. Hundreds more fighters had come down from the hills, and slowly, their line was advancing forward and circling in on the soldiers.

"I have to go back for Mom," Sohan yelled as the last of the kids had crossed the wall.

"I'm coming," Emmy answered. There was no question she'd go.

"No," he pleaded. "You take Nora and go with the others. It's too dangerous."

She firmly shook her head. "You know I can't. Besides, I think I know where to go."

He looked at her with curious eyes.

"I can feel her," she explained.

"Then I'm coming too," Nora declared.

Emmy nodded, reaching out for her sister's hand. "We'll stay together."

Sohan didn't argue any further. They had no time.

She didn't know why she knew this, but there was just one thought in her head: they had to go back to the main building, the one with Stryker's office. She didn't know what would happen after that, but that was where they needed to go now.

"Stay right behind me, okay?" They nodded. Sohan took a deep breath and kissed Emmy and Nora on their heads. "Here we go."

He jumped out from behind the bricks and ran toward the buildings. The girls followed, their heads lowered and hands together. To their right, the rebel fighters had gotten closer and only about a stone's throw away. As they ran along the wall, being careful to stay away from the battle, something broke in the soldiers' line, and men charged forward to meet the rebels in direct combat.

Shots and bombs still fired, causing bright flames to burst up in the snow, but a huge jumble of bodies thrashed against each other in the middle of the camp. People fell left and right; bright, red stains seeped through the white snow where they lay on the ground, some still moaning and yelling undecipherable things.

"Don't look," she told Nora, whose startled eyes looked back in fear. Emmy squeezed her hand. She nodded. "Just stay with me."

They were nearing the soldiers' main line, which now stood largely empty except for a few men manning the big guns. They kept their bodies as low as possible, hiding behind anything that would provide cover along the way. As they approached the building behind the trenches, Sohan yelled, "Look.".

At the end of his gaze were two familiar figures—Leona and Alex—who had just emerged from a door on the other end of the building.

Emmy waved her arms to get their attention, but they were too far away. They tiptoed along the building, trying to hide from the remaining soldiers.

"You stay here." Sohan jumped out from behind the corner before Emmy could answer, almost running. He picked up a rifle from the ground and crept over to the building. Leona soon recognized her husband in the distance. Her eyes searched for a moment, looking for her daughters, but she hurried forward to meet him.

Nora and Emmy watched, holding their breath, as the two carefully made their way toward each other. The girls' eyes were glued to the tips of the parents' heads as they bobbed up and down above the sandbags and dirt. When they finally reached one another and resumed their journey back to the girls, Emmy and Nora looked at each other and laughed, excited. But it was too early to celebrate.

Gunshots fired behind the lines, followed by an explosion. One of the big machine gun posts, where the soldiers had been firing rocket launchers, had blown up.

"Where'd they go?" Nora asked, full of worry.

"I don't know. I can't see them." There was no sign of her parents.

Emmy was about to jump out when she saw her dad's face peek out from under the trenches and go back down again. His hand came up next, motioning as if to say, he was okay. She exhaled in relief.

In a couple of minutes another explosion took place behind the line, where the remaining heavy artillery fired. Sohan's hand popped up again, though. They were helping the rebel fighters by disabling the big guns. Already the battle had gotten much quieter, even though the rebel rockets still fired.

But the explosions had caught the attention of other Party soldiers, who ran out of the building firing at the infiltrators. Sohan and Alex fired back as they ran, but this slowed them down and attracted even more attention to their whereabouts. A couple of soldiers ran after them, followed by another familiar face—Stryker. She could hardly see his face in the distance, but he wildly fired his pistol after her parents.

Shit. The man did not give up. But Emmy could only watch, her fists clenched and body tight with worry, as her parents made their way forward.

Like a miracle, Sohan, Leona, and Alex made it safely to where the girls waited.

"Mom!" they both cried and embraced their mother.

"We have to go, now," Sohan yelled, grabbing Nora's hand and running toward the broken wall.

Without a word the rest of them followed, running as fast as they could. Shots fired behind them, and bullets hit the ground, barely missing them. But all Emmy was aware of was the sound of her footsteps and the push of her heavy breath, with its steam rising in front of her like thick smoke. There was no time to look back. She just ran, pushing her legs and lungs as much as she could for what felt like eternity. The shots continued.

They were almost there. The ocean behind the wall looked as wide as ever. Alex ran up front, followed by Sohan and Nora still holding hands, with Leona and Emmy trailing behind. They only needed another minute, maybe less.

Alex safely climbed over the broken wall and reached the other side. Sohan and Nora were next, about to climb over, when Nora screamed and fell to the ground. A bullet had grazed her leg; blood gushed. Leona gasped and instinctively threw herself over her daughter. Emmy also fell to her knees. Their mother quickly opened her coat and ripped a length of her thin, cotton skirt, using the strap to tie around Nora's wound. When she finished, Sohan lifted Nora's little body and started the climb toward the beach.

Another bullet nearly hit and bounced off a rock right next to Sohan. Emmy turned to the direction of the shot. There stood Stryker, no more than twenty feet away, aiming his pistol again with a bizarre and tortured expression on his face.

"No!" Emmy yelled.

He fired.

Sohan and Nora stumbled to the ground. Before she even realized, Emmy charged toward Stryker, running with a force that she never knew she had. He was aiming his pistol again.

I won't let you. She knew this with every cell in her body. Enormous heat burned inside; only a single thought echoed through her entire being. *I won't let you.*

Like an arrow she ran, all of her fierce energy aimed at her target. As she neared, he looked at her, and their eyes met. His face moved into a terrible grin, and he adjusted his aim—for her. She ran harder and closed her eyes. She was about to hit him like a truck.

Two shots fired as their bodies collided, and they both hit the ground. With a bone-breaking thump, everything went dark in her world.

{ 45 }

December 21

A huge bonfire burned brightly, lighting up the dark forest. A number of smaller fires also burned, surrounded by smaller groups of people talking, drinking, and celebrating. A small band with a fiddle, a banjo, and a cello played a joyful tune; small children danced, encouraged by happy parents.

Nearly everyone at Innisfree was out for the rebel's first victory against the Party. They had freed thousands of people and hundreds of children and had done some real damage to the Party's secret operations. Madame Alande stood near the main fire, surrounded by various members of the Council, receiving congratulations from members and affiliates from near and far.

Emmy watched the scene quietly, sitting by one of the smaller fires away from the busy crowds. Chris and Alex sat with her, quietly sipping beer and also watching. Chris had a cast on his left leg, having been injured from the battle. He was expected to heal fully in time, and for the time being, the worst part of it was enduring the residents' good-natured tease about walking with a cane.

So much had happened in such a short period of time. Emmy would have wondered if any of it had really happened at all, if it wasn't for the physical proof in front of her eyes. It all felt like a dream. She felt a pat on her back.

"You okay?" Chris looked at her with concern.

She nodded.

"Wish I could celebrate with them," he said, looking at the happy people, "but we lost many."

"But you saved us," she said softly. She smiled. "You're my hero in that regard."

"Hey, what about me?" Alex chimed in.

Emmy smiled at him too. "You too. You're also my hero."

She wanted to feel happier. After all, it was over, and she and her family were now free. But like Chris, she remembered those who didn't make it, who'd perished on that remote island where she never wanted to set foot again in her life. And she was painfully aware of the giant hole in her heart.

She pulled her knees closer to her chest and watched the flames dance in the air. The smell and the crackling of burning wood reminded her of Bath, of the giant hearth in her mom's kitchen.

"Hey, look what I got here." Finn walked toward them waving a folded newspaper in his hand. He had a smirk on his face as he sat next to her and handed her the paper.

"Finn," Pablo was the first one to spot him from far away and run to his side.

He had become the little boy's hero since returning from the island, where, as far as he understood, battles were hard-fought and enemies were defeated. If Pablo had looked up to him before, now he worshipped him.

Pablo wasn't alone, either. Most of the little ones at Innisfree had come to love Finn, especially since he told the stories with drama and flare, any time anyone asked. He was the favorite among all. Of course, he was often not the main hero of the stories he told, but unlike Chris or Emmy, he enjoyed the storytelling.

"Tell us the story again."

"You want to hear that *again*?" Finn teased, playing hard-to-get.

"Start with when Emmy was captured and you were looking for her." Pablo settled in front of him, making himself comfortable. Other kids gathered, settling in for a raptured story time.

Bree walked over, smiling and happy to have Finn back, with two drinks in her hand. She handed one to him and sat next to him.

"I don't think I should tell it again." He frowned and feigned boredom.

"Yes," the children screamed.

"Okay, you asked for it." He cleared his throat and adjusted his body to position himself for the best view for the kids, his hands raised in front of him. He usually became very animated with these stories, using his hands and arms to describe the far-away island, the harsh forests, and the scary soldiers.

"The day that Chris had to go back for reinforcements, the winds were cold and harsh, and it hurt to keep our eyes open," he started. "Emmy and I had to find a spot where we could get a good view of the camp, which was huge and filled with RP soldiers everywhere. The soldiers were big and burly, every single one of them, and carried at least three kinds of weapons at all times."

Soon all of Innisfree's children had gathered there, their eyes sparkling and mouths ajar. The scene made Emmy smile. Chris and Alex listened too. She'd heard the story a hundred times by now, begrudgingly, but still found it amusing. Finn was a great storyteller, much better than she could ever be. People—adults and children alike—asked her questions too sometimes, but she couldn't bring herself to talk about it. She got all choked up and lost her words.

As he continued his story for a captivated audience, she glanced at the paper in her hand. It was folded to show a single newspaper article, "Fallen Rational Party Reeducation Camp Found Riddled with Rights Violations."

It read:

The ruling Rational Party of The New Republic was dealt a blow last week when the first of its reeducation camps, which started as an experiment to eradicate religious beliefs from the minds of its citizens, was attacked and captured by unidentified rebel forces opposed to its policies. Nearly two hundred soldiers are reported to have been killed in the attack, including the camp's Interim Director Sweeney Stryker, in addition to three hundred severely wounded soldiers who are now being treated at Seven Hills Military Hospital outside Alexandria. It is unclear how many rebel fighters were injured or killed in the attack, as authorities found no bodies onsite.

Residents of the surrounding area, a rural region known for its fishing industry, say that they had no idea that the Party had built a reeducation camp on Wick Island, even though they had been fishing nearby for the past two years.

A resident, speaking on condition of anonymity, told The Republic Times, "It's a horrible thing that they did there. We rescued many children who started to swim across the freezing water. They were really weak and scared. Many looked like they hadn't been fed for months."

He said a number of fishing boats rescued the fleeing children from the ocean and the island as fighting ensued. The children were later reunited with their parents, who were set free by the rebel forces, he said. Residents describe a heartwarming but sad scene, in which not all parents could find their children, who were believed to have been killed during the fight.

"The soldiers used children as human shields and shot at them." The anonymous source described the scene as "cruel and appalling." All of the families left with the rebels before Party authorities could retake charge of the

area, residents say. They also claim that they didn't see or meet any of the rebel fighters.

An initial review of the camp's facilities by human rights experts showed that the Rational Party had engaged in torture and execution of its inmates, although it is unclear how many may have been killed. Administrative records of the camp had been burnt by the time the journalists arrived at the site. Party officials say it was caused by the rebels' bombings. Despite the lack of records, some experts argue that remaining evidence paints a vastly different picture of the camp's operations than were previously described by Party officials, who have consistently maintained that it treated the religious followers humanely.

John Middleton, an official Rational Party spokesperson, denied allegations of torture and executions at the camp. "The Rational Party doesn't engage in torture, nor do we kill people without legal due process. These are all hearsay, made up by rogue militia who call themselves rebels but are really out to destabilize our country for their own gain. Rest assured that we're doing everything we can to find every last one of them and bring them to justice."

The Ministry of Mental Hygiene is also launching a formal investigation into the matter.

"Do you think people will care?" Emmy interrupted Finn from his story. She handed the paper to Chris. "I mean, people out there?"

Finn looked at her for a second, confused, but quickly smiled. "I hope so."

"Come on," Pablo whined. He sat up straight, eager for the story to continue. "This is the good part. Then what happened?"

"All right, where was I?" Finn rubbed his hands together.

"You saw the director run after Emmy's family to the wall," another child yelled.

"Right," Finn said. "They were running and running. Bullets were flying right next to them, and bombs were exploding everywhere. *Boom! Boom!*" He waved his arms in big circles. "Then they were almost there, just about to cross the broken wall to the beach, where all these children were getting rescued by the fishing boats. Her dad was carrying Nora in his arms because she got shot in the leg. Emmy and her mom were right behind them. Chris and I were fighting these big, muscular soldiers on the ground when we saw Emmy being chased by this tall, skinny, ugly man who kept on shooting at them. We ran after them. Then the ugly man shot Emmy's father, and he fell to the ground. Emmy ran full-force at this man, who was now aiming for her, and I'd never seen anyone who ran that fast."

Everyone's heads turned toward Emmy, their eyes big and sparkling in wonder, before they went back to Finn.

"She looked like a bull, from what I saw," he continued in an incredulous voice. She smacked him hard on his shoulder.

"What?" he protested, smirking, and continued. "But at the same time, Chris drew his gun and aimed for this guy. Then, *bam!* She ran into him just as Chris fired, and they both fell to the ground real hard. I mean, she must have hit him at like, eighty miles an hour. But we weren't sure who was shot. Neither of them moved."

Pausing, he looked at her tenderly before turning back to the kids.

"I thought she was dead, and it was just horrible, thinking we couldn't save her. So we ran over and checked her body and shook her real hard. And as you can see, Emmy wasn't shot." He smiled.

"It was the ugly man," someone shouted.

"Chris got him right here." Finn pointed his index finger to the middle of his forehead. "And he was long dead by the time we got there."

A quiet murmur spread among the children.

"How many did you save?" Pablo asked.

"Thousands," he answered, "and hundreds of children just like you." He took a deep breath. "A lot died too. I don't want you to forget. We were lucky, but almost a hundred of our fighters lost their lives. Never forget that, okay?"

The children nodded and applauded.

"Go play now. And no more stories," Finn yelled. But Emmy knew she'd hear it again.

As children slowly scattered away, she saw two familiar faces walking slowly toward her. Leona was helping Nora walk on a cane, slowly limping toward her. She got up and helped them both sit near the fire.

"You just missed Finn's story time," she said to Nora.

"He did it again?" The little girl frowned.

"I can do it again if you want," Finn teased. "Just say the word."

Everyone laughed.

Emmy leaned her head on her mother's shoulder and hugged her. A ball formed in her throat, and her heart was sore. "I miss him, Mom. Wish he was here too."

"Me too, honey." Leona held her close. "But you know what? I just talked to him on the other side. And he says it's wonderful there. He misses us too, but he's always with us." She kissed her daughter's head. "And Grandma says hello."

Emmy laughed, closing her eyes. Tears rolled down her face.

NOTE TO READERS

If you liked *The Magical Awakening of Emmy Sukar*, please:

- LEAVE A REVIEW where you bought the copy. This makes it much easier for others to find it!

- SIGN UP FOR UPDATES on the upcoming release of The Limitless Series, Book II. You can do that and check out other information on the author's webpage, at solkwon.com.

Thank you so much for reading *The Magical Awakening* and please feel free to send me comments through my website!

ABOUT THE AUTHOR

Sol Kwon is the author of *The Magical Awakening of Emmy Sukar,* her debut novel. She lives in Washington, DC, with her husband and a Westie named Chester. She meditates almost every day and loves to explore the layers of her mind, body and spirit, which inspired the story of *The Magical Awakening.* Sol grew up reading all kinds of books, from the philosophical *Sophie's World* to passionate poetry by W.B. Yeats. While most of her professional career has involved writing about corporate social responsibility, she discovered her love for writing fiction when she began *The Magical Awakening* in 2013. Sol is a member of the Society of Children's Writers and Illustrators (SCBWI) and The Writers' Center.